"MANY OF THOSE *who are now writing novels were only children during the Civil War. Through the eyes of children they saw, calmly, atrocious things. They forgot them. But there was a moment in their lives, as they grew up, in which they suddenly remembered them again. And they remembered them more and more as their bones grew harder and their blood richer. Not to forget them, for that is impossible, but to set them aside they have turned to writing fiction. After the first wave, the fleeting, journalistic wave that told of crimes and statistics . . . the second wave comes, the slower and more powerful one: the one that tells what is destroyed and awakened in our consciences."*

This was the statement made by Juan Goytisolo at the age of eighteen about the new literature that he envisioned in Spain. Born in Barcelona in 1931, Goytisolo lived in the Republican zone during the Civil War. He studied at universities in Barcelona, Madrid, and Paris. In 1951 he founded a literary group, "Turia," and in 1952 he won the "Joven Literatura" prize for his story "The World of Mirrors."

His first novel, *The Young Assassins*, was the runner-up for the Nadal Prize, but did not meet censorship requirements. A slightly cut version was published in Spain; restored to its original, from which the present translation was made, the novel has appeared in France and in Germany.

Today at twenty-eight "Juan Goytisolo is already considered an elder, the front-rank man in the new literary generation."* He divides his time between Paris and Barcelona and his home on the Costa Brava in northern Catalonia, devoting himself to his writing.

Photograph by

**
*

THE YOUNG ASSASSINS

**
*

THE YOUNG

BY

TRANSLATED FROM THE

ASSASSINS

JUAN GOYTISOLO

SPANISH BY JOHN RUST

* * * * *

Alfred A. Knopf   New York   1959

L. C. Catalog card number: 59–6221

© Alfred A. Knopf, Inc., 1958

THIS IS A BORZOI BOOK,
PUBLISHED BY ALFRED A. KNOPF, INC.

FIRST AMERICAN EDITION

Originally published in Spain in 1954 as JUEGOS DE MANOS by Ediciones Destino, S. L.

We return to the place as the guilty one
always returns to the scene of his crime.

E · M · S

The Principal Characters

*
* *
*

EDUARDO URIBE (*Tánger*): *a weak-willed lush with a love for make-believe; David's cousin; sidekick of Raúl; a hanger-on, but not really one of the gang.*

*

THE GANG

RAÚL RIVERA: *a medical student in Madrid from Arucas, Las Palmas, in the Canary Islands; a handsome, physical boy with the look of a* chulo (*youth of lower class, usually unemployed, who spends time in bars or on streets, affects flashy clothes, and often engages in questionable activities*).

LUIS PÁEZ: *a tough little kid who has quit engineering school and is the despair of his conventional bourgeois parents with whom he lives in Madrid.*

CORTÉZAR: *another tough boy, usually playing second to others in gang.*

AGUSTÍN MENDOZA: *the ringleader and backbone of the gang; a boy from Barcelona who is living on his own as a painter in a Madrid studio.*

DAVID: *a law student from a prominent Barcelona family; grandson of an Indian (a Spaniard who has returned to Spain after making a fortune in the West Indies); a sensitive boy, once a model student, who has been greatly influenced by Agustín.*

ANA: *the only one of the gang not of a wealthy bourgeois family; a dedicated revolutionist.*

✻

GLORIA PÁEZ: *once David's girl, now in love with Jaime Betancourt.*

DON SIDONIA: *a Madrid lawyer; father of Luis and Gloria.*

DOÑA CECILIA: *his wife.*

LOLA: *Agustín's mistress.*

PLANAS: *Raúl's roommate at the* residencia (*an off-campus dormitory for students*).

FRANCISCO GUARNER: *a Madrid politician.*

✻

JAIME BETANCOURT: *a young law student from Las Palmas; now in jail for illegal possession of concealed weapons.*

ENRIQUE SUAREZ: *boy from the Canaries, now living in Madrid.*

GERARDO: *another youth from the Canaries.*

THE YOUNG ASSASSINS

I

I t was still raining when they went out into the street. The drops falling from the eaves splashed onto the slate ledge, and along the curb the mouths of the sewers gulped down the water from the street.

They stopped in the doorway, undecided as to whether they should go on, while the man with the doughnuts grumbled and complained that the damages had been insufficiently compensated for.

"Let's go now! Get out of here! If I said it . . ."

The ashen light of the dawn was suffusing the atmosphere with indefinable sadness.

The fog was turning yellowish around the globes of the street lamps. The buildings that lined the narrow street looked like wooden fronts put up for the filming of a movie. There were no signs of life.

"I'm cold."

Eduardo Uribe, "Tánger," freed himself from the arms of the girls and pounded on the door that had just been closed.

"Open up! Open up!"

The breath that came out of the corners of his mouth looked like cigarette smoke. It was cold; he wanted a quick drink.

The girls immediately surrounded him, putting their arms around him, solicitous and fearful at the possibility of another fight.

"Let's go, Tánger, can't you see they're closed? There's nobody in there now."

"Come along with us, honey. We'll take you home where there's a good bed. The important thing is to get warm."

But Uribe wouldn't have anybody quiet him down. The bodies pushing against him infuriated him. He broke away from them violently.

"Let me alone! I don't like anybody touching me. What I want is to get in here."

Again raising his fist, he beat on the metal door.

"Open up! Open!"

The smallest of the three girls, the one who had caused the fight, was still crying and trying to pull him away.

"Come on, honey, please. . . ."

Uribe turned around, furious.

"I'm not your honey and I never was."

Another rain of knocks on the door.

"Watchman! Watchman! Come and open this door!"

The narrow street was empty. It was drizzling. A woman stuck her head out of the window of one of the neighboring houses.

"Hey, you good-for-nothings! This is a fine time of night to be making so much noise and waking up the whole neighborhood."

The girls turned toward the intruder.

"Shut up yourself. Nobody asked you to butt in."

A new insult. Another. A bang: the noise of a shutter slammed shut.

"Well, at last. . . ."

Leaning against a lamppost, Raúl Rivera watched the spectacle with indifference.

He was solid-looking, robust and chunky; a little older than Eduardo Uribe, he had thick curly hair and a big black mustache. Dressed flashily, he wore his jacket unbuttoned; his pants were full of dust. His shirt was open too, and his badly knotted tie hung limp. His face looked faded and gray, as if his bloodless skin had absorbed the indefinite shade of the last shreds of the fog. Leaning against the lamppost, with his hat pushed back and a cigarette between his lips, he was trying to remain apart from the little group, which he was watching nonetheless.

"It's useless," he said.

One of the girls, the fattest one, gave him a scornful look.

"Nobody's talking to you, either. The whole thing's your fault. You didn't have to hit him—you could have come to some kind of an understanding."

She stopped for a moment and pointed to Uribe.

"If you were really his friend, you wouldn't have been looking for trouble, and you wouldn't have insulted him the way you did, for not getting into the fight."

Raúl Rivera forced a bitter smile.

"Sure. Now it's all my fault. That's really good! It'll teach me not to mess around with women."

With his hands on his hips and the smoke coiling around in front of his face, he was the living image of outraged dignity.

"Yes. It's the same old story: He's just the poor little, mixed-up kid, and I'm the one who gets him into scrapes." He was talking to himself, not to the girl, who he neither desired nor would have wanted as a friend, talking in the sorrowful tones of one who enjoys torturing himself. "I knock myself out for him," he thought, "and as if that wasn't enough, now it turns out I'm to blame." These aftermaths often left him masochistic.

Uribe, meanwhile, continued to pound on the door of the bakery.

"Open up! Open up!"

"We can't go on like this," he thought.

But it wasn't the first time he had said this to himself, and realizing the fact he became furious. As always, the evening had ended badly. Every time they went to Lavapiés, things turned out badly. Uribe would sing. They'd both get drunk. And when they were drunk, somebody, almost always Uribe, started a quarrel. And Raúl would have to use the power of his fists to mollify the anger of the attackers while Uribe stood by, laughing and enjoying it all like a child.

"Next time, I don't care if there are fifteen of them, I'll let them destroy him," he thought with satisfaction. His relationship with Uribe was a strange one; a mixture, in varying proportions, of admiration and contempt.

Usually he amused himself by insulting Uribe, making fun of his mannerisms and gestures, speaking with repugnance of his habits, and delighting in playing practical jokes on him. But on the other hand, Raúl couldn't get along without Uribe, whom he kept constantly at his side, wanting always to chew the fat with him, feeling happy each time Uribe launched him on a new fight.

Raúl's failing, or his virtue, was his prodigious physical strength. Whenever he got into a fight, no matter with whom, he won—inevitably.

That's what made him penitent after the final blow. So he would turn on Uribe, insult him, call him a coward and a fairy. Then he would promise himself that he would reform and punish Uribe, sometimes going so far as to beat him up.

Immediately afterwards he would be sorry. Choking with the humiliation he had caused his friend, in less than an hour he would be begging him, with tears in his eyes, to forgive him, and he would stroke Uribe's hair and embrace him. And they would go on as though nothing had hap-

pened, until Raúl left with one of the girls and Uribe
would roll home with the last of the drunks. But tonight
Raúl didn't go so far as to hit him. Leaning against the
lamppost, hands on his hips, Raúl felt both humiliated and
hurt.

Uribe, seeing that no one was responding to his knocking, sat on the curb and looked with tired, sullen eyes down
between his knees at the stream of water in the gutter.

The girls were talking in a huddle, deciding what should
be done. They spoke quite loud, not caring whether they
were being heard or not, since their two friends were obviously drunk.

"We gotta get a taxi."

"At this hour? It's impossible."

"There ought to be a cab stand here somewhere."

"We'd do better to go look. Maybe on Atocha Street."

"Think he'll want to?"

"Phooey, we'll drag him."

They looked at Raúl.

The dying light of the street lamp filtered its yellowish
halo down on the paleness of the youth's face, so that the
wrinkles, caught in the vertical light, stood out fine and
intermeshed.

It had stopped raining; but from the balconies of the
neighboring houses the paint, soaked by the rain, dripped
a gummy secretion onto the sidewalk, like mascara
smeared by tears, and the brick pavement seemed to absorb the wavering light of the dawn mixed with the pale
foam oozing from the walls.

The street was still deserted and it seemed as though the
damp asphalt absorbed the sounds made by their footsteps.
In the distance the guttural commands of a man could be
heard, accompanied by the nervous clatter of slipping
hoofs.

The small girl went up to Uribe and pulled him to her by his lapels.

"Come on, Tánger," she said. "You'll freeze to death if you stay that way any longer without moving."

Uribe did not budge.

The girl hesitated a moment, not knowing what to do; a door across the street had just opened, and a flabby-cheeked boy contemplated the scene with curiosity.

"Tánger." She took hold of him by the shoulders and managed to get him to his feet.

Uribe looked at her half dazed and rubbed his eyes indolently.

"Phew," he said. "These female gorillas!"

They started walking.

"And what about him?" They were going past the lamp-post against which Raúl Rivera was still leaning, and Uribe pointed at him.

The girl pulled him again by the sleeve; Uribe was the one who had the money. Raúl did not interest her.

"Bah! Let him rot there. You've seen how he treated you. He insulted you. He's a fine friend!"

Uribe turned around again and looked insolently at Raúl, who stood there with his cigarette drooping obliquely across his chin, smiling bitterly.

For a few seconds Uribe hesitated, enjoying his power. Then, remembering the insults he'd suffered only a little while ago, he pouted. "All right. Let's go."

He said it as if he possessed some magical, all-embracing power over his friend, but had capriciously refused to use it. He offered his arm to the two gorillas and turned his back on Raúl disdainfully.

At almost the same moment Raúl flicked away his cigarette, buttoned up his jacket, and with a brisk step walked off in the opposite direction.

Uribe and the girls climbed the steep incline of the street in silence. A cool wind caused some papers to dance on the surface of the puddles and drew from their throats, when they breathed, filmy wisps of gauze.

Uribe smiled. The brief rest he had taken sitting on the curb had been refreshing. The row of uniform building-fronts gave him the impression that the houses were advancing along with him. As usual, his feet were leading him to some unknown place, and he was content to follow his own footsteps. The effects of the drinks had worn off, and the daylight awakened in him his foolishness and his love for dressing up.

"The nuptial fishes," he said.

The phrase had sprung to his mind; he'd read it in some poem or other, and it delighted him.

"I say: the nuptial fishes."

The girls looked at him, stunned.

"Come on, laugh! We must be gay at the fish's funeral."

He stopped in the middle of the sidewalk and took out of his pocket a small mirror framed in mother-of-pearl.

"Hi, old friend," he said to his image in the glass.

He studied himself; in the crude light of day his face seemed aged. It looked as though an artist had amused himself drawing numerous clusters of tiny crow's feet on his forehead, around his eyes, in the corners of his mouth. When he arched his eyebrows while gesticulating, it seemed something was sucking the flesh from behind his brow, creating deep lines there, as though they had been made by running make-up.

"I look old, and I am sad," he murmured.

On a sudden impulse he smashed the mirror on the sidewalk, studding it with a myriad of tiny stars.

The girls stooped to pick up the ruined frame.

"Oh, and it was so pretty!"

Uribe, with a vague look on his face, was talking with himself: "I must sparkle, be brilliant. . . . I like footlights and music. Otherwise, I hate these female gorillas."

He went over to the short girl and slapped her familiarly on the back. "Know of any place that's open?"

"Now? At this hour?"

"Yes. Any place, a bar or a café. Some place where there are people."

At first they did not answer him.

"Near here . . . on Atocha Street," one of them said.

Uribe took her arm. "I'll find a man for you, sweetie. A better one than I would be. I promise."

They turned the corner.

A gust of cool air rippled the puddles. The few passers-by on the sidewalk were walking fast. The wind blew; the day promised more rain.

* * *

A harsh light chiseled out the furnishings of the room: the bare walls painted a light gray, the American desk with its sharp angles, the modern, chromium chairs. On the lamp was an opaque globe. On the desk the paperweight, the ashtray, and the writing materials seemed to shine with a light of their own, independent of that which filtered in the windows through the curtains. Don Jerónimo was a little over fifty; his face was a mass of pink bulges, and in the middle of his fat chin nestled a dimple the size of a pea. Behind his glasses his eyes shone indulgently.

"So you're Páez's son? Well, well! Who'd have thought it! A grown-up man, already! How is your father? We're old friends. I don't know if you know. We went around together, the same gang. Then Life. . . . You know how it is. Each one goes his own way. One marries. And your mother? I saw her last year, at the Charity Ball. Gay as ever . . ."

Luis Páez smiled from ear to ear. "Soon as they see a chance to make a speech, how these guys run on!" he thought, and then changed his expression. Cortézar, on his left, watched him out of the corner of his eye. "He's really got a face of cement. To have to put up with characters like this Don Jerónimo! How nauseating! Well, anything for the cause!" And he watched while Luis Páez nodded his head attentively and smiled sweetly.

"And you? Going to college, already! Well, I'll be— These young bucks. Nothing like being twenty, I always say. What are you studying? Medicine, perhaps? Law, of course? Like your Dad . . . quite a boy! You fellows are insatiable. In my day we didn't study so much; all we thought about was having a good time. Except your father, believe me! Always the model student. When I tell you that he never even once went to a dance . . ."

While he talked, the folds of fat in his neck rippled like jelly. His whole being spelled dynamism, cheerfulness. Seeing him there outlined in the swivel chair, Luis Páez suddenly recalled the model: in an economics journal that his father subscribed to. A fat man, half bald, wearing glasses, was waving his hand in the air like a fairy godmother: "Smile! It will increase your business." Mentally, Luis Páez sent him to hell, but his smile did not disappear.

"And you want to get your driver's license. Fine, fine. So you like mechanics. Ah, young fellows these days are interested in everything. Ever driven before? Yes, of course. Been driving long? Gabriel tells me your test was okay. How old are you?"

"Eighteen," replied Luis, while he put on an expression that displayed all those positive virtues so desirable in a smart and alert young person: interest, respect, sympathy, admiration for his elders, and so forth.

"And do you have your father's signed consent with you? We can't issue permits to people under twenty-one, unless . . ."

Blah, blah, blah! The tortoise-shell glasses completed his triumphant air: "There's nothing like a smile to . . ." From the start Luis had been waiting for this moment, and the look of consternation on his face was really quite touching. "Why, no, I didn't know that. Before he left, my father told me it was all arranged. I had no idea that—"

"Is your father out of town?"

"Yes, he left two weeks ago."

He remembered the formula and rearranged his smile. It should be, he thought, sad and melancholy, like the smile of an ordinarily careful young man when he makes an error; and at the same time it should reflect an expression of serene confidence in the all-embracing power of his elders. Luis was sorry that he did not have a mirror to see his reflection; but judging from Cortézar's expression, he was doing all right.

"That's too bad," said Don Jerónimo.

The caressing eyes of the boy turned on him in a plea for help. "Oh, and here I thought that everything was in order."

There was such disappointment in his voice that the man felt himself hesitating: Maybe just this once. It was cruel to disappoint a young fellow who wants to learn something useful. He had always said it: Never stand in the way of anybody who wants to get ahead.

"Well, I'll see what can be done. The regulation is quite clear: no licenses issued to minors without parents' consent. But in the case of a lifelong friend like your father . . ."

He had gotten up and from the door he gave him an encouraging smile. "Wait just a moment. I think Gabriel has your papers."

As soon as they were alone, Luis Páez sneered: "Ever seen such an ass? 'Ah, you young fellows of today are insatiable. Your father . . .' What a damned fool!"

"God, how he went on and on! If I were he, I'd start writing my memoirs," Cortézar added.

" 'I'll see what I can do, I'll see what can be done. . . .' I'd like to show him a thing or two."

"Shut up! Not so loud. He might hear you."

"Let him hear me! The hell with him."

Luis took a cigarette out of his pocket and lit up.

"Guys like that make me sick."

"Shut up!" said Cortézar.

Luis picked up an ashtray from the table and put it into his pocket.

"What are you doing?"

"I'm taking it. They're getting rather scarce around home."

"Don't be a fool. He'll notice it."

"So what? He's not going to frisk us on the way out."

Luis was ashamed of the act he had just had to put on, and this gesture might help to redeem him.

"You're crazy," said Cortézar.

Cortézar contemplated in amazement the cool audacity of his friend. Luis Páez paid no attention to him. He leaned back in his chair with a cigarette between his lips and took a look around him. The light filtering through the curtains was cloudy, like lemonade. On a table lay an open copy of a society magazine. He turned the pages at random: "In his manorial residence on Serrano Street, the Marquess of Leriga received outstanding members of Madrid society. Photographs: A corner of the drawing-room. Observe the

Louis XV console. Another detail: Flemish tapestry embroidered in gold." He thrust out his lower lip. And then the voice of his friend interrupted Luis's brooding.

"We still don't have the thousand pesetas. Until we have them in our pocket, we can't do a thing."

"Don't worry. We'll have them," Luis answered.

"I'd like to know how we're going to get it."

"We got the driver's license, didn't we? You didn't see how we'd get that, either."

"Money's different. And we're not going to find anybody who'll lend it to us."

"I tell you, *we'll get it*. Before the week's up, we'll have rented the car."

"Unless, of course, you're the one who is going to make it his business to get it. . . ."

"And who said I wouldn't?"

Luis yawned and turned toward the window. Outside, the air had condensed, and the light was becoming more and more pale. An oppressive silence paralyzed the trees and plants. Motionless, like a photographic plate, the street offered the absurdity of people walking. He let the curtain fall back.

"Say," said Cortézar, "what if the old guy should run into your old man?"

Luis Páez reassured him. "Once I have the license . . ."

He stopped suddenly, and the smile of a few moments before flashed across his face. Don Jerónimo had come back with the card in his hand. Before sitting down, Don Jerónimo turned the chair to an angle of thirty-degrees. "As you see, everything has a remedy. If one really makes up his mind to something, sooner or later he gets it." He smiled. "My friend, it's all taken care of. We've filled in the form, and your father can sign it as soon as he gets back."

The boy smiled at him with disarming humility.

"Thank you so much."

While the man stamped his signature on the license, the two boys exchanged a look of triumph.

"Nothing like helping out young people when they show they want to get ahead."

Blah, blah, blah! Wrinkles, dimples, folds, bulges, fat, fat, fat. The man talked on with a new burst of enthusiasm. Trapped in the ring of his glasses, his pupils seemed like blue marbles in the milky cornea. In a friendly voice he asked Luis Páez if he would be taking "Dad" out in the car. "Whores," thought Luis Páez, "I'll pile a whole bunch of whores into it." He squeezed the soft, spongy hand and left the office promising to return soon with his father.

Several days before, the battle of nerves he had been waging at home had reached an intolerable intensity. The water was always left running in the bathroom, the upholstery of the living-room was burned, the rug covered with butts. He still remembered what had happened last Christmas: the tree that his mother, Doña Cecilia, had bought, the lights, the ornaments, and the angel hair. She had put the presents on the table: one at each place, where they usually sat; and each with a card, on which she had written: *Papa, Mama, Luis.* . . . She had even turned off the ceiling light to make the room more cozy. And his father, Don Sidonio, who had walked in and given him a hug, was wearing a little paper hat fastened under his chin with a rubber band; he opened the champagne, talked his head off, and wanted to show in every way possible that he had forgotten about his rage of the night before. He had really believed that Luis had enrolled that fall in engineering school. The discovery of Luis's deceit had been pretty tough on him; it was understandable. Maybe he was just a bit old-fashioned. "Yes, that must be it," he would say in that bitter voice of his that he always used in his daily subterfuge, which Doña Cecilia knew so well: "In my day it would have been considered a terrible thing to lie to our parents. When I think of your poor grandfather, I shudder. He would have died of shame if I had done a thing like that to him. Yes, I'm getting old, I guess." And he had looked at Luis in the hope that he would retract or compromise and the situation could be saved. "No," thought Luis, "no, no, and no." A fierce pride kept him from it. But on this particular Christmas everything had been forgotten: Don Sidonio had welcomed the prodigal son with champagne. He wore a paper hat on his head and played with the children. Such a palaver! Luis could still hear his voice: "Open your package, Gloria." "What did you get, children?" And their shouting: "Oh, thank you, Daddy, thank you, Daddy." The happy family. Playing at being happily married. And Luis? Wasn't he going to open his present, to please his poor mother? No. And if his father ordered him to? He couldn't care less. To hell with it all. With everybody. He was going out. Going where? He didn't know. He was going out to supper. Some friends were waiting for him. Friends? Hoodlums, that's what they were: thieves, anarchists, a bunch of bums. Under his little paper hat, Don Sidonio was choking. Golden bubbles of champagne rose to the top of the glass; slices of fruits, peelings, crescents, floated aimlessly in the punch bowl. Luis's brothers and sisters looked at him wide-eyed, their mouths open. Doña Cecilia begged them to be quiet, reminding them that it was Christmas.

The ringing of the doorbell interrupted them; down the hall someone they did not know walked noisily, as though shuffling along a sidewalk covered with dry leaves, and approached the dining-room. *Never in my life have I felt so sharp a pain as in that moment. Is it possible that a*

whole lifetime of labor can end up in something like this?
Is it possible, my God, is it possible? And Tánger had burst
into the room, drunk, playing with a yoyo and blowing a
little trumpet, boldly defying the norms of decorum and
decency: "My case transcends middle-class morality."
Tánger went through that whole infinite gamut of nuances
he knew—and knows—how to give to his expression, when
he dresses up like a witch or a pansy, and dedicates himself to regaling the audience with reliquaries of flowers,
faded souvenirs extracted from between the pages of old
missals, placed there by hundred-year-old grandmothers
who had died in odor of sanctity, aroma of the past which
disintegrated between his fingers. And he, Luis, was fascinated by what was going to happen, by what was at that
very moment already happening, thanks to the devil at his
side who was helping him to win the round.

"My dear sir, *dear*, yes, because dear is that son of yours
whom I admire so much, and to whom I am bound by so
many deep-seated ties. I hope you will find it possible to
pardon my presence at such an intimate family reunion,
especially taking into consideration my present state,
which, not to employ an injurious term that might offend
the ladies present, I shall call lamentable." And with his
twisted face, and his bright eyes dancing, and hiccough-
ing in his drunkenness, he had tossed the yoyo in front
of their very noses: "Come on, you bum, the gorillas are
waiting outside for us."

And Luis had felt himself, for the last time, split in two—
caught between the past that clung to his mother's tearless
eyes and to the farce of the happy home, and the dum-
founded being that he was, gazing at the fantastic face of
Uribe with his clowning gestures and waxen lips. Without
quite knowing how, Luis had found himself out in the street.
Yes, they could all go to hell. His father did not want to

understand him; he deluded himself. The hell with all of
them; the old man, the kids, the mother. And Uribe, clinging to his arm, surprised by his serious mien, said: "I put
my foot in it, eh kid? Guess I said some things I shouldn't
have said. You'll forgive me, won't you? Oh, say that you
will! I'll just die of grief if you won't."

How fresh it all was in his memory, and yet, how remote!
He had come through the test strengthened, almost invul-
nerable. "Siegfried's bath," he joked. From that day on he
began to see everything in a different light: "The world is
an exchange of favors." One had to beware of affection, for
beneath the surface there's always something murky.

Don Sidonio tried to tell him about the struggles he had
had to pay for his own education: "Ask your mother." And
Doña Cecilia, caught between the two, always in her role
of accomplice, talked on monotonously of fleeting inter-
views, long sleepless nights, hours stolen from sleep, little
bricks of the future home, of the prosperity that he was
enjoying. Just as the little swallows build their nests with
the bits of materials they carry in their bills, so had this
man, his father, put up the walls of their home, formed the
protective shell that safeguarded their innocent sleep, the
nutritious bread that sustained their bodies, and the warp
and woof of the cloth that covered them in winter. That
was all. Doubtless Luis was abnormal if he considered this
to be of little account. He thought: "My father is a piece
of soulless flesh." Only Agustín Mendoza was right: "To be
a man . . ." There were so few men. "It is difficult to
show something new. We find everything done for us. We
are never really ourselves." Yes, the water was left running;
the chairs were burned; the discord at home went on. His
parents were always silent, and although he did not hear
them when they went to bed, he knew that Don Sidonio
was conspiring: "What does he do when he goes out? What

does he do? Where does he get the money?" Whispering
voices, fragments of words, dead echoes, drowned immediately afterwards in quantities of shame, in a sea of resignation, in the absolute certainty that in the end they could
change nothing.

Cortézar had just taken his arm, and his touch made
Luis Páez jump slightly.

"Sorry," he said, "what was that you were saying? I was
thinking about something else and wasn't listening."

They went on walking, in silence, in the direction of
the garage.

* * *

Raúl Rivera stopped in the doorway for a moment; with
his hat thrown back, his jacket unbuttoned, and his cigarette dangling from his lips, he had the loose look of a
chulo. And, like a *chulo*, he held his arms akimbo. His shirt
was stained with wine. His tie was hanging halfway out of
his pocket, just where he had stuffed it when he was arguing with the women. He had walked all the way from the
bar, and tiny beads of sweat speckled his forehead.

On the way back his thoughts had turned gloomy, cruel.
The cowards! He had beat them up one after the other, and
sent them all running; and now, he didn't even remember
how many of them there had been. He saw only the picture of the tallest one, holding his nose with his handkerchief to stop the flow of blood. The blonde woman,
offended at his insults, was crying. The proprietor was
picking up the chairs. Everybody looked at him with accusing eyes. Once again he had played "Raúl"—the drunken
binge, the fight, the quarrel with the women—and all on
account of that fairy, Tánger. "Yes: fairy; because that's
what he is. I swear to God he is. A guy lifts a hand to help
him out and that's the thanks he gets for it." He had it

coming to him. Maybe now he'd learn to keep his nose out of other people's business.

His hands, accustomed to the semi-darkness of the bedroom, found the catch without difficulty. He opened the window. The light put the outlines of the different objects into precise relief and brought back to him the faithful image of that room whose details he knew by heart. Everything was there in forced motionlessness, like a family group in front of a camera: the mirrored wardrobe where he could see in the glass Planas's bed, empty, and Raúl, himself, the black sheep of the family who wasted Papa's money and wasn't passing a single course, going to bed drunk again after a night of debauchery. Oh, enough of all this!

He began to undress, exasperated. His movements, brusque and tense, came from an insufferable physical tension. His eyes, standing out like two light spots in a photographic negative, gave to his face, so full of life and fury, a wild, impenetrable brutishness.

The sight of his own naked body reawakened his fighting blood. His muscles strained and pulled. His fists clenched instinctively. He looked around hoping to find somebody he could take his anger out on, but Planas was nowhere to be seen.

In Las Palmas when he came home at dawn to the *pension* where he slept, the faithful concierge would smile at him sweetly: "So early, and up already? Well, the early bird catches the worm." Raúl had always thought of her as the epitome of malice, but she was easier to take than the patient silence of his roommate, whom he would wake as he rolled in half drunk. "If he'd only shout or something—" At least that's what Raúl did those mornings that Planas awakened him. It wouldn't have hurt Planas any to do the same. But Planas kept quiet. And to Raúl's mind came a whole world of sighing and resigned people for whom each trial meant another line in their faded face, who prayed in silence for the salvation of the sinners, and who passed through life like the beneficent beings to whom one pays no attention.

The worst of it—yes, the worst of it—was that his repulsion made him suffer. Accustomed as he was to mutual respect, the cold spectacle of Planas's disdain confused him. Once about a month ago, after a long series of bowing and scraping, like a pet cat before accepting a morsel, he asked Planas if he had anything against him. Against him? Why, no; nothing at all. Or rather, yes; many things. For example? Well . . . No, it wasn't worth trying to explain; he wouldn't understand. And if he made an effort to understand? No, not even then. And if he begged him? Not then, either. Oh, stop it! What I want is that you let me alone. If only Planas would return his insults, or give him some motive to justify his aversion. Raúl took him by the lapels one day: "Insult me! Be a man! Show me at least that you've got some red blood in your veins."

No, Planas never answered back. Then Raúl saw in Planas his father, as he had been ten years before, but with the older-looking face of his last visit home. "Well-brought-up children do not talk back at table." Across from him his uncle was explaining that the density of the population of Belgium was greater than that of Spain. "Pay attention, Raúl." That's what Planas always said to him, too. He looked at the empty bed and tried to picture him there. Sometimes, for no reason at all, he would make scathing remarks just to provoke Planas. He would say, for example, that Planas did not bathe often enough; he smelled bad; his odor sickened him. "You ought to use talcum powder." Planas listened to him, crushed. He nodded his head and the next day hastened to correct the defect. "I hope you no longer have cause for complaint," he said. And he searched Raúl's eyes for approval.

It was enough to drive a man crazy. It seemed as though Planas annoyed him deliberately. The whole day he would sit there in the room, studying, with the gentle look of a domesticated animal. His methodical behavior infuriated Raúl. Every one of his acts, judged independently by Raúl, deserved a special reprimand. For example, when Planas went to bed, he closed his eyes immediately and crossed his hands over his chest. One day when Raúl was feeling hungover and disgusted with himself, the sight of Planas in bed was just too much for him, and he blew his top.

"You don't sleep," he shouted at him, "you merely comply with your obligation to sleep."

Planas sat up in bed, his eyes wide with surprise; but, as usual, he made no comment. "He wants to rob me of my very reason for being," thought Raúl. "He'll end up by driving me out. Now, with his gaze fixed on the wrinkled sheets, he felt the fury mounting inside his head. Oh, what he wouldn't give to shake up that flabby body. Imagining it, he felt the muscles in his arms grow taut, felt himself turning hard as a rock.

Last night before going to Agustín Mendoza's studio, he had sent a distressful telegram to his family: NOBODY CAN LIVE ON AIR. Signed: YOUR VÍA CRUCIS. And now it seemed to him that the telegram wouldn't help matters either. He had no future. He wasn't studying. The assistant in anatomy had flunked him for the sixth time. The last time he had gone out of the classroom with the firm resolve to get down to work from that day on. Tánger was waiting for him outside, and when he heard that Raúl had failed, he had offered to buy him a few drinks. That was over three months ago and since then Raúl hadn't read a page. "If

I could only get a hold of some money." In Arucas his life
had been organized; his future was a readymade suit to
which he had only to adapt himself; with his medical
degree he would live in his parents' home and marry any
one of the well-fixed girls of the town. He was sure of
being happy, if by happiness he meant, as his father did,
peace and quiet and no worry about the future. "It's a
matter of organizing life, like a long-term insurance policy."
In school he had shown a taste for work and the will to
study. His perseverance functioned without the slightest
ruffle. When he worked, he worked for a precise and practical purpose. He had become used to the idea of being a
good, honest bourgeois, and the idea did not bother him in
the least; on the contrary, he got a secret pleasure out of
accepting it.

The years in Madrid had passed very quickly. At times
he felt a certain sense of detachment from the peaceful existence of the Canaries, but he attributed this indifference
to distance and the amount of time that he had spent away
from the islands. "I have only to go back," Raúl thought,
"and everything will be as it always was. My real life has
its roots there." His father wrote him long letters filled with
affectionate phrases, giving him the latest news of the
town, plus numerous commentaries; and he would answer
with pious lies, speaking of his studies and his work in the
laboratory.

The year before, during the summer vacation, Raúl
finally decided to pack his bags. Without letting his family
know, he took the boat for home. But even during the
crossing, a part of him refused to admit the reality of his
return. It was useless to try to tell himself: "I'll be a doctor
in Arucas: Waiting for me are my parents, my practice, and
the woman I am going to marry." He had the feeling that
someone else was saying all this. When he arrived at Las

Palmas, he gave the taxi-driver his grandfather's address. "The die is cast," he thought. He was going home: the taxi was taking him there; but not for a single moment did the idea occur to him that he was going to see his own family. He had the conviction that he would not find anybody there. The visit seemed to him a kind of rite: an expediency in order to live in peace with himself. Standing in front of his house, the bandage fell from his eyes. There was a light in the living-room, and the radio was on. He remained motionless in front of the iron fence, but he could not make up his mind to go in. The house gave him the impression of having shrunk, choked as it was between the other, newer buildings flanking it. He went up furtively to the window, like a burglar, and looked in. His father was standing there; at the window, protected by the darkness, he could observe him as he would have watched a stranger: thin, wrinkled, shorter than Raúl had remembered him— and it seemed as if, during his son's absence, his father had been replaced by a substitute. Raúl's grandfather was reading the newspaper in his armchair, and his sister was leafing through some old photographs. *They've changed. The city, the atmosphere, the family are strangers to me. I cannot go back into that house: it is not mine.* And through the windowpane fragments of conversation and familiar voices reached his ears. He would have remained there indefinitely, if the taxi-driver had not shouted to him from the gate: "Make up your mind, my friend, one way or the other. I can't wait all night." Of course. Naturally. He paid the fare and picked up his bags. His forehead was covered with perspiration, and his hands shook. The dining-room light obsessed him. The night fragrance of the wisteria produced in him a peculiar intoxication. With a great effort, he managed to ring the doorbell.

That was all over a year ago, and Raúl thought he could still smell the wisteria. But no; it was that insane perfume that Tánger had given him for his birthday. He had left the bottle open. With a brusque motion, he hid it in the drawer and locked it up.

He looked at his watch and saw that it was almost ten. An overpowering desire to sleep had taken hold of him. His eyes smarted. His temples pulsed achingly. He could not stop thinking about the telegram, Tánger Uribe, the fight, and the necessity of getting some money, no matter how.

The walls, grayish in the morning light, impinged upon him with the sharpness of their angles. It seemed as though a multitude of human beings, posted in the dark corners of the room, were stabbing him with their piercing eyes. He saw them dancing among the shadows of the pictures on the walls, leaping from chair to chair, tiny and distrustful.

Frightened, Raúl adjusted the window-shutters, took the box of sleeping pills, swallowed three of them, and closed his eyes. Drawn up in a ball, he buried his head under the sheets and lay motionless, like a puppet, fallen among the silent sticks of furniture that watched him in silence.

*   *   *

Although she arrived two minutes before the hour agreed upon, Enrique Suárez was waiting for her on the corner. As soon as he caught sight of her, he went quickly over to meet her. They shook hands.

There was hardly anybody in the bar at that hour. Almost all the tables were empty. They could, therefore, talk comfortably, without anyone bothering them. Before exchanging a word, Enrique offered her his pack of cigarettes. Cloria took one, and the boy lighted a match.

"Thanks."

The waiter had come over to them: a ridiculous old man, half bald, who spoke in a monotone.

"There are crabs, clams, oysters, grilled shrimp, tripe, fried birds. . . ."

Enrique looked at her inquiringly.

"I'll have some clams," said Gloria.

"Good. Make it two orders. With lemon."

They kept looking at the waiter until he finally left them. Then Gloria raised her head.

"Well?"

Enrique Suárez hesitated a few moments.

"Nothing new yet," he said.

As if moved by some irrepressible force, the girl's hands played with the toothpicks: she broke them into bits.

"Have you located him?"

"No. He must still be incommunicado."

"And Gerardo?"

"I went to see him this morning. But the matter is much more serious than we thought at first. He can't do anything, either."

Gloria swallowed hard: her face expressed an unconquerable anguish. Her eyes shining, she begged Enrique to help her.

"Have they found out about it yet at his *residencia?*"

"We invented an excuse," said Enrique Suárez.

They stopped talking while the waiter served the clams. Gloria picked up a piece of lemon and squeezed it over the shells.

"Can't something be done?"

Enrique stopped her with a gesture: "Look here: Gerardo doesn't think so. If you've read the morning papers you know how they're handling holdup cases now. They're putting on the pressure, and anybody caught within these next few weeks will stay locked-up for some time. We don't know yet what measures they'll take: they may give them a public trial, and then—"

"But he hasn't done anything," stammered the girl.

"I know it," replied Enrique, "but he's going to have to prove it. And they may not believe him."

Gloria could hardly believe her ears. "Is it that serious?"

Enrique was picking up toothpicks now, too, and breaking them nervously in his fingers.

"You must understand me. I'm not saying that the case is so serious. You know how those things go. Most likely they'll let him go right away, but it's just possible that they'll make him stand trial, which would be quite disagreeable."

The girl listened to him in consternation. "If we only knew who was going to handle the case. Maybe my father, through some friend—"

"Your father? And how would you manage to convince him?"

Gloria bit her lips. "Very simple. By telling him the whole story."

"The whole story? You're mad!"

"I'd threaten him with a public scandal, for example. You don't know him. Before he'd let me tell the world what happened he'd be perfectly capable of hanging himself."

"What if he paid no attention to you?"

The girl gulped again. "I'd carry out the threat. I'd tell everybody that I love Jaime and that two weeks ago I gave myself to him."

The palm of her hand was filled with the remains of the toothpicks, and she threw them on the floor.

"Listen, Gloria. Whatever happens, you must face things calmly. You know perfectly well that what you say is impossible. Jaime would be the first one to stop you, if he knew. You'd only make him angry, and you'd gain nothing."

Absorbed in thought, Gloria looked down at her white, delicate hands, and sat twisting them as though they were small independent creatures with lives of their own. "I love him," she murmured.

Enrique looked away from her for a moment. "I know, Gloria. I'm a friend of his, too, and I know how these things can hurt. Poor Jaime was getting along badly enough with his family before this thing happened. It's too much having this land on him as well. If they find out about it, they'll make him go back to the Canaries."

"Do you really think so?" Gloria had paled.

"I know them. They'll stop sending him money so that he'll have to go home if he doesn't want to starve to death."

Everything came tumbling down over her ears. It seemed absurd to her that she should be here doing nothing, while everything conspired to keep her from Jaime. Her nervous fingers kept playing with the toothpicks.

"We've got to do something," she murmured.

Enrique ate his clams in silence. "Gerardo mentioned something about a bond," he began. He saw that Gloria raised her eyes, hopefully, and he added: "That's the ordinary procedure in such cases. You pay, and everything is taken care of." He smiled sadly. "But for us the system might as well not exist. We couldn't possibly pay."

"How much does it amount to?"

Enrique Suárez made a vague gesture. "I don't know. A thousand, fifteen hundred, perhaps."

"What about you? Do you have anything?"

The boy shook his head. "No. I'm not getting along so well with my family, either; they never send me a cent any more."

"And the boys at the *residencia?*"

"I asked around this morning; they don't have a penny."

No. There was no way of saving him: they'd keep him in jail a couple of months, and when he got out he'd go with his family to the ends of the earth somewhere. While she was thinking this, she felt a wave of rebellion surge in her throat. Impulsively, she took Enrique's hand.

"I . . . I'll get whatever is needed," she said.

The boy arched his eyebrows in surprise. "You?"

Gloria's decision had sprung from her lips before she had even formulated it. Now she was surprised at the assurance with which she had spoken.

"Yes. One way or another . . . I'll get it."

Enrique had his doubts. "Do you intend to ask your father for it?"

She shook her head. "No, he wouldn't give it to me, but that doesn't make any difference. I'll get the money together somehow—tonight if necessary. How big a hurry is there?"

"I don't know. The sooner we have it— In any case, I'll ask Gerardo. By that time he'll have found out about the details of getting the bond, and this afternoon . . ."

Gloria buried her sharp nails into the palms of her hands: there were no more toothpicks left.

"All right. If you see him, tell him that we'll have the money tomorrow morning."

She had stood up, propelled by some strange urgency, and her eyes sparkled. Enrique Suárez got up, too.

"And how are you going about getting the money?"

Gloria herself had no idea as yet. "I don't know. But don't worry. Within a few hours I'll have it in my hands."

Enrique looked at her doubtfully. "I hope you're not going to do anything foolish. Jaime would be the first to object, you know."

"Bah! He'll never know. I'll never tell him that I was the one who got the money."

Enrique hesitated. "All right. You're old enough to know what you're doing."

The waiter came with the check, and Enrique paid him hastily, telling him to keep the change. The waiter bowed, and they left.

Outside a harsh light devoured the façades of the buildings, and the wind swept the clouds over the rooftops. For a few moments they stood on the corner without speaking.

"When will you be talking to Gerardo?" she asked.

"This afternoon."

"Fine! I'll telephone your house at five o'clock. I'll probably have the money by then. And you do everything you can to get in touch with him." She hesitated a few seconds. "But remember one thing: my name is not to be mixed up in this business. Jaime must not know anything about the money. I know that if he found out he'd never forgive me."

"Don't worry."

They shook hands. Then as Enrique put his hand on her shoulder affectionately, the girl smiled at him sadly. Her eyes—the pupils had become as small as pinheads—avoided him.

"Until five, then," he said.

They separated. Gloria went up Claudio Coello Street; Enrique Suárez, toward the Castellana.

*   *   *

Bang! Bang! "We are shadows, relics of the past, ghosts terrorized by the scorn of the world, and the fragile memory of our splendid past. Dethroned archangels, perpetually sterile, our destiny is to hate the species. We trans-

form ourselves like Proteus. We are Icaruses." Bang! Bang!
"We sowed flowers of geometric petals and astral semi-
circles. . . ." Once again. Oh, it was unbearable. Stop!
Enough! Enough! He covered his ears with his hands.
"Come on, Tánger, don't pretend to be asleep. I know
perfectly well that you're still awake." Please. He got up
and looked around the room, his eyes still heavy with
sleep. He hadn't been in bed a half-hour, and his friends
were already bothering him. "All right, all right! I'm coming." He opened the door and looked up at Cortézar irri-
tably.

"Okay, would you mind telling me what you want? This
is a fine time to be coming around waking a guy up."

Without saying a word, Cortézar put his hand under
Tánger's chin and drew his eyes toward the window. He
parted the curtains. Uribe, still wearing his velvet jacket
with the double row of mother-of-pearl buttons and the
fur collar turned up around his ears, had the pale, somno-
lent look of one who hasn't slept a wink all night.

"One o'clock! You call that early?"

It was the first time that Cortézar had gone to Uribe's
room since they had met, and his eyes were as wide with
surprise as all the others' had been on first seeing the place.
Although the room was big, there was scarcely a square
foot of unused space. The walls, despite the twelve-foot
ceiling, were literally covered with pictures, newspaper-
clippings, shawls, bullfight posters, lanterns, and masks.
The ceiling was of carved wood, and by means of cleverly
concealed hooks a number of caravels and ships plowed
through the air like a real flotilla, miraculously maintaining
itself aloft. On the bed a leopard skin spread its head and
paws with a protective air, and the various endtables and
stands were covered with a strange assortment of objects
that seemed to have been strewn like seeds and in growing

had acquired monstrous proportions: glass balls, pieces of lacquer, stuffed birds, and a music box with the golden emblem of liberty on it.

The ritual of having people in was one of Tánger Uribe's favorite pastimes. He would show people the paper accordions that covered the lightbulbs; the masks lit up, too, for he had placed little bulbs wrapped in red silk behind their empty eyes. And if a visitor asked, not without a touch of irony, whether he had anything else to show, Uribe would open one by one the little drawers of the *vargueño* where he kept hidden a whole world of sorcerer's materials: talismans; horseshoes; all of the astral stones—topaz, garnet, zircon, lapis lazuli, ruby, sapphire, coral, and amber—and in a variety of colored envelopes the ingredients for San Cipriano's recipe, astrological tables, as well as the necessary paraphernalia for casting a spell on a hen, or making the devil appear in a scarlet frock coat trimmed with galloons, a yellow vest, and checked pants. But Cortézar's arrival that morning had put Uribe in a bad mood, and he had no desire to show his treasures to anybody. He rubbed his eyes and with raised eyebrows stared at his friend.

On returning home, Uribe had found a note from his landlady on the bed. "Srta. Ana would like to see you this afternoon. Says to call her at 67218." All right. So he must do it. But shouldn't he let Agustín know first? Maybe he was not aware of the step the girl had taken; it would be better to avoid complications.

He caressed the soft fur of his lapels with the palm of his hand, meditatively. "Bah!" he said to himself, "To hell with her. I don't give a damn." He couldn't go to see her. He was too drunk. He looked at Cortézar, who at that moment was holding in his hands a glass ball: with its colored stripes, transparent, it created the illusion that the light was originating from within itself. Cortézar had come to talk. Who knows what he had to say? An unreasonable fear made Tánger take the lead.

"I stole this ball in Barcelona one day in a very curious way. I was coming back from a day in the country and was going toward my home when I noticed some colored balls in a store window. Although I didn't have any money, I went in without hesitation. The proprietress, a woman from Ampurdán, had a nervous tic: every few seconds she would close her eyes. I was sitting across from her with my knapsack open between my legs, in such a way that I blocked her view of the table where she kept the balls; each time the woman closed her eyes, I removed a ball."

With his shoulders hunched up and his arms pasted to his sides, he held between his delicate fingers a dying cigarette. Again the impression that Cortézar had come to tell him something took hold of him: a piece of news, some wild escapade of one of the leper sessions, maybe. Perhaps Cortézar had not gone himself and just wanted to find out what had happened. "I hope that's it," he thought. "I hope, I hope, I hope!" He stopped to take a breath, or really to stall for time to make up another story. The incidents of the early morning had humiliated him, and now he felt an irresistible need to have his revenge somehow on fate.

"When I stole for the first time," Uribe said, "I was sixteen years old, and I was in love with a beautiful girl. From my little Arab friends I had learned the essentials of being a good pickpocket. The girl wanted a present and I didn't have any money. One day my mother presented me to the wife of the American consul: an affectionate, blonde woman with exquisite manners. In those days I was an innocent little boy, with the face of a little clay saint. I let her embrace me. A few seconds later, when she withdrew, I had in my possession her famous diamond necklace."

His white hand fished into Cortézar's cigarette case and extracted a flattened cigarette, which he placed between his lips.

"But the story doesn't end there: My mother had seen me. I was trembling. I was afraid of her punishment and was already planning to run away. 'When the consul's wife leaves,' I thought, 'she'll kill me.' I let her take me to the door and bowed my head in resignation: a Christian martyr in front of a lion couldn't have suffered as much. I heard her return, her footsteps coming closer and closer. I closed my eyes. And you can imagine my surprise when I realized my mother was embracing me. 'My son,' she said, 'you're cleverer than I had ever imagined. I would never have been able to do it alone.' Not paying any attention to my tears, she put the necklace around her neck. All she said was: 'We'll have to change the design a little. What a pity!' "

He stopped, exhausted. Half an hour before, in the hall, he had been assailed by two creditors. Following his usual practice, he had decided to ignore them. "I don't know who you are or what you are talking about." With great affectation he had taken a pair of gold scissors from his pocket and started to pare a fingernail. "Creatures like me, we have come into the world for the sole purpose of sparkling. Like the butterflies and the centaurs. In short, you annoy me." But the creditors hadn't paid any attention to him and had raised a great fuss with Doña Asunción. *Poor but honest Doña Asunción, whose life has been and is a perpetual Vía Crucis.* Remembering the scene, he put his hand to his head.

"Oh, it's all so horrible."

He discovered that Cortézar was looking at him, and he realized that he wasn't alone. Of course. How foolish! He had opened the door himself for Cortézar less than ten minutes ago. He had tried to go to sleep: he was sleepy; he needed to rest. A man in America had gone for nine years without sleeping. That man . . .

"I can see you haven't closed your eyes all night," said Cortézar. "May I ask what you all have been up to?"

Uribe's face lit up. So that was all.

"Some whores on Manuel Becerra Street . . ."

He forced a smile, as if he were going to tell something very funny, but he stopped himself. "Oh, well! That's hardly any of your business."

Cortézar looked at him questioningly.

"I decided to come here because I thought Raúl Rivera would be with you. We had agreed that the first thing this morning I would call for him at his house to go with Luis Páez to get the license. But he hadn't come in yet. Maybe he's home by this time."

"Perhaps," said Uribe.

"Where did you leave him?"

"I don't know. Honestly. If I knew, I'd tell you, but I've forgotten."

"Did you do a lot of drinking?"

"I guess so. As a matter of fact, I . . ."

"And your cousin?"

"Cousin?"

"David."

"Oh, David. I don't know. I lost track of him shortly after midnight."

Whenever anybody spoke of David, Uribe forgot that David was his cousin. He should be more on his guard; they'd take him for a fool. *David is a boy of very refined sensibilities.* "His grandmother and my mother. Or was it his grandmother and my grandmother? It's so mixed up."

Cortézar picked up a pistol that was on the table. "Yours? I suppose it's not loaded."

He held it rather gingerly. The barrel was short and the butt was inlaid with mother-of-pearl: little roseate circles painted in enamel.

"It's so romantic," Uribe explained. "Instead of cartridges, it shoots artificial flowers, photographs of Naples and Vesuvius, and pairs of lovers."

Once again he felt his conscience weighted with the memory of his drunkenness and with it the need to tell lies; two hours earlier in a bar on Manuel Becerra Street he had run out on the three whores. The place where he had taken them had two exits, and he had escaped by the back one. "By this time they're probably beginning to miss me." In a frameless mirror—there were dozens of them in his room—he saw himself and knew that he was drunk. He was aware of his audience. He was on stage. Cortézar, with a bored air, lit a cigarette.

"Páez got the license," he said. "Now the only thing he needs is the money to rent the car."

"Car?" Again Uribe was confused. A moment ago there had budded forth in his brain a sheaf of memories. Alcohol. A fight. Raúl's insults. He looked at his watch. One-fifteen. It was late; he must take a walk before lunch.

He got ready to go out. On the table the landlady's note was demanding his attention. He looked away from it. No. He ought to answer. He took out his fountain pen: "If Srta. Ana calls, tell her that I'm dead." He took a pin and stuck the note on the door.

The madness again. He repeated it aloud: "Dead."

He took a package of cigarettes and slipped it into his pocket with extreme care. Cortézar was waiting for him at the door.

"All right. Let's go."

❋   ❋   ❋

"You mean: kill him all by yourself?"

Agustín Mendoza, with his knees braced against the edge of the table, tilted his chair back. "It strikes me as rather touching. How should I say . . . romantic." He stopped a moment, and then added in a mocking tone: "But it won't do."

Ana was seated across from him on the other side of the table, her look lost in the contortions of the flames. The fuses had just blown out, leaving the whole landing dark, and Agustín had lighted a candle.

"You think that you'd be prepared to do it alone, right?" Agustín said, his head cocked to one side, giving her a quick glance.

"Yes."

"And you'd even let yourself get arrested, if necessary, or you'd commit suicide, perhaps."

When Agustín spoke like that, Ana didn't know where he was leading her. She began to regret having spoken. *Now it was too late.*

"That hasn't anything to do with it."

"Yes, it has."

Agustín's hand reached out hesitatingly toward the canary cage that Lola had recently given him. It was a small cage made of different colored wires, and when the door was opened the bird hesitated a few seconds before taking flight.

"They'd arrest you in no time at all."

"Impossible. I have it all thought out."

Agustín cut her off with a movement of his head. "No. You haven't anything thought out. And if you try to pull it off the way you would have it, I wouldn't give two cents for your hide."

He stopped just as he was going to form another

sentence and watched the bird attentively: motionless, hunched up on one of the bars, he was a sad helpless sight, like a stuffed bird, or a withered flower.

"I don't understand," said Ana.

"To put it briefly, your plan is childish."

"Childish?"

"Yes. Any amateur with a grain of intelligence would have thought of the same thing: lack of motive. In your effort to do something different, all you've succeeded in doing is to call attention to yourself."

We've got to cool off that head a little, he thought. The girl has ideas, but she's got to put them in order. Curiously, he was thirsty again. That sweet liquor of Uribe's was devilish.

"Listen to me. We'd better talk calmly. You come here with a bona-fide offer, and I discuss it with you. I'll name you a price, if you wish. The whole business, the way you put it, doesn't interest me or anybody else. Whatever you may have against the gentleman is something that concerns you alone, and I have nothing to do with . . ."

He lit his pipe unhurriedly and enjoyed it a while before continuing.

"Who'd care about helping you if there was nothing to gain? Look, for your own sake, the motive has to be disguised. The theft, for example. You say that this woman has spoken to you about the safe. Splendid! There's the element that can change the whole aspect of the case. In order to exact your own virtues from others, you have to pay them a good price."

Ana watched him, perplexed. "No. I don't see what advantage you can gain from it, unless you'd do it for the money. And in that case . . ."

"And in that case?" said Agustín.

The girl bit her lip. "Nothing. I didn't say anything."

Agustín Mendoza toyed with his pipe.

"Listen here, it's a question of covering up your tracks. Give them a false scent. If you do it alone, you'll find yourself up a blind alley. You know the concierge. They would immediately suspect subversive activity. Within two weeks, at most, they'd catch up with you. And I have no desire to be a martyr, I assure you. I'm interested in the case for several reasons, but I don't want to get skinned in such a stupid manner. Besides, the money—"

He made a gesture with his hand. Over the dark bottle of champagne the candle projected a hesitating light. Against the walls the shadows, like terrified specters, recoiled covering their faces with their hands.

"If they arrest you, you'll have gained nothing but a nice little trip to Africa—or rather a longish one. And that's exactly what will happen unless you take my advice."

The embellished panorama of the room, with its bottle, its candle, and Agustín Mendoza in the background, projected itself in the dark circles of her eyes, as on the inverse lens of a spyglass.

"I've thought it out very carefully," said Ana. "The apartment is not watched, and once in the street—"

"You're wrong there." Years ago he had taken part in a burglary with some of his pals, and he had put forth then the same theories he was repeating now. "And I'll tell you why in just a few words. You've spoken of the maid, but if you don't compromise her in some definite way, nobody will guarantee that she'll keep quiet. You've already left a witness who at any given moment can turn against you. If you intend to kill him all by yourself, you don't need me. I don't need to know anything, even though I am one of the group."

The lights had just come on again, and in one second the room was restored to its precise outlines. The bird,

THE YOUNG ASSASSINS   40

motionless and surprised, was watching them. Agustín blew out the candle in one puff and continued talking: "You never know what the other guy is thinking and what he could say behind your back. To trust is to be blind-folded. How do you know, for example, that I haven't a loose tongue and that I might not shoot my mouth off about it? So far you've left two loopholes. Unless, of course," he added with an arrogant look, "you've already talked to somebody else."

"No," said Ana, "I haven't said anything."

"Good! Two are enough."

"I'd deny it," said Ana. "If there's no proof . . ."

"Please! Don't be so naïve. You'd confess, like anybody else. You know what happened to those boys from the Canaries."

He said it just to humiliate her. Two hours ago, after she had tried in vain to get in touch with him through Uribe, Ana had presented herself at his studio, sure that she had planned something on a grand scale. In a few minutes Agustín Mendoza had reduced her exultation into confusion and shame.

"If my plan strikes you as so bad, tell me what you would do in my place."

She said this in a sharp tone, obviously annoyed, which wiped the smile off Agustín's face. A light fluttering of wings claimed his attention for a few seconds; the bird had just perched on the lampshade and was balancing there most precariously.

"In order to pull a job like that, you need several, not one. While one is doing the work, the others are covering up his tracks. And at this point another factor enters in. Any of us has a great advantage over you. We're not sus-pect. Nobody's going to be suspicious of the sons of wealthy bourgeois. Particularly in the case of theft."

Ana played nervously with the paintbrushes that lay scattered on top of the table.

"Will you talk to your comrades about it?"

"Yes, if you still want me to come in on it. And believe me: the worst thing is to beat about the bush. We have to be fast and efficient. The one who does the killing has to think only about hiding himself long enough to be able to get outside. On the corner a car will be waiting for him, ready to go, and ten minutes later it will leave him at the other end of Madrid. And if necessary, there will be more than ten people to swear that at that particular hour he was in Carabanchel, playing dice. It will be done like that, or not at all."

Ana lowered her head. "Then?"

"To begin with, let the others know."

"Who?"

"Rivera, Cortézar, David, Páez. . . ."

"Do you think that . . . ?"

"It's up to them. I think they've all been waiting for something like this. If they're not interested, they can always back out."

The girl hesitated. "Wouldn't it be better . . . if just the two of us?"

"No. Nothing half-baked. We take it seriously or not at all."

"All right, then. You should know. You know them better than I do."

In the silence that suddenly fell upon the room, Lola's canary let forth a note that sounded unreal, almost fantastic.

✻   ✻   ✻

Señor Páez's famous stamp collection had disappeared from his study. On his way home from the office that afternoon, Don Sidonio had acquired some very rare specimens of the United States of Venezuela from a collector on Marqués de Cubas Street. When he went to put them in his album, he was astonished to find that it had been stolen. The lock of the drawer showed signs of having been forced in a very amateurish manner, by a thief who, moreover, had not even bothered to cover up his tracks.

Don Sidonio, who was a man of habit, thought it was his duty to discuss the matter with his wife, before preliminary investigation. He feared strongly that the investigation would not take long, as he had for several months now been suspicious of his own son. The boy . . .

With the envelope of stamps in his hand, he went to the kitchen where his wife was preparing the dessert for dinner.

"Cecilia."

His wife, who at the moment was taking same cakes out of the oven, looked at him questioningly.

"My stamp collection has disappeared."

She seemed not to understand. "Your stamps?"

"Yes. Someone stole them this afternoon. They forced the lock on the drawer and took the whole album."

Doña Cecilia took time to wipe her hands. They were full of dough which she rubbed off on her apron.

"When did you first notice it?"

Sidonio hesitated a moment: "Just now. But come to think of it, I remember having heard something peculiar down there this afternoon while I was taking my siesta." He interrupted himself for a few seconds. "But maybe I was just dreaming."

Without saying anything more, he went with his wife to the study. Together they studied the forced lock, the splinters of wood. The thief had not touched some old documents and a portfolio of water colors. Two Havana cigars were also missing.

"Do you think that possibly . . . ?" said Cecilia.

Her husband paused again before answering. "I don't know."

Without exchanging a word, they had come to an agreement: their suspicions hurt each of them, but they did not see how they could avoid them.

"We might go and see," said Sidonio.

In the boy's room Doña Cecilia turned on the light, and they found the room was, as always, in complete disorder—the bed unmade and soiled, and the floor littered with cigarette butts and paper. Doña Cecilia looked around with an air of resignation.

"All day I wear myself out over this. But there's no way of keeping a pigsty clean."

Her husband, meanwhile, had bent over and picked up off the floor mat a cigar butt, which he held in the palm of his hand.

"What's that?" asked his wife.

"Looks like one of mine."

Her presence in her son's room while he was not there made Cecilia ashamed of her suspicions. Because of her natural indulgence, she attributed her son's mistakes to his lack of experience. "Young people are all alike," she said to herself. And she could not help having a certain admiration for him.

"Oh, all cigars are alike."

Don Sidonio put the butt to his nose and took a good sniff. "No; no, they're not. I know what I'm talking about."

But she would not give in for inwardly she accused herself of condemning her son on insufficient evidence, and she wished to absolve herself.

"The fact that it's the same brand doesn't prove any-thing," she said. "Maybe he buys your brand."

She immediately regretted having spoken. Officially, since last year when Luis had refused to go back to school, neither one of them had given him anything. Occasionally she would slip him five pesetas, which he pocketed without even saying thanks. According to his principles, others were obligated to him, and there was no reason to thank them for their services. But as a general rule, they never gave him anything, and yet Luis always had money at his disposal. He smoked expensive cigarettes, had a good many telephone calls, and led quite an active social life. So, although the question was often on the tips of their tongues, neither she nor her husband dared to say anything to him—and now her words struck her as being inept. The question had also sprung to her husband's mind.

"*Buy*, did you say? I'd like to know where he gets the money."

Cecilia did not answer: with her head lowered she pre-tended to be looking at the butts crushed into the rug.

Her husband walked from one end of the room to the other with the envelope of stamps in his hand. "That's just it. Where does he get the money? He doesn't work; he doesn't do anything. At home we don't give him a cent; and yet he doesn't deprive himself of a single thing. He goes to the movies, he smokes, buys a lot of cheap novels."

He pointed to the pile of books stacked on the table: socialistic plays, communistic and French novels.

"These books. They're to blame for everything. They distract him, fill his head with crazy ideas, waste his time." He turned to his wife and looked her straight in the eye. "Maybe you can tell me how he gets his money?"

His question was charged with reproach, and Doña Cecilia said nothing.

"No. You don't know either. But you prefer to ignore it." He corrected himself: "We prefer not to know the answer. We see him come back from the movies, go out with cheap women, buy books and cigarettes; and we don't say anything to him about it. As if it were the most natural thing in the world for a kid his age to carry a wallet filled with money. If the boy has money, we must find out where he gets it."

His wife looked at him in consternation. "But, Sidonio! You're talking as if you knew beyond a doubt that it was he who took the album. Until he comes home we cannot know for sure. Maybe it wasn't he."

Don Sidonio shrugged his shoulders. "Oh, no? Tell me who it could have been, then. The maid? Grandma? Gloria? Or one of the little kids?"

Cecilia bowed her head. "No; I don't say that. What I mean is that perhaps he didn't steal it. You know how Luis is. Maybe he wanted to look at the collection, and when he found the case locked . . ."

The explanation did not hold water. Before she finished, Cecilia realized that not even she herself believed it.

Don Sidonio noticed her confusion and decided to take advantage of it and return to his attack: "*Look* at it? Since when has he showed any interest in stamps? Since when has he been interested in anything at all worthwhile? We've spoiled him by indulging him, always making excuses for him: 'Oh, poor boy, he'll be angry. Don't say anything to him, he'll get sore.' Now you see how he thanks us: he listens to us the way he would listen to rain falling, and in the end he does exactly what he damn well pleases."

He felt annoyed with himself for his weakness of character, and every time he got angry, he would swear that he would be inflexible with the boy. But he knew only too well that Luis had lost respect for his authority, for when confronted, Luis did not spare him the truth of his intense scorn. The realization of his own impotence exasperated him.

His wife, as always, bore the brunt of these invectives which were supposedly directed at Luis, but which, in reality were addressed to himself. On Cecilia's face one could read resignation. The idea of suffering the reproaches that Luis really deserved made her feel closer to her son.

"The point is, we cannot go on like this. I'm tired of being tolerant, and I won't take it any more. He can do anything he wants—outside with his band of anarchists. It's all the same to me. But in my home—no. I'm tired of having these smart-alecks come in and out as if this were their own house, cluttering up the hall with cigarette butts, messing up the bathroom, and leaving the place like a barnyard. To think we've come to this! Outside with the anarchists! They have no business in my home. The government is already going far enough tolerating them on the streets."

He had been raising his voice little by little, and the two younger children, sensing that a quarrel or a fight was going on, were peering in at the door, wide-eyed. Doña Cecilia sent them on their way.

"Go along, children! This is no place for you to be. Go on, now, beat it!"

The little cropped heads disappeared into the thin air as if by magic, but from the hallway came their giggles and whispers. Doña Cecilia tried to calm her husband.

"Yes, of course. We simply must do something. But we must be careful. If we hurry, things will be even worse.

We run the risk in this case of alienating the boy completely and then having it turn out that we were mistaken. Look, leave it up to me. If the boy has taken the album, he'll tell mc so. Wc cannot make a scene without being absolutely certain what really happened."

The old, traditional reasons rose to her lips. Whenever Don Sidonio got angry with Luis, she was always the one to come between them: "Let's try to be calm. Just be calm." On his part, Don Sidonio played at letting himself be won over. He pretended to accept as valid the arguments that covered up his cowardice, and in unloading onto his wife's shoulders the responsibility of making decisions about the boy, he thought he was complying, at the same time, with his obligation toward his son and with the necessity of procrastinating with his wife.

He let Cecilia repeat the well-known arguments and contented himself with saying: "All right. Do as you please. If you want to go on ruining the child, go ahead. But don't say that I didn't warn you."

Then, without bothering to search the dresser drawers for his album, he left his son's room.

When Luis got home the family was already seated at the table: following his usual pattern of behavior, he entered without saying hello and took his place without a word.

As a general rule, he carried a book or newspaper with him, and between courses he would read, oblivious to the rest of the family's conversation. This time, although he was not reading, he managed to show a complete indifference to the talk going on around him. He merely ate each course as it was placed before him, never once raising his glance.

While the soup was being served, his father had asked: "Is it cold out?"

But Luis did not deign to answer. And Doña Cecilia had preferred not to press the point. She knew that if he had answered, he would have let go with some impertinent remark; and she was afraid that Sidonio would lose his temper. With the greatest tact possible, she tried to change the subject.

Luis did not mind lying if the lie was going to benefit him in some way. He often lied, and, moreover, he did not even take the trouble to cover it up. He couldn't care less what any member of his family might think of him. He knew how to get along perfectly well without the approval of others. And if they did not like it, so much the worse for them. When Doña Cecilia asked him just as they were finishing dessert if he had borrowed the album, she had taken it for granted that he would say no; and she was astonished when the boy, after glancing briefly around the table, said indifferently: "Yes. I took it."

Don Sidonio could not believe his ears. The tone in which Luis had answered was intended to be provocative, and he was on the verge of raising his voice, but his wife raised her hand to stop him.

"And what did you do with it?"

Luis shrugged his shoulders.

"I sold it."

Doña Cecilia turned pale.

"Sold it? To whom?"

"That's none of your business."

His answer left no room for doubt, and Luis considered the incident closed. Let them do what they pleased, they'd get no more out of him.

The painful silence was suddenly interrupted by a sharp noise. Don Sidonio had gotten up from the table and, red with fury, left the room, slamming the door behind him.

Luis took Gloria's arm as they left the dining-room. His sister was pale as wax, and when Luis looked her straight in the eye she lowered her head submissively.

"What did you do with it?" he said.

He got no answer.

*   *   *

Careful. *Careful.* CAREFUL. He was shaking one of the cab-drivers and did not have time to turn around: he received the blow right square in the face, and it laid him out flat: stars, strange flowers with geometric petals, lights like flashes from a broken mirror. He had started the fight with several drinks in him, and he woke up in his *residencia* with his face all black and blue—a leather mask dented and scuffed. At first he had a hard time understanding what had happened: he was sure that he had done all right; his arms and his fists were as good as ever. But when he looked at himself in the mirror he did not understand. Little by little he felt that something was tumbling down within: the myth. The booziness had not left him yet completely, and an undefinable sadness saturated him, as if he were a sponge. He was stretched out on the bed with his face covered with crosses of bandages, his skin smeared with tincture of iodine, and when Uribe came to see him he greeted him with a bitter smile. "They got me, Tánger. I was drunk and they attacked me from behind, but they beat me up." He spoke with a sad voice that he did not recognize as his own; Raúl Rivera, prostrate on a bed, licking his wounds. For ten days now he had not been able to leave the house, and during those ten days Tánger had stayed with him, not leaving his side for a moment: beefsteaks, wild honey, melted paraffin, tallow, pomade, and other ungents whose secrets only Tánger knew. He was superstitious, and he believed in all kinds of charms and talismans.

From his bed Raúl watched his strange maneuvers calmly, and when he saw that his wounds were healing on the strength of Tánger's concoctions, he began to be convinced that Uribe had magical powers. "What would become of the world," he said, "if we didn't hide its harshness? All we want to do is to hide and someone, someone not ourselves, surrounds us and gives us a name. How long are we to run down the paths of anguish?" Raúl had finished by laughing: his full lips parted, showing his white teeth and healthy red gums. *Yes, how long? how long?*

This had been several weeks ago, and since then a good deal of water had gone over the dam. Now, with a great wealth of gestures, Raúl was narrating the incident of the night in the tavern. He still had a bandage on one of his hands which called for an explanation.

"What was the fight all about?" asked David.

Raúl, his hat thrown back on his head (for he did not even take it off in the bars), let the smoke twist its curls around his face.

"About?" he said. And he loosened his tie with his hairy hands. "For what other reason if not for that fairy there?"

He pointed to Uribe, looking like a wax doll, wrapped up in his green velvet jacket with the fur collar. With his white incredibly small hand, he was distributing blessings.

Agustín Mendoza, after ordering a round of drinks, took an empty seat at the head of the table.

"What did he do?" he asked.

Raúl leaned back in his chair, his cigarette dividing his freshly shaven chin in two. "What do you suppose? Same as always. Started the fight and then beat it. But, by God, this time he got the worst of it."

And with the vehemence that always accompanied a recital of his exploits, he explained what had happened.

"And to top it off," he said, "that little souse not only did not even thank me, but got offended when I called a spade a spade. I'd slugged two guys, and he never lifted a finger. Besides, it was all his fault: it was only natural to tell him what I thought of him when I finished. But no. Monsieur Uribe pretended that he was above all that sort of thing, and left like a coward without even saying good-by."

The livid light of the lamps made Uribe's face even paler than usual.

"I went with the gorillas," he said.

Raúl sneered at him. "For all the good you get out of a woman," he said.

Uribe took an artificial flower out of his pocket and placed it affectedly in his lapel.

"They simply adore me," he replied. "As soon as they speak to me, they're taken with me. I offer them magic: the alchemy of colors. I make love to them in rooms illuminated with violet-colored lights, and I tie colored bows on their teats. One ugly old whore, I wrapped a green gauze veil around her face and made her believe that she was young and beautiful. And after it is all over, I kiss their hands as if they had given me their maiden-head, and I put a bouquet of white roses on their pillows. And they love me because I make them believe they're different. I deceive them. I give them magic."

The images flashed in his brain like fireworks. When he talked like that, even Raúl Rivera could not help admiring him.

"That morning, however," put in Cortézar, "you gave them the slip."

Uribe shrugged his shoulders, in excuse. "Yes. I hate

the morning so." And at these words his waxen, doll-like face, accentuated by his little white hands, assumed an unreal, almost fantastic look. "In the light of day those women are so coarse and ordinary: they have such rough skin, and their mouths are toothless, like syphilitics. I had some precious masks in my pocket—delicate little masks of silk with puzzling smiles; I suggested to them that we make paper lampshades and put up colored lanterns. I also had some transparent wings, like dragonfly wings, but they wouldn't go along with me. *They were too real, and they were horrible.*"

He had lowered his voice as he went on talking and when he finished he looked up at Agustín Mendoza a moment: "Tell me," he said, "have you seen Ana?"

Agustín had filled his pipe, which he usually smoked only after supper. He was having difficulty lighting it.

"Yes. She came to the studio."

"What did she want?"

"Nothing special."

"I do hope you did not mention me. She telephoned me, but I was drunk and I don't know what kind of a message I must have left for her."

"Forget it!" Agustín spoke with indifference, trying to make it understood that the subject was of no special interest to him. He had bought the evening paper as he left the studio, and now he laid it on the table unfolded. Bold headlines told of the latest revolutionary plot.

Little Luis Páez leaned over to read the paper—his blond curls falling over his forehead in ringlets.

"You all want to know something?" he said suddenly. "They've arrested Jaime Betancourt, that friend of my sister, the guy from the Canaries, a couple of days ago."

Rivera looked at him with sudden interest. "Betancourt? How do you know?"

Luis took a cigarette from the case that David was holding out to him.

"She told me so herself. She was desperately worried, because she thought they were going to prosecute. Apparently they picked him up, him and four others in an apartment on Carrera de San Jerónimo for unlawful possession of arms."

He stopped a second to measure the effect of his story; he knew that David was in love with his sister Gloria and wanted to know how he would take it. "He looks stunned," he thought.

"I'd never have dreamed that Jaime would have become a revolutionary," said Raúl. "In Las Palmas we went to school together, and he got the prize every year for good behavior. His family, like mine, are very conservative rightists."

With his hat thrown back, his eyebrows arched, his thick mustache in form of a W, and his eyes round as two black balls, his face showed such astonishment that someone started to laugh.

"And how did they get pinched?" asked Cortézar.

Luis Páez shrugged his shoulders. "I don't know. Apparently, my sister isn't very well informed. Seems they'd hidden in the apartment a small store of arms, and someone squealed. When the police entered they went straight to the place where the arms were: behind a picture of Little Jesus of Prague, which they'd just put there to throw them off."

"Who are the others?"

"Gloria doesn't know that, either. Although I think that one of them is Zin, that anarchist artist with the burned hands."

The news left Raúl Rivera stupefied. He threw his head back, pursed his lips, and kept turning his cigarette around in his fingers. As always when he tried to explain to himself something that he did not understand, and which perhaps humiliated him, he smiled bitterly.

"I've known him ever since he was this high"—and his hands separated about the length of a fetus. "We went to school together every morning. He was only a skinny little kid who never played during recess and was afraid of everything: of playing hooky, of wrestling Canary-Islander fashion, and even of swimming in the bay."

Uribe raised the furry lapels of his velvet jacket. "In other words," he said, "he was more intelligent than you."

"Yes, he was more intelligent, but also more peace-loving, more quiet. And somewhat cowardly, too. I remember one time he got me mad and I roughed him up."

"You're always roughing people up," said Uribe. "You don't have to tell us. We know."

The pupils of Raúl's eyes, etched against the white, looked like two black pinholes. "Aw, shut up, once and for all, will you?" he cried.

He took enough time to expel the smoke that he had stored up in his lungs and then went on: "Three months ago I saw him in a café on the Gran Vía. He had the same inoffensive look that he'd always had, and when he told me he was studying law I just took it for granted he was a good student. I even kidded him about his academic success. And we shook hands like old friends. Now it turns out that they've locked him up."

The news had humiliated him. He was saying "Now it turns out that they've locked him up" in the same tone that somebody else would say "And now it turns out that he's a better man than I am."

"Looks like the news annoys you," Cortézar observed ironically.

Rivera hesitated a few seconds. "Well, I wouldn't go so far as to say it annoys me. But I'll admit it does surprise me. It's just that he had such an inoffensvie look about him that I thought him incapable of getting into any kind of scrape like that."

Agustín Mendoza had folded the evening paper in such a way that its headlines were visible to all.

"The truth is," he said, "no one dares to commit himself in a definite way. None of us, for example, has ever done anything to call attention to himself."

He remembered that in a clandestine magazine which they had published the year before—and had brought out just the one issue—the editorial had said: "An ideology which does not transform its postulates into immediate action is false and harmful."

"Yes," little Luis Páez pointed out, "we're wasting time."

The events of the last few days had aroused his indignation, and he too felt the necessity of doing something positive. "We've been talking about 'doing something' for quite some time now, and we let the others get ahead of us."

Agustín Mendoza drained his glass of gin.

"Yes. That's the trouble," he said. "Neither we nor Zin's gang have done anything worthwhile. When we founded *Atica*, we preached action, and Rudy, Jorge, and his gang laughed at us because they thought us incapable of acting. And in a way they were right. The fact that they don't act either is no excuse, but rather all the more reason for us to do so. All we need now for everything to go on as usual is to return to our respective homes and be received as lost sheep."

He had stopped to pour himself another drink and glanced at his audience. Uribe was the only one who was not listening: with his head turned aside, he was whispering something mysterious in the ear of his neighbor, a blond boy with a seraphic look, whose name was Angel. His appearance, thought Agustín, corresponds exactly with his name. I can just see him dressed in a white tunic, walking about heaven with a flower in his hand.

"Don't you agree?" Agustín asked David.

The boy moistened his lips with his tongue before answering: his face was pale, as if powdered with flour, and he had delicate hands which were never still for a moment.

"Yes," David answered. "At home the banquet and the guests await us. Everything is ready for the return of the prodigal son: the ox, the relatives, the servants. It may even be that our fathers are waiting for us at the bend of the road."

"Yes," said Agustín, "and that is exactly what must not happen."

"But that is what most probably will happen," Luis Páez interrupted. "And we will possess again that which is our birthright." He had spoken a few times with Ana and had learned his lesson well. "Every generation has done the same. The parents try to warn their sons: and the children pay no attention: they stray. They play at living, and in the end they return to the fold, their eyes red with tears. The happy ending, of course. In the final analysis, none of us has really given up anything or really broken off."

He had spoken with such vehemence that even some of the good middle-class people at neighboring tables had stopped talking to listen to him.

"Yes. That's it. We're parasites," said Cortézar. "What else can we be?"

"First of all," replied Agustín in a soft, low voice, "cut the cables. If we want to be logical and if we hope to go ahead, we have to burn our ships."

He noticed that all eyes were on him: eyes that in the

light of the gaslamps, which lent them a livid phosphores-
cence, seemed almost ghostlike.

"Only some irrevocable and definite act that would compromise us forever can prove that we're not just playing.
An act that we cannot back out of or escape from. Up to
now we've been satisfied with just talking. And it is absolutely necessary that after committing this act we can say:
it's done now; there's no way out."

"The important thing is," put in David, "to determine
the nature of the act."

Luis lit a cigarette. "The end is obvious, but we still
have to decide on the means."

"Yes," said Uribe, "what form should our action take?"

He had asked his question in a casual way without even
turning around, for at that moment he was savoring the
response he was getting from the blond boy. He put forth
his tiny celluloid hands in a gesture of protest, as if he were
scandalized at what he had just heard. Raúl shot him a
look—a look that came from the deep pinholes of his eyes.

"Well, it won't be by going around letting everybody
pinch your ass, you big fairy," he said.

The remark caused a rather general disturbance in the
café.

"All right, now. Shut up, both of you," interrupted Cortézar. "We didn't come here to talk about asses. And if you
want to discuss that sort of thing you had better do it some
place else."

Raúl, with an offended look, unbuttoned his collar. "I
didn't say that with the idea of deliberately annoying anybody," he said. "I was only trying to make things clear to
him."

There was a pause—just enough time for everyone to
turn a curious and questioning glance on Agustín Mendoza.

"Yes, that's the point," Agustín said, "to determine the nature of the act to be committed. That is really the only problem."

He fingered his chin for a few moments. He was facing the light: framed by his beard and by his hair, his face stood out unbelievably white.

"Our past experience ought to have taught us something: that where there are hierarchies there's deceit. Only a small group, well organized, can act efficiently."

Little Luis Páez's eyes sparkled. "How?"

Agustín hesitated a few seconds. He began to think that maybe he had gone too far, that he'd better stop now. "That's more than enough for today," he said to himself.

"We'll determine the method later, by mutual agreement. To begin with, what matters is the individual factor. If each one of us is sure of himself, there's no problem. Now, if anyone has scruples of any kind whatsoever, the door's always open. Weaklings have no place in a group like ours. But once committed, you've got to know how to stick with it to the end."

For a moment he thought about the dreariness of his lonely evenings: sleep, lassitude, alcohol. Lola had promised to come and see him tomorrow: he felt imprisoned in the labyrinth that he himself had made.

There was a long silence, interrupted suddenly by a muffled exclamation. Uribe had pulled the flower out of his boutonniere and was using it to point at the boy with the seraphic look.

"Oh, look at him! Just look at him!"

He had assumed the tragic pose of his best scenes. Drawn, pale, hardly separating his hands from his body, like an awkward puppet, he pointed with his artificial flower at the boy. Uribe's velvet coat was too small for him, and it made him look thinner than he was.

"He just made me an indecent proposal," he exclaimed.

This unexpected outburst had released the tension, and Agustín felt much relieved. The men at the other table were laughing and looking at them.

The boy, terribly upset, protested. "I— What I meant—"

Uribe covered his ears. "Oh, stop! Enough! Enough!"

Carrying a cardboard tray, like the ones used in candy stores, Uribe began to circulate from table to table. He knew that Raúl was watching him, and this made him feel even wilder.

"Bad leg . . . Hey. Bad leg."

The other customers didn't know what was going on, but they grinned broadly at him.

"Yes. The leg. A bit lame . . . from birth."

When he got to the middle of the floor, under the brilliant glare of the ring of gaslights, his face took on a look of anguish.

"He's going to do an imitation of a gangster picture," Agustín, with a look of amusement, explained to the people at the other tables.

Fragile and greenish, the little figure in the velvet coat crumpled with a tragic look on his face.

"Oh, Johnny, I didn't mean to do it, I swear I didn't. I never meant to hurt you. When I fired— Oh, I didn't know it was you, Johnny. Remember those days in the Rockies, when we used to play under the pine trees? We were like brothers, Johnny. I— Oh, I swear it. No! Johnny! Johnny!"

He had let himself fall to the floor, playing the grief-stricken, and then immediately he leaped up again with a bound.

"Oh, I'm so drunk!"

Everybody applauded. Even Raúl. The manager of the place, who at first had been afraid that the exhibition might annoy the customers, had been all ready to tell

Uribe to stop; but seeing the hit he had made, he now hastened to congratulate him.

"Here, have a drink. It's on the house."

Uribe lifted his glass exultantly.

The group broke up. Cortézar was the first to get up, and the rest quickly followed. Uribe's act had made them all talkative. As soon as they were in the street, the clown took Rivera's arm. "Oh, Raúl," he said, "were you really angry?"

And seeing that his companion, still offended, did not bother to answer, he took up a song: " 'Let us flee! The moon is our accomplice . . .' "

On the glistening asphalt pavement of the street, they parted from the rest of the group. And in the silence of his friend, Uribe understood that he had been forgiven.

"I'll tell you what," he said, "let's go some place and get drunk!"

✳ ✳ II ✳ ✳

For Gloria, life was turning out very differently from
what her parents had led her to expect. The girl had
made this discovery a good many years ago, and even
now, looking back on her childhood, she was surprised at
how faithfully her memory served her. In those days Don
Sidonio used to take them to a village in the province of
Guadalajara: it was there, during the summer vacations,
that she had found out that the world was not confined to
the four walls of their apartment and that the image of it
which her brother offered her was neither worse nor more
boring than the life she led at home. In the gray village of
Guadalajara, a place of refuge for snakes and lizards,
where only a few morning-glories and geraniums lent a
desperate note of color, Luis had initiated her into the
secrets of his gang: a world of power and cruelty in which
the ruse was a natural recourse and the lie a weapon of
combat. In the abandoned barn on the hill, among rusty
farm implements and disemboweled, empty sacks, the
meetings of The Crabs were held—the terrorizing gang
that broke street lights, stole from the fruit stands in the
streets, forced open the alms box in church, and persecuted
lone couples seeking solitude in the shady corners of the
Casino garden. The All-Powerful Brothers wore masks and
hoods, carried knives and daggers. To be initiated in the
Mysteries meant submitting to a series of tests, designed

to challenge the newcomer's talents: steal a pitcher from the old Ceramics-vendor, pull the chains off the door of the seafood restaurant, let the air out of the tires of the post-office clerk's bicycle that had been left standing out in front of the hotel, and carry out a series of more or less capricious deeds ranging from the well-nigh impossible to the foolish and defiant.

Out of deference to her sex, Gloria was admitted without initiation, and once she'd become the All-Powerful Sister she presided several times over the baptism of new initiates. Luis—Falcon Eye, with his silk mask, his wide belt, and his whip (a water-closet chain), administered justice to the obstinate candidate. She had also assisted in torturing the barber's son: the gang had made a few incisions on his arm with a knife previously sterilized with a candle that she had held over the mouth of a beer bottle, and the boy, thus branded, was set free, after taking an oath of silence.

A hundred yards from their meeting-ground, but in effect really a hundred miles, Don Sidonio and Doña Cecilia, seated in their living-room rockers, browsed through magazines and newspapers. Every day the father would reproach Luis with the same charges: that he did not study, that he showed himself unworthy of the summer vacation which, at great sacrifice, Don Sidonio had provided. Was this the result of the education he had received? Yes, that was it. What use was it, then, to have him in an expensive private school? None. Mathematics, physics, geometry—nothing did him any good. The children's grandmother, always there with a little white cap on her head, like those in an illustrated cover for a book of fairy tales, spoke to Gloria of a soft, quilted world where the plants were grateful for being watered and animals rewarded the children who petted them. She told, also, of the poor children who had no mothers, whom one should love and pity; and there were the images of fat and gluttonous-looking saints to whom one should pray and entrust oneself. But Luis had taught Gloria to despise them. With his little friends he would urinate on the pots of carnations, which the next day would look burned, and which the sweet tears of Grandmama could not revive; they set traps for birds and poured cement down ant-holes. They followed beggars and threw stones at them; dirtied up the paralytic boy of the candy store with cow dung.

Coming back to Madrid was like coming back to another world. Luis in those days demanded payments for certain concessions on his part: to behave as he should at table when there were guests, 5 pesetas; for not singing in the hallway when Grandmama was sleeping, 1.50. Gloria would watch him and say nothing. One day the four children emptied the stuffings of a pillow in the patio of the house, and Don Sidonio locked them up in their room for all afternoon. So Luis undressed them, and all of them stood naked on the balcony of their window. It was winter, and they stood there crying: "We're so cold!" While the passers-by, amazed, began to gather under the window. "It's Papa. He's punishing us." A few minutes later the neighbors entered the house en masse, and Don Sidonio had a pretty uncomfortable time of it.

"What you have done today surpasses anything I might have imagined. You've lost all sense of shame. Is it possible that you're my own flesh and blood?" And when, for the first time in Gloria's experience, he slammed the door, the cuckoo clock started its mocking calls and the phonograph, stuck in the middle of a record, continued spinning like a heavy, obstinate insect. For a moment it seemed as though time had stopped and that in the frozen second the cuckoo calls and the buzzing of the spinning record constituted the only sign of life in a house where the kind of quarrels one does not forgive had just settled down like an invasion of pale, dirty bats. Their grandmother, with her breviary on her lap, read aloud: "'Who *shall be* he who shall say that *something* came to pass that the Lord did not command?'" And everybody turned in her direction because they did not recognize her voice, just as if this new shadow which Gloria felt had spoken through her grandmother's mouth and had summarized, although incompletely, her own opinion. Five years had passed since that time, and Gloria had never been able to forget the incident.

Luis had grown up in shamelessness. "Yes, in *shamelessness,* because in order to break with everybody and everything, in order to play with what others value and respect, it is necessary to have great strength"—these were words that Gloria associated with the "Don't get so excited, Sidonio: the boy is still just a youngster," which formed the background music for the farce in which, for several years now, they all took part. Luis was this and much more: "A pioneer, to whom you should be grateful because he has enabled you to create a life of your own," Jaime Betancourt had told her. "That's the advantage of being the younger." It was true. Her response of a week ago apropos of those cursed stamps was a good test. She had tried to thank him, not only for that, no, but also for having gotten her out of "that society, where," as Jaime said, "even the concept of life is handed down to you, as a loan." But when she wanted to do it, her ideas had become all mixed up in her head until they were nothing but a jumble. She had failed. Jaime had spoken to her of something like "the tragedy of the moral narrowness of the environment," but she was not so sure. Just in case, she preferred to keep silent.

And the debt remained standing. It was useless to hover around him. Luis paid no attention to her. Or, as Jaime would put it: "He went to his objective direct." She waited until the rest of the family had left, and when finally he spoke to her, it seemed as though a miracle had taken place.

"Come on out for a walk," he said, "I want to talk to you about something."

"Just as you wish."

They put on their coats in silence. In the doorway Doña Cecilia warned: "Button up tight. It's very windy out."

They went out into the street. Gloria walked to the right, without saying a word, mildly excited. She looked down at her brother's feet, which were opening up a pathway through the dry chestnut leaves, and answered with a shudder the question that she had been waiting for impatiently.

"What did you do with the stamps?"

She cleared her throat before answering. "I gave them to Enrique Suárez. He sold them to a collector."

"How much did they give you for them?"

"I don't know. Not much. Six hundred pesetas, I guess."

"Were they for Betancourt?"

"Yes. Why?"

"He's still in jail."

The girl avoided his gaze. She seemed confused.

"It didn't do any good. Apparently in cases such as this a bond does not work, but Gerardo says that they will release him pretty soon anyway. Another guy who was accused of the same thing, the illegal possession of concealed weapons, they let go at the end of ten days."

Luis lit a cigarette. He stopped in a doorway to protect the flame that was about to go out in the hollow of his hands.

"And the money?"

"The six hundred pesetas?"

"Yes."

Gloria's face was filled with consternation. "Do you need them?"

Luis spat out a piece of tobacco. "Yes."

They continued walking, in silence, for a few seconds. "I . . . that same day I gave them to Gerardo."

"You said yourself that they were not necessary."

"Yes, but there were the debts."

She stopped for a few seconds, ashamed.

"His family does not send him anything. They're on the outs with him and want him to go back. He never would have accepted them, but since I knew through Gerardo that he was in trouble . . ."

She gave Luis a pleading look.

"You're stupid," he said.

The boy took the cigarette from between his lips and threw it on the ground.

"You're just a stupid girl."

"But he owed a lot of money," she said.

Her brother paid no attention to her. "He owed . . . he owed. Go tell it to your grandmother! She'll believe you."

Gloria's cheeks had turned scarlet. "Perhaps . . . maybe they haven't paid it yet. If you wish, I'll go this afternoon and see Gerardo, and I'll tell him that I need it. I'll tell him that—"

"Five hundred pesetas is what I need right now. If they're going to give you fifty cents back, you can keep them for yourself."

"If you want me to, I'll—"

"I don't want anything. I just thought I'd ask a favor of you, that's all. If you don't want to, it's no business of mine."

He spoke in a hard voice, *in that hard voice of one who denies his home, who does not recognize his own father or mother, and who sinks deeper and deeper into shamelessness. Oh, Lord, how long shall I have to bear it?*

"I—I assure you I do not have the money. I gave it to Gerardo, believe me. If you wish, you can ask him right now, by phone. There's one over there in that bar."

Oysters. Canapés. We deliver. . . . Again Don Sidonio's words invaded her brain: "Without morality, without decency, how can a man develop into something in life? How?"

"Excuses—anyone can make them up. I, too, could have let the family accuse you, and excused myself later. I'd like to know what good that would have done you."

They had come to Alcalá Street and were heading down toward Plaza Cibeles, walking along the iron fence of Retiro Park.

"Yes, I could have washed my hands of the whole thing, and I didn't do it. I could also explain to them tonight the whole business about the stamp album, and tell them about the people you're mixed up with, and then ask you to forgive me."

He was smiling scornfully, and he quickened his step a little. Gloria almost had to run to keep up with him. She felt herself the most unhappy girl in the world and was on the point of breaking into tears.

"Okay. It's all right. The best thing for you to do now is to go on your way."

He looked straight ahead as he spoke, without even glancing at her. Then, seeing that she was not leaving, his expression seemed to become a little more gentle. He adjusted his pace to hers and took her arm.

"Hell! Forget everything I've said. It's not important."

Against the pale blue sky the leaves of the trees were

turning a soft yellow. Over the rooftops a few whitish clouds stretched a thin wisp of silk. They walked along in silence for a while longer.

"Oh, I almost forgot," said Luis suddenly, "one of these days you must call up David, the sooner the better."

The remark, made with affected casualness, greatly surprised Gloria. Six months ago—yes, it was in May—Luis had met them together in the street, and when she got home he had riddled her with questions. "Why is he running after you?" She did not answer him. Always, when she quarreled with Luis, she preferred to let him do the talking. Her brother never tried to convince anybody of anything: he was satisfied with having the last word, shutting up the other guy. She answered only that when someone came up and greeted her, she couldn't quite send him away coldly. *Besides, David is not my type. He may be in love with me. Perhaps. I like him as a friend, yes, like a very good friend, but—* And Luis had interrupted her thoughts to speak with the scorn that only he knew how to put into words: "David, oh, the Very Perfume of Goodness." And now Luis himself was asking her to contact him.

"What's gotten into you?"

She said it with the fear that her brother might answer her with some kind of insult, and she was surprised when she heard him say: "I think he's in love with you."

"In love with me? I haven't seen him for months."

"That doesn't make any difference. From now on you must go out with him, until you hear further from me."

When he spoke like that, in that dry voice so unconcerned about what the other person might be thinking, Gloria could not help admiring him.

"We haven't seen each other for a long time, and I think—"

"What you think doesn't interest me in the least. I'm asking a favor of you, that's all."

She lowered her head, confused.

"Yes, of course. I only meant that if you were to call him it would be much easier."

"Just as you like. This very afternoon I'll invite him over to the house. Once he is there, you'll find a way to approach him."

The memory of her activities in the gang of the All-Powerful Brothers rose to the surface of her mind. They would send her into the danger zones as an ambushed emissary, and she would transmit the information she obtained from the enemy.

"Am I to find out something?"

Luis shook his head. "No. All you have to do is go out with him. I warn you, he knows all about Jaime, so it's best you don't bring that up. The only thing you have to do," he added with an ironic smile, "is to show him some affection."

"She's got something," he used to say, "that I daresay is unique. She makes herself loved by everybody around her." The year before, Don Sidonio had invited to dinner a young fellow with a brilliant future—someone he would have liked to see her marry some day. Luis, the cross that Don Sidonio had borne on his shoulders since the boy was four years old, had asked the guest if he were rich, if his father had a good income, and he had praised, burlesquing them, the domestic virtues of his sister. "The outcast, because it is necessary to be an outcast in order to . . ." This time Gloria let the remark go by. They had gone as far as the post office, where her brother got ready to leave her.

"Okay. We'll talk about it later. I'll call him this afternoon."

"Are you leaving?"

"Yes. I have something to do."

"And the money? Because if you wish—"

"Forget it. I'll find it somewhere else."

He went off whistling. In the first café along the Gran Vía, he went down to the washroom, asked the lady attendant for a telephone slug, and deposited it into the box.

"May I speak with David?"

"Who's calling, please?"

"Páez."

He put the receiver down on the table and eyed the woman attendant. She was looking for something in the folds of her skirt and was muttering to herself. After a minute he put his ear to the receiver.

"David? It's Páez. Listen: Tomorrow afternoon Cortézar is coming over to my place. He has some tickets for a show, and I thought you might be interested in going along."

"What are they giving? Anything good?"

"I don't know. He didn't say."

"What time are you expecting him?"

"At six."

"Okay. I'll be there."

"Fine, I'll be looking for you."

"Okay."

Luis cut off just when David was beginning to thank him. He went up the steps two at a time. He was smiling. "Now," he thought, "the only thing I need is the money."

As soon as he reached the street, he hailed a cab.

"Take me to Noviciado."

In the cab he unfolded the handkerchief in which he had put his grandmother's wedding ring and the baptismal medals of his younger brother and sister, and analyzed the goods with a critical eye.

"Now, we'll see what we can get for this junk."

He knocked on the glass partition and told the driver to step on it.

*   *   *

The servant girl had given her the information that very morning, after a struggle of two hours in which it looked as if she, Ana, were going to get the worst of it. The maid had a tall, dark boyfriend, who witnessed the interview with a distrustful air: he was a Manchegan peasant with skin like baked clay, and he kept turning his beret in his hands. Paula had been won over, Ana reported later, only after overcoming a thousand inner resistances which were obvious by the nervous twitching of her lips, her fidgeting fingers, the muscles that palpitated at skin surface, fears that . . .

" 'Yes,' " Ana went on, "she said to me, 'I'm willing, provided nothing happens to the Señor. You don't know how good he has been to me. I have been with him for six years now and have never had the least reprimand. Believe me. He's a real gentleman—that one—who knows how to be grateful for everything; and he never overlooks a single attention. I would never be able to forgive myself if anything serious should happen to him. You understand what I mean: it's one thing to steal, but to do harm, to kill, say. . . . Don't count on me for anything like that. I am a quiet woman, who wants to marry and have children, and the best way to do that is to avoid complications.' She went on telling me how clean and orderly she had been since she was a child, and about how a deceased grandmother had instilled in her love for one's neighbor and for the humble things in life. 'Although I'm just a simple country girl, I have an extraordinary love for family life.' "

Ana had ensnared her in a rosary of tranquilizing, soft words, which implied a recognition of and tribute to her integrity, giving her all kinds of guarantees, praising the naturalness of her sentiments, and exhorting her to keep her heart always pure and white.

"It was a real test of praise and courtesy. From the beginning I realized the boyfriend was on my side. It was enough to see his face: narrow forehead, enormous lips, thick brushlike mustache, and liquid eyes that shone with greediness. He did have, it's true, a handsome physique, narrow in the hips and wide in the shoulders, but he had the brains of a mosquito. I pretended to be speaking to Paula, but actually I was directing my words at him: I made a point of convincing him, to fight his innate wariness. She looked at me fixedly. She is one of those heavy-set women with a starchy face who are continually invoking the heavenly powers and proclaiming their virtue to the four winds. 'The present case is different,' I told her, 'you must marry; you cannot wait any longer.' And she let herself be caressed by my warm smiles; her obtuse brow plowed with wrinkles, she seemed to be devouring them."

While she spoke she stopped pacing up and down and sat in the armchair usually occupied by Agustín's models. In order to do so, she had to remove dried paintbrushes and one of the daggers which Agustín had forgotten to put away. Leaning against the easel with an air of indolence, he looked at her as if he were about to sketch her.

On the table in a bowl of yellow water a few withered roses floated. "A gift from a lady friend," Agustín had said. In the corners where the ceiling fell obliquely to about a foot from the floor there were some folders showing a number of dance projects, and a tutu of silk gauze lay on one of the old sea chests.

"You don't mind if I mix some colors?" Agustín had said.

She shook her head: her dense face, of pale complexion,

seemed to absorb the leaden light of the afternoon and to incorporate it into her skin. Through the unbuttoned sweater, her blouse revealed her high-set breasts, which seemed beautifully formed.

She explained how, at a certain moment, everything had almost slipped through her hands, and the effort she had had to make to gain control, paying out rope like a fisherman, so that the game should have time to exhaust itself.

" 'Here it is six years I've been working for Señor Guarner,' the girl said to me—and, immediately, from the tone of the voice, I put her in that class of people who speculate on sentiments the way they would on merchandise, and I knew she was getting ready to ask a higher price. 'Six years, you know, is a very long time, and even though it isn't one's own house, it's natural to get attached, to become so familiar with the furniture you end up thinking of it as your own. Besides, the gentleman has always been so kind to me. Not a year has passed but what he has given me a present for either Christmas or Epiphany. Look. These earrings he gave me last year. They're gold.' You should have heard her voice: she breathed the kind of tenderness that makes people feel sorry for telling their troubles, nursing their wounds. I let her go on to her heart's content. The boyfriend was at her side, frowning, obstinately agreeing with a nod of his head. The time before, we had agreed to pay her 2,000 pesetas, and Paula did not think this was enough. . . ."

A bargaining began which, according to Ana, had lasted the whole morning. Ana had insisted upon holding to the original figure. The girl speculated on the danger, continued to speak of her feelings toward the old man and the pain that the betrayal of his confidence was causing her.

"I had promised them ten per cent of the profits that we

would make. That amount, plus the advance payment, would enable them to buy themselves a little house in Puertollano, which is where the boyfriend lives. Paula said to me that if the robbery should fail then they'd be without their ten per cent; and then she added, how could she be sure that, instead of ten per cent, she wasn't getting only eight, or six, or even five per cent. I answered her that, in that case, the boyfriend could take part in the robbery. 'Oh, no; not that,' she said. 'We don't want to get mixed up in this affair. My fiancé is an honorable man who just needs money to establish himself, but he is not the adventurous type.' By the time we're pulling the job, she wants to be in Puertollano. Although she has served in the house for six years, and has won the confidence of the old man, she's afraid that her departure a few days before the crime may cause some suspicion."

Ana reached over and took one of the petals that were floating in the yellow water. Her eyes when she looked at Agustín were like two fans in dizzy motion. Leaning against the easel, Agustín Mendoza was drawing, not uttering a word.

"We'd just about reached a dead-end in the conversation, and I went back to the same point. I was getting ready to raise the figure when the boyfriend looked at me with a very strange expression. His eyes shone as he asked me if I had the money with me. I told him I did. Then he turned toward the girl. 'Go on. Give it to her.' Paula hesitated a moment, but she could not help giving in. She took the paper out of her change purse and handed it to me."

As if by reflex action, Ana opened the clasp of her own purse and unfolded the paper.

"The combination is RAY-12. Guarner keeps the key in the pocket of his vest. Once we have the combination, the lock will offer no difficulties. Paula has also given me a sketch of the office, showing the place where the safe is built into the wall. She had already told me all the rest: how to get an interview, the people that are in the house—"

She stopped talking, because she thought Agustín was about to say something; but it was only a yawn. The atmosphere of the studio had become unreal. Now the tutu seemed to be eating up the afternoon light. Ana's body, erect in the armchair, projected a fragile shadow across the floor. Her fingers left the crescents of their nails on the withered petals.

"The day after tomorrow the girl will definitely leave the house, so that when we go into action we'll have a clear field."

Ana recalled that years ago, when she was only fifteen, her father kept in the kitchen a knife, the sharp blade of which had fascinated her. When no one could see her, she would look at it avidly. She wondered just how much resistance human flesh would offer to its keen edge, and she imagined it would be enough to place the point of the blade on the skin in order for the body, attracted by the inevitability of the crime, to rush forward to meet the hilt.

The juvenile gang to which she had belonged had lived, in their own way, the confusion that floated in the atmosphere of those years: they ran through rubbish piles and alleys, armed with knives, shouting and giving guttural orders, absorbing voraciously the gestures of their elders when they attacked. Tato, the boldest of them, had in one slash ripped open the throat of a cat. The blood had gushed forth, red, like the pulp of a wild fruit, and she and her comrades, drunk with enthusiasm, had bathed their hands in it, then stoned an old beggar woman, and returned home filled with excitement.

All that belonged to the past, but now Ana felt she was reliving those days.

"Yes," she said softly, "the moment for decision has arrived."

She had put her hand to her forehead in an attitude of reflection. Agustín placed his pencil in the jar.

"I think the individual problem is more important."

He stopped a moment to observe the effect of his words. "Don't you think so?"

His words floated in the air like ghosts. The notes of a piano terribly out of tune could be heard through the patio window. Outside the wind slashed through the rain obliquely. Agustín, who was near the window, looked out indifferently: the drops bubbled in pools, and on the panes ribbons of water joined together capriciously.

Now, once again, Ana had stopped talking. The lampshade of fluted paper in the middle of the dark desolation of the room gave a note of color—the only residue of light to which the dying afternoon clung obstinately. In the bowl of yellow water there were no more petals. Only a few discolored brushes showed their unkempt bristles over the edge of the bowl. The girl stood up and went over to look at the drawing.

"Is that me?" she asked.

Agustín did not answer.

✻ ✻ ✻

In spite of all his efforts, his mind held fast to the memories of that last afternoon, the details of which he relived with painful insistence. Two days before, Luis had asked him if he wanted to go to the movies, and when he arrived at Luis's house he had been met by his sister.

"I've come to see Luis."

Gloria went to look for him in his room.

"I think he's gone out. If you'll wait a moment, I'll go and see."

No. There was nobody anywhere. Gloria was dressed in street clothes.

"I was just going for a walk," she said.

"Let's go together, then."

She walked along without speaking, even though David led her along the paths they both knew so well. Everything reminded them of their rare summer walks together: the thicket of trees, shrubs, and vines; the trunks of the chestnut trees where several months before they had carved their initials with a penknife. They sat down on a stone bench set in the bushiest part, and there Gloria threw her head back and looked up toward the sky.

The leaves of the chestnut trees, membranous like the wings of a dragonfly, stood out flatly against a changing sky. Above them the birds, almost invisible, traced little black W's in the air. For almost an hour he had been asking Gloria questions, which she had answered only absent-mindedly.

The afternoon left him with a curious impression. The attitude of the girl was cold, almost indifferent, and though they had spoken of many things, she did so in a mechanical, forced way. Yet, at the same time, he detected a certain abandon on her part that confused him. "If only I had had the courage to kiss her." But, as always happened in such circumstances, he lacked the strength.

Now, while he was writing in his diary, the memory of the day before left in him a bitter aftertaste. A mixed feeling made up of hope, annoyance, and bitterness, settled in his heart.

The way in which Gloria had spoken of men of action infuriated him. He thought of Jaime Betancourt, of his activities, of his being in jail. Perhaps she considered him more of a man and for that reason loved him. He looked with anger out across the skyline which he could barely see through the curtain.

His room opened on a vast perspective of chimneys, dormers, and rooftops. Against the lead-gray sky, the garrets of the neighboring houses stood out in a two-dimensional relief, like a photograph. David was bent over his oilcloth notebook with pen in hand, and when somebody knocked at the door he answered without looking up: "Come in!"

It was Gloria: she was wearing a black, tight-fitting suit which made her look more of a woman than she really was and through which the curves of her body insinuated themselves boldly. In his embarrassment, David noticed she was smiling at him.

"It's you."

He jumped to his feet and took her hand cordially. He had on a dirty shirt and a pair of dark bedroom slippers.

"I was working," he said.

His voice came out with difficulty, and he had to clear his throat.

She picked up a paperweight—a glass swan of a curious shape—which she held between her fingers, as if weighing it.

"Yours?"

David smiled, embarrassed. It seemed that all intelligence escaped him, leaving him empty, dead.

"If you'd like to have it . . . I have lots of others at home. They're from Majorca."

Gloria put it down on the table. She began to pull off voluptuously and provocatively the black silk gloves she was wearing. Across the oilcloth notebook left on the blotter, a title was written in pencil and she read: "Diary. Do you keep a diary?"

"Well, you see—" David hastened to take it from her, gently but firmly. "When I have nothing to do, I pass the time scribbling in it. Nothing of any importance. When I've filled it, I'll throw it away."

Fortunately the diary did not interest her further. With a half-smile on her face, she took a look around the room: the engravings on the walls, the collection of canes that his father had given him. She stopped in front of a machete with a silver handle.

"And this?"

"It was my grandfather's. He brought it back from Cuba."

David's heart was beating fast. He felt the girl's subtle perfume reaching him. He kept his gaze fixed on the back of her neck, left bare by her upswept hair.

"I like it," said Gloria.

David was just about to say "You can have it, if you like it," but was able to stop himself in time. "Take it easy, take it easy," he thought. Irritated, he realized that his bed was still unmade and his pajamas were lying on the floor.

"Everything's a mess," he apologized. "The cleaning-woman hasn't been in yet this morning, and the bed is still unmade."

"Oh, I don't mind. I like to see it like this, everything upset. I've walked under the arcade on this street often, and I always wondered what these houses were like inside. When I came up, I couldn't find your door. I nearly stumbled coming up the stairs."

"Yes, you can hardly see."

She went over to the window and looked at the landscape of rooftops.

"I had no idea you lived in such a beautiful place," she said. "This morning I thought I'd ask Luis for your address, and as soon as I had it, I decided to come and visit you."

When she turned her back to him, he buttoned the collar of his shirt and straightened the knot of his tie. He felt at once happy and dissatisfied, wavering between the desire to appear bold and the fear that was taking hold of him in the presence of this girl.

Gloria asked him some questions about the buildings that could be seen from there. She did not seem uneasy in the least, as if her visit were the most natural thing in the world.

On the table there were a bottle of wine and some dirty empty glasses. David went to the washstand to wash them.

"I'd really like to offer you something better, but unless I step out for a moment and get something you'll have to be satisfied with a glass of Cazalla."

"Give me some Cazalla; that will do. Here, within these walls, it's the most appropriate drink."

Her very forwardness shocked him. Months ago when she began to interest him, Gloria was only a little girl. Now her manners were those of a woman, and David felt disconcerted.

He handed her a glass, which she held between her fingers without raising it to her lips. As she took it from him, her nails scraped him lightly.

"Do you mind if I make myself comfortable?"

"Of course not."

She sat on top of the table and rested her feet on the back of a chair.

Looking at her as she drank, David thought that the girl had all the grace of a young animal. Her movements were gentle, precise. He had not as yet gotten over his surprise, and inwardly he was trying to figure out the reasons for her visit. But he did not dare ask. He was afraid of breaking the spell.

"Ordinarily girls don't care for Cazalla," he said when she handed the glass back to him.

"No. But I'm no ordinary girl."

Mechanically he refilled her glass.

"I hope you don't intend to get me drunk," she said.

David blushed slightly. "If you don't feel like drinking it, don't."

"Oh, don't take offense."

The low-cut black suit left her throat bare. In one of her lapels Gloria had put a flower, and the petals lay unfolded on her skin.

"May I?"

He was surprised at his own audacity. Taking a step forward, David bent over to smell the flower. His face brushed against her throat. Gloria, smiling, stroked his hair. Again he felt the scraping of her sharp nails. In spite of himself, his body stiffened, and he thought: "No, it can't be." His hand, independent of his body, had rested on her shoulder: his fingers pressing into the soft skin. He took her in his arms brutally. She felt the shock of his lips, of his hair. Then she separated herself from him.

"Please," she said, "that's enough."

She had withdrawn toward the table and was looking at him coldly.

Disheveled and pale, David inspired pity more than anything else. It wasn't honest of her to lead him on when he least expected it, only to cut him off suddenly: David was the kind that gives up easily.

She took a compact out of her bag and powdered her nose. Imagining that Luis was watching them, she forced herself to smile at him indifferently.

"I had come to visit you, not to have you kiss me," she said.

The boy lowered his head.

"I'm sorry. Forgive me."

There was a moment of silence, and Gloria said: "Tidy yourself up a bit. We had better go out."

*   *   *

A few weeks earlier Agustín Mendoza had asked Ana the source of her aversion toward Guarner. When she left the juvenile gang with which she had been associated, Ana had laid out her plan to him in great detail, and Agustín had the impression that she had been meditating on this plan for some time now, just looking for the opportunity of carrying it out.

The idea, she confessed to him, dated from a childhood memory of something that had happened many years ago. It was the day of the inauguration of a housing-project near her parents' house. Since dawn—the images paraded before her eyes like a newsreel—the neighborhood had been all decked out. The *Señor Delegado*, it was announced, was coming to visit. A brigade of workers washed the façades, swept the sidewalks, arranged the hangings, the carpets, and the pennants. The *procurador*, who was from Aravaca, had acquired from the mayor the triumphal arch used on these special solemn occasions and had placed it across the street from the school. It was of green rush, carefully interwoven, and decorated with laurel and Spanish broom, with a wooden panchart in the middle. Two hours before the painters had hurriedly erased the inscription reading: "Blessed Be Your Purity," which the people of Aravaca had put there years ago in homage to the local patron saint and which, from that time on, had greeted all illustrious guests visiting the town. Those in charge had intended to leave it like that, but the *procurador*—a pinkish gentleman with layers of fat under his chin—was of the opinion that it was not dignified enough. In its place they inscribed: *"Viva el Señor Delegado,"* and draped a pennant with the national colors above it.

The whole neighborhood was alive with holiday celebration. Some employees, with official emblems on their sleeves, distributed chocolates, almonds, and candies among the noisy bunch of kids that crowded around the *procurador,* yelling, heckling, and following him about. The people waved little paper flags. The neighbors stetched between their houses thick nets of paper streamers. The children, imagining this was a carnival, asked their parents if there were going to be fireworks and if, as part of the finale, balloons were going to be sent up. They, too, wanted to dress up, just as the fine gentlemen of the reception committee, who, in their Prince Alberts and striped trousers, with their voluminous stomachs and rounded hips, looked in profile vaguely like pigeons. They could be seen running here and there, stumbling over each other, in pursuit of the men with the emblems on their sleeves.

Ana—it was curious how she recalled it after so many years, as though it were engraved on her memory in burning images—wore a blue little coat with a round collar. Before going out into the street she had been given two little flags, which she held stiffly upright, one in each hand, at the level of her face: WE SAY YES. Her round pupils popped out of the orbit of her eyes, like openmouthed fish. Seen from afar, her face was a white disk with three garish holes in the middle: the blue eyes and a sticky piece of candy that the men with the emblems had stuck in her mouth as she passed; a red candy stick that looked like a pipe one puts in the mouth of a snowman.

Suddenly from the other end of the street the cheering

started. People appeared on their balconies, threw flowers, and applauded. The children all shouted: *"Viva el Señor Delegado!"* Ana, too, with her little flags, one in each hand, stood up straight and shouted: *"Viva! Viva!"* The red candy stick stuck to her lips, and she could scarcely speak. She took the candy out of her mouth. *"Viva! Viva!"* It was a great day; the children all had their little flags.

"Mine is red," she explained; "red, yellow, and then red again."

The boy beside her looked at her for a moment in scorn.

"Yes, of course! So is mine. They're all alike."

"But your candy is green," Ana said then, "and mine is red."

"That's true," the boy answered, "so it is."

The delegate came toward her. He was wearing a black frock coat, like all the rest, and responded to the cheers of the people with a slight bow of the head. His face had etched itself on her memory indelibly: the bland look, the measured step, the small black beard that he fingered during the pauses in his speech. In the crowd of frock coats he seemed a being from another planet, finer and more delicate.

Ana applauded frantically. When he passed under the arch the joy of the crowd came forth like a howl. How the children shouted! Ana had dropped her candy, and she bent down to pick it up, wiped off the dirt with her sleeve, and continued applauding. A few minutes later she saw him up on the platform under the flags that waved gaily in the wind.

The pennants fluttered from the eaves of the recently inaugurated buildings. A scarlet carpeting covered the platform. The people crowded in to hear the speech, and Ana took the candy out of her mouth. A silence ensued. The microphone and the loudspeakers rasped hoarsely. It was hard to tell whether the delegate was clearing his throat or whether the noises were coming from the inside of the microphone. The people hesitated, conjecturing. Ana stood with her mouth open, sucking on her candy and waving her little flags. He began his speech; she did not understand it, but the voice pleased her; it was soft and well modulated.

"You can tell a mile off that he's a gentleman," her mother had said.

And then all of a sudden, during one of the pauses, a strange fanfare was heard coming from down the street. The eyes of the crowd turned inevitably in that direction, Ana's, too, round with surprise. Shouts, protests, curses were heard all over.

"They're here already."

"Who?"

"The revolutionaries."

Her candy fell out of her mouth, but this time she did not bother to pick it up. A barrage of whistles interrupted the words of the delegate. From every side—Ana was not aware of the differences—volleys of insults were hurled: "Get out of here, get out! Sons of bitches!" The children ran from one side to the other, all excited. Some applauded.

The boy at her side asked her: "Are they getting ready to shoot the fireworks off?"

"Looks like it."

"The balloons, the balloons!"

Before she realized what she was doing, Ana had run along with the rest of the kids, laughing and pushing. She, too, shouted: "Viva! Viva!" Some young fellows had climbed upon the balconies of the houses and were throwing the flags down into the street. "Stop them! Stop them!" the people shouted. The children, wild with excitement, fell on the spoils, fought among themselves, ran after one another screaming. Someone handed out leaflets: DOWN WITH OPPRESSION. The children howled: "Down! Down!" Without knowing quite how, Ana found herself with a handful of the leaflets. She put them together with the WE-SAY-YES flags and started to wave them in the air.

On the platform the man went on with his speech. The crowd immediately around him listened in a religious silence, although nobody could really keep track of what he was saying. The loudspeakers were functioning well enough; but although faces were turned toward the platform, all eyes, like mechanical lenses that could be focused at will, looked in the direction of the other end of the street, where the disturbance was coming from.

There the confusion was getting worse and worse. The further away the crowd was from the platform, the more boldly people turned their backs on the delegate. A block further down they were forgetting to keep their composure: they participated in the noise, applauded, hissed. The enemies—her father had called them that—paraded along the avenue. They were poorly dressed young fellows carrying posters, which they stuck on the trees and walls of the houses. TO ALL WORKERS OF THE CITY AND OF THE COUNTRY, SOCIALISTS, MEN! Below there was something in fine print which Ana could not understand: so far, her mother had taught her only the capital letters. The parade, however, had filled her with enthusiasm. Six months before, from a rooftop, she had seen the Krone Circus parade—something like this, only on a smaller scale.

The contingency, under the shadow of the *guardia civil*, continued its march along a parallel street in closed ranks: WE, THE FIGHT. ENOUGH! Ana did not understand what the banners said, but she applauded enthusiastically. The men's hands were dirty, and they raised their fists in the air. There were also some poorly dressed women with them, shouting and laughing. Some kids ran between the ranks with their insignia of combat: colored ribbons, little flags that fluttered wildly in the breeze.

Bringing up the rear was a tiny gypsy who was playing a drum that was bigger than he was: tam-tam. At his side a little gypsy girl in a dirty flowered dress danced and sang, holding her hands way above her head, playing invisible castanets. Ana noticed, in astonishment, that she was barefoot. Her dark feet turned and twisted nimbly in the dust of the street. Her emaciated figure presented itself to the public, bowed, and threw kisses, and wound around the little gypsy boy.

Ana was still holding the little flags crossed over her breast as though she were about to give some signals; but her face was frozen in astonishment. The little gypsy girl, so dirty, fascinated her. When she passed by, Ana longed to talk to her, to kiss her. And it seemed to her that the shining eyes of the gypsy girl were fixed on her, too.

They were leaving. With their flags waving in the wind, they disappeared down the avenue. How Ana stared at them! Come back, come back! She wanted to follow them. The drummer boy ran, and the little gypsy girl raised her skirts and showed her behind to the spectators. Their little bodies were filled with life. Ana began to weep, and repeated their cries: "Down! Down!" The slogans on the posters were mixed in her mind with the words of the delegate. Tears ran down her cheeks. She did not understand anything. She was only eight years old.

"The delegate," Ana told Agustín Mendoza, "was Francisco Guarner, and as time passed, he epitomized for me all that I hated most. He is kind, tender, and friendly with children. He represents the whole thing: superficiality and education, money and manners."

She told how she had furtively followed his career for many years now. Guarner was a decorative figure, a fashion plate, a stuffed shirt, but in the eyes of a bourgeoisie—the closed world of the parents from which they felt themselves so detached—he was the incarnation of the old-fashioned way, of good manners, and the peaceful concept of life, of all that that the young people who sensed the uprising and the imminence of the fight hoped to stamp out forever. "To kill him," she said, "would be the equivalent of giving the death blow to the concept of life that he represents." "The atmosphere," Francisco Guarner himself had written, "is filled with blood. It seems the young smell it from far off. It is strange. Undoubtedly I am getting old." And he concluded the article that had caused a sensation among the parents: "In my day everything was different. In those days we at least had decent manners." Ana had handed the clipping to Agustín with an air of triumph, and when he asked her if her rebellion dated from that time, she replied with a gesture of the hand.

"It was much later," she said. "I remained for a long time still under the absolute influence of my mother, and for seven years or more I lived the stifling existence of the mediocre. My mother was absurd, inconsistent, and generous. Her teachings had something infinitely consoling, like those respectable manuals on how to conquer timidness or the art of succeeding in business. Her ideas were grotesque, devoid of all significance, like so many empty shells. 'Have confidence in yourself.' Or else: 'You must act according to your nature in order to fulfill your own potential.' And her words, spoken with a tone of conviction, quietly slipped into my ears, without leaving the slightest trace.

"The manuals on education which she bought had thrown her into a sea of confusion, and I was the one who paid for it. She made a great effort to make a successful woman out of me and tried in this way to fight my timidity, only succeeding, as a matter of fact, in increasing it. She made me put on my school uniform to visit the rich women in whose houses she had once served years before, and there she would present me as a very intelligent and educated girl, 'much above the level of the rest of the girls of her age.'

"Sometimes she took me to a strange house where, according to her, some exquisite little boys 'were dying to become my friends.' It was useless for me to resist. Mama was as firm as a rock. She never let go of any idea once she had gotten it into her head. So I had to go calling at places where I knew I wasn't wanted; climb the steps that led me to the oracular door, press the bell that invariably made me tremble pitifully. More than once the owner of the house, seeing how undone I was, asked me if I was ill.

"Other times, it was I who had to receive the visit of some boy all dressed up in his Sunday best, evidently brought by force, with whom my mother wanted me to be intimate friends. I could imagine the scene that had been made in his house when the boy had resisted going and the mother had insisted: 'See here, you've got to go whether you like it or not; you must go there and at least pretend to be friendly. I promised it to the poor woman and you cannot let me down now. The fact that she is a little girl who has no money is no reason for you to despise her. After all, she is your own age. Maybe you'll have fun playing together.' When I thought about all this, my timidity increased. I felt myself blushing, and it cost me a superhuman effort to say even a single word.

"My mother harbored the illusion that my destiny should be different from hers. She did not want me to ever learn to cook, and she became indignant when I would say that, in the end, I would end up being a factory worker, just as she did. 'That's not true,' she would exclaim, 'I swear by all that's holy that you will not spend your life in a factory. You have the makings of an artist and the manners of a lady.' And almost without realizing it, the two of us launched into a preposterous, wild argument: she, determined to prove to me that I was intelligent, and I, firmly resolved to preserve my mediocrity. I made her suffer: 'You know very well that what you say is not true.' And I: 'It is useless for you to try to fool yourself. I am like the others; just as homely and as common as any of them.' And between the two of us there was my father, who watched us with disgust, excluded, as he was, from the circle of our emotions.

"My mother was more ambitious and more intelligent than my father, who was, after all, a simple carpenter; he respected and accepted her natural superiority as an established fact. He had given over to her entirely the task of bringing me up, and I never saw him cross over the boundary lines that he voluntarily had imposed upon himself. Mama was grateful to him for this understanding, and when she spoke of him, she always referred to him as 'your poor father.' She also took it upon herself to excuse him if, on occasion, he hurt her feelings. She attributed his bad humor to overwork, although now that I think of it I believe I detected a kind of complacency in her pity and a kind of secret desire to keep him apart from us. For my mother was at heart a very selfish woman who could not stand to have me show any affection for anyone else, and when she referred to us, the exclusion of Papa was taken for granted: 'Just you and I, my dear child!' she would say. 'The rest do not matter.'

"Eight years ago, when I was fifteen, I went on Sunday mornings to a catechism class with young rich girls who were assisting the parish priest. The girls were of the highest social rank; they met with us in nice, clean classrooms, became our friends, and showered us with gifts of toys and candy. My mother, whose dream it was to get me into the rich girls' world, made me attend class every Sunday, and in spite of myself I had to please her in this.

"It was there that I met a girl named Celeste. She was tall and thin, elegant and well educated, and I think that from the very first day I had a crush on her. To me, she represented the highest ideal of my life: the possibility of becoming a famous dancer. She took dancing lessons every day, and one time she showed me several photographs of herself dressed in a Greek toga.

"From then on life changed completely for me. Each week I waited feverishly for Sunday to arrive so that I could see her again, drink in the musical ring of her voice and the delicate perfume that emanated from her body. She, too, was conscious of the admiration she awakened in me, and honored me with preferential treatment. I was her favorite. I called her 'Señorita Celeste,' but she insisted that I should not call her señorita. 'For goodness' sake, Ana,' she would say, 'if we are to be friends, we certainly shall have to call each other by our first names. Just call me Celeste.'

"Celeste symbolized for me the fulfillment of my hope: she was a person from a select class, whose very presence filled me with happiness. Little by little I got in the habit of counting the days of the week by the days that separated me from her. On Sunday mornings I would get up at dawn. I put on my horrible school uniform and ran as fast as I could to the parish center, my heart overflowing with happiness.

"What Celeste might possibly be doing during the rest of the week had me terribly worried, and as I did not dare ask her, I was only letting myself be guided by certain signs. I considered her as being in a forbidden and hermetically closed territory to which I would never have access. Whenever I thought about it, the tenuousness of our relationship put my heart on edge: the idea occurred to me that Celeste might not ever come again, and it seemed as though my world would tumble. Mentally I promised myself to ask her. When I was not in her presence, I spoke easily and sensibly; people considered me brilliant and bold. But as soon as I was near her, all that front disappeared: I could hardly manage to stammer out a word.

"The situation would have gone on indefinitely, perhaps, if Celeste herself had not suspected what was happening. One day she put her perfumed face close to mine and asked me if I loved her. My heart rang out like a bell within my breast: I had to make a terrific effort to get out the word 'Yes.' Then Celeste took my hands in hers and asked me with a smile to come visit her any afternoon. 'We all love you so much,' she said. And behind her I saw forming a multitude of faces, all pleasant and tenderly predisposed toward me. Before leaving, she made me promise that I would go to see her, and from the door of her car she turned around one last time and threw me a kiss.

"As she did not show up in the classroom the following Sunday, two days later I screwed up my courage and went to visit her in her apartment on Velázquez Street. At home I put a lilac ribbon in my hair the best way I knew how, and my mother gave me a red leather bag to carry, one she used for change when she went to the market.

"Thus decked out, my heart pounding, I stood in front of the terrifying front door, and I remember standing there for quite a long while with my ear to the door—at the risk of being surprised in such a ridiculous position. When I finally knocked, a nervous shudder shook my whole body. As in a trance, I let myself be led by a uniformed maid into the small parlor where I did not dare to sit down, feeling more and more homely and insignificant. I stood waiting for some time, filled at once with happiness and with panic. When Celeste appeared I very nearly broke down, sobbing.

"Dressed in a sheer silk suit with a tiny lace collar, she was more beautiful than I had ever seen her. 'Well! What a surprise!' she said, but I felt instinctively that my presence there annoyed her. Nevertheless, she kissed me on both cheeks and made me sit down in one of the big chairs.

"Her eyes scanned me from head to foot in a hastiness that betrayed her impatience. 'Well, well, so you finally decided to come and see me.' She went to get some candy for me, and during the pause I noticed some fruits on the sideboard: they were round, enormous, and highly polished, very much of a rich house; it looked as if the maid had taken great pleasure in shining them up.

"Then I heard voices in the next room, and through the doorway I saw a group of girls, elegantly dressed, who were looking at me in some astonishment. A ridiculous idea occurred to me: they had gathered there, lying in ambush for my entrance. And I felt the color rush to my face.

"Celeste, too, was somewhat embarrassed, and felt obliged to apologize. 'It's one of the girls from the cate-

chism class,' she said, 'who has been so sweet as to come
and see me. Ana, dear, go in and give them all a nice kiss.'
I went from tenderness to tenderness, as one passes from
hand to hand, suffering the damp contact of their caresses
as they brushed my skin. Celeste smiled at me benevo-
lently. 'Her ambition is to be a dancer.' I felt their glances
go toward my straight legs, and while they asked me
stupid questions, I felt a flame of hatred kindling within
me. I wanted to die right there on the spot and be swallowed up by the earth.

"I supposed that everybody but me had someone to
encourage them, and as I walked home, among the crowds
in the streets, I felt myself a flower of an unknown species
whose pollen was of interest to no one.

"A few days later an old friend of my father's came to
visit us at home. He had just been laid off because of
recent strikes and—as far as I could gather—he was active
in a band of leftists. I heard him arguing with my father
after supper, and that night I could not sleep. I had heard
him say that in the future world charity would be abol-
ished, and although the meaning of the phrase escaped
me, there was something in it that bothered and confused
me.

"As soon as I got up the next day I approached my
father suddenly.

" 'What is it that the revolutionists want?' I asked.

"My father was not a very intelligent man. He hesitated
a few moments before answering, and finally he said:
'They want to destroy the existing order. They preach
revolution.'

"I was beginning to understand, and I asked: 'And you?
Are you a revolutionist?'

"Papa filled his pipe.

" 'No. No, I'm not. I think that each one should try to rise in the world through his own efforts.'

"I interrupted him: 'And what about those who cannot?'

"He didn't know what to answer, and he turned around and walked away.

"The talk left me both depressed and excited. I vaguely felt that I could be useful in something, but I could not imagine how. That night I approached my father again.

" 'The revolutionists . . . do they kill their enemies?'

" 'Yes,' he answered. 'They don't mind a bit causing bloodshed.'

"The prestige of the party immediately went up in my mind. 'There are those who kill,' I said to myself, 'and those who let themselves be killed.' And I felt passionately that I belonged to the first group.

" 'And why aren't they fighting now?'

"Papa's glance traveled absent-mindedly around the room. He was very far from suspecting the importance that these minutes were having for me.

" 'They're probably waiting for the right moment to strike.'

"The idea of a conspiracy, still secret but probably working silently, thrilled me.

" 'And you,' I insisted, 'would you be on their side if they started something?'

"I knew that the question was going to annoy him, but I asked it, anyway.

" 'Well, you see, it's like this,' he said. 'When one gets old he doesn't bother himself with those things so much. All he wants is to be let alone. So far as I can make out, changes only make things worse.'

" 'And yet you were a revolutionary some years ago. Mama told me so one day.'

"My father remained silent a while.

" 'Yes. When I was young.'

"Dismayed, I ran off and took refuge in my bedroom. I stretched out on the bed but the irresistible necessity to act kept me from being still for even a moment. Unable to contain myself, I hastened to tell my mother about it.

" 'Mama, I want to work in a factory.'

"I remember that she looked at me for a few seconds, astonished and bewildered, not understanding.

" 'You what? You're crazy!'

"But I had already made up my mind to it.

" 'Yes, I am going to work in a factory.'

"There was no way of making her understand, and that very afternoon I ran away from home.

"Two weeks later I took a job in a clock factory. The gesture represented for me the complete repudiation of my childhood. It had been a very unhappy one, and I wanted to make it impossible for any other girl in the future to be exposed to a Celeste. It was about this time that I had begun to feel, as if in a dream, the desire to kill. Only through bloodshed, I told myself, can one attain the right to be a revolutionary. I imagined then that all real men had to their credit at least one death and—"

She stopped a few seconds as if groping for the right words. In front of her, Agustín Mendoza had set up against the easel the sketch of a dwarfed and deformed dancer who was trying vainly to take off into the air.

"The rest you already know," she said. "There is nothing I could tell you that you don't already know."

*　*　*

"I swear to God I'll do it."

Raúl Rivera struck the wooden table with his fist: he

was in shirt sleeves, with his hat thrown back; and a cigarette that had gone out hung from his lips.

"In that case," said Enrique Suárez, "all you have to do is prove it."

Raúl clapped his hands.

"Claudio!"

The man behind the counter looked at him with small, keen eyes.

"What can I do for you, Don Raúl?"

"Do you have an empty bottle?"

"Yes, sir. Must it be of some particular brand?"

Raúl threw his cigarette on the floor and smashed it with his heel.

"It doesn't matter. It's for an experiment."

Claudio searched about hurriedly among the cases; he was wearing a white apron tied around at the waist, like a local barber; in the center of his ash-colored eyes his pupils glowed like embers. Raúl had been a customer of his for more than a year, now; from the *residencia,* which was near by, he paid him a visit every morning. Of all Claudio's clients, Raúl was the one who spent the most money.

"Looks like your family finally remembered you, Don Raúl," he said.

Raúl, as usual, joked about it. "It can't always be lean years, you know."

Claudio handed him an amontillado wine bottle.

"This one all right?"

Raúl took it in his hands. "It has a pretty thick bottom, but it'll do."

Gerardo, Suárez, and the other Canaries watched him without saying anything.

"Fill it up with water," he said.

Claudio obeyed; he was used to Raúl's exhibitions, and

he entered in with good grace. He handed him the bottle filled to the brim.

"Good! Now, give me a rag of some kind to hold it with."

Gerardo gave him his handkerchief.

"Okay."

He folded it in half and wound it around the neck of the bottle.

"That's so I won't cut myself."

The clientele of the establishment, a strange mixture of students from the Residencia de Isaac Peral and truck-drivers from a near-by garage, looked at him with curiosity.

"Want to try it?" he said to Enrique Suárez.

Enrique nodded no. "Let Gerardo do it."

"Okay, here," and he handed him the bottle. "All you have to do is hit it hard with the palm of your right hand, and the bottom will fly out and break into bits."

Gerardo, a pale, but robust young man, hesitated: "What if I cut myself?"

Raúl Rivera smiled. Beneath his thick black mustache his lips curled, round and brutal.

"Try it."

"If you have to break the bottle," said Claudio, "maybe you had better go out in the street and do it."

"Just as you wish."

The group went out of the bar. In the street some dark men with gunny sacks folded over their heads were unloading coal from a truck. From her usual place on the corner the old beggar woman, to whom Raúl gave all his small change, smiled at them with wooden lips.

"With one blow, did you say?"

"That depends on you."

Raúl leaned against the wall with his arms crossed over

his chest and his legs spread apart. In the sunlight his eyes shone like two balls of smoked glass.

Gerardo took hold of the bottle with his left hand and hit the mouth of it with the palm of his right. He hit it squarely, but the bottom did not budge.

"Like that?" he asked.

Raúl smiled. "Yes, but harder."

Gerardo handed the bottle over to him. "Nobody could break it like that."

"Try again."

"Hell, no. Once is enough."

He looked at the palm of his hand, where the mouth of the bottle had left an impression: a pink circle that was getting redder and redder. Raúl Rivera took the bottle. He put his cigarette down on a little shelf just inside the doorway and unloosened the kerchief around his neck.

"See if I can't do it."

The art of taking a hold of the bottle, of shaking it as though it held some miracle-producing elixir, and of describing a gesture in the air with the palm of his hand, brief as a flash, took on, as Raúl performed, an obscure and almost sacred significance: like the ceremonies that demand a certain ritual. He struck the bottle.

The bottom flew out broken to bits: the water spilled all over the sidewalk. All the onlookers broke into cheers.

"A drink for everybody," said Raúl.

They went in the bar. While Raúl Rivera went to the washroom the rest of the Canaries sat down at one of the tables toward the rear, where two fellow Canaries and a girl were discussing politics with the *proletario*.

"I wouldn't be so sure."

"I tell you, it will all end up in so much eyewash."

They showed Gerardo the headlines about the trial of the revolutionaries.

"You don't think they'll do anything to him?"

The *proletario* smiled scornfully.

"They'll end up by shooting some worker who happened to be passing by. The big fish never get caught."

Gerardo shrugged his shoulders.

"That's what I think."

That morning Jaime Betancourt and another comrade had been set free. With Gloria Páez and the other guy's girlfriend, the Canaries had all gone to meet them at the gate of the jail: the young ex-prisoners had just shaved and looked about as always. Perhaps a little more pale than usual.

"Like a rather boring vacation," said Jaime. "As soon as they had us under arrest they didn't know what to do with us, and they didn't know what excuse to make to let us go."

His words, the irony in them, had given them back their optimism.

"I'll bet that what they'll probably do is to eliminate some worker, and that'll be the end of that."

"Yes," said the *proletario*, "it's always the most unfortunate people who pay."

They moved over in order to make room for Raúl. One of the Canaries, the smallest of the group, rested his elbow on top of the table.

"And what did he tell you?"

"Who?"

"What do you mean, who? Betancourt, of course!"

"Nothing. They had a pretty soft time of it, I guess. Apparently his family hasn't even found out about it. When he got back to his *residencia* he found a notice from the post office that they were holding a money order for him."

The *proletario* spat on the floor, scornfully. "Nothing ever happens to you kids. You just go on having a good time. The spectacle of poverty has always amused well-fed stomachs."

The Canaries did not pay any attention to him. They were used to his reproaches; they knew them by heart. His anger was particularly directed toward the contributors to *Atica*.

"You guys don't have a *people*," he said to them. "You're just a bunch of bourgeois with leftist ideas. You don't have any atmosphere of your own. What you do doesn't do the slightest good. You work in a vacuum. You write for a non-existent public."

The little Canary asked again: "Where is he now?"

Gerardo turned toward Raúl and smiled mockingly. "He went off with your friend Luis Páez's sister, of course. She behaved like a heroine."

He was caressing the bills in his pants pocket: there were still two hundred pesetas left.

"I don't know her," said Raúl.

The Canaries burst out laughing.

"No reason why you should."

Raúl emptied his glass in one draught.

"I know her brother. He's a friend of Agustín."

"Yes, we know all about it. The girl, you know, has a lot of confidence in us."

"Yes, a great deal of confidence."

They smiled contemptuously. Raúl began to feel annoyed. "Some sort of secret?"

His position vis-à-vis the Canaries was one of misgiving and distrust. All of his countrymen had separated from the group because of the publication of *Atica*. And since then they had been living at swords' points.

Enrique Suárez pretended to be looking with profound interest at the wine that remained in the bottom of his glass.

"Lose something?" asked Raúl.

"No, why?"

"You were looking at the glass so intently."

Gerardo laughed.

"Do you know David, that well-educated Catalonian who's a friend of Agustín Mendoza?"

Raúl nodded affirmatively. The suspicion that his friends might be amusing themselves at his expense increased his boastfulness. "Sure."

As Gerardo began to speak, a small dimple formed in his chin. "If you see him, tell him he better be careful, unless he wants to get his fingers burned."

"We understand he's sticking his nose in other people's business."

"You mean Gloria."

"Yes, Gloria."

The conceited tone of his former comrades exasperated him. Just because they ran out into the street the day of the strike and ran like a pack of greyhounds, they imagine they're a bunch of heroes, he thought. It was too much.

"I believe David's quite free to go out with whom he pleases."

He raised his hand to his neck and played with the little silver medal that he was wearing.

"Gloria's a smart one," said the other Canary. "And if she tires of him, she'll do him dirty."

"If she hasn't already done so by now."

"Yes, if she hasn't already done so."

There was an exchange of looks around the table.

"You're all filthy-minded," said the other girl. "Gloria isn't that kind. She's not a bad sort."

"No. Tell us that she's just a sweet, innocent little girl, and we'll believe you."

"Oh, sure. She's a saint."

The girl shrugged her shoulders. "You all exaggerate."

"Women always like to defend one another," said the *proletario*. "No doubt it's because they don't have a clear conscience."

Everybody laughed. Gerardo with his flat face came forward: his lips were pink and looked as if they were lacquered.

"Look here, let's just forget it. We only wanted to warn you, because he's a friend of yours. But one thing: you might tell Agustín Mendoza that he shouldn't play with fire."

The blood rushed to Raúl's face.

"I don't know what you mean."

"I mean just what I say. If he wants his big deal to remain secret, he'd better be more careful and not be exhibiting himself with her in the streets."

"I still don't get you."

"You're not going to tell me that you don't know Ana? I've seen you together several times."

"Can you tell me what all this has to do with Luis Páez's sister?"

Gerardo shrugged his shoulders.

"Nothing. Nothing whatsoever."

"As far as I'm concerned," said Enrique Suárez, "you can do what you please. But I repeat that the moment seems to me to be ill-chosen. You should have shown your face several months ago."

During the days of the strike Raúl had been living near Atocha in the apartment of a nurse from the clinic, with whom he was running around at the time.

"I admit that I've done absolutely nothing," he said,

"but at least I haven't made a fool of myself, like some of you have."

This time Enrique Suárez's outburst really burned Raúl. "And if you call all that sissy-stuff that you did 'showing your face,' then I'm San Luis de Gonzaga."

"At least we went down into the street," said Enrique.

"Well, you might just as well have stayed home. I don't think that the revolution would have suffered any."

The *proletario* approved with a nod of the head.

"Raúl's right. It would be better if bourgeois types like all of you would stay home and wait for them to come and butcher you. The world would be better off for it."

"You, too, instead of getting drunk all the time, could do something a little more practical," said the little Canary.

The *proletario* spat into his glass.

"Nobody was talking to you."

"He's right," said the girl. "You're useless, too."

"I guess we're all a bunch of parasites," concluded the *proletario*.

* * *

There was something attractive about Raúl's body: women liked the loose swaying of his limbs, which gave him a disjointed appearance when he walked. Factory girls would often turn around to look at him in the street, and as Raúl felt their eyes on him, he could not help taking a kind of delight in it.

That morning in the dispensary, where he practiced occasionally, he had had further proof. While he was preparing the injection for a patient the woman's attitude immediately attracted his attention. She was young, had an attractive face, and her eyes looked at him with the gentleness of a tamed animal. Almost without realizing it, Raúl surprised himself by kissing her on the neck, on the lips, and all over her body. The woman, he remembered now, smiled at him gratefully; they hadn't exchanged a word. He did not even know her name. In the next room a man had been waiting for her, who gave her his arm as they left.

"Believe me! She was a marvelous woman. I didn't know what to say. I wanted the earth to swallow me up; the fellow who was with her asked me how much he owed. I had to tell him that he owed me ten-fifty."

"Did you accept it?"

"Of course; I had to."

"And the woman, what was she doing meanwhile?"

Raúl pushed his hat back. "She was the perfect cynic. Hanging on the arm of the fellow, she looked at me as if she had never seen me before. She called me 'Doctor.' When they left she did not even shake hands."

In the dark corner of the room Eduardo Uribe was playing solitaire. Apparently he was not the least bit interested in what the rest were saying. Occasionally he would pour himself a glass of a lilac-colored liquor and sip at it.

"The gentleman makes them all fall in love with him," he said in a falsetto voice.

Ana turned around somewhat surprised: she did not know his clownish voice, and for a moment she thought that someone had just come in.

"He's just irresistible."

Cortézar looked at him in annoyance.

"If you're drunk, the best thing you can do is to shut up."

Uribe emptied his glass in one swallow. "*Sursum corda.* Let us lift our hearts."

He plunged his nose into the bottle as though he were savoring its bouquet, but seeing that Cortézar kept watching him, he quit. "You may go on. I assure you that you are not interrupting my game of solitaire."

Cortézar turned to Raúl.

"Well, as I was saying, did you ask the Canaries any questions?"

Rivera stroked his thick mustache—a gesture that had become a habit. "No. I didn't ask them any questions. Gerardo asked me if I knew Ana. I told him I did. And that was when he warned me that we should be careful."

At the other end of the room the shrill voice rose again.

"False! False! Mr. Raúl Rivera did not see Gerardo or anybody like him. The gentleman was very busy at that moment with a beautiful gorilla-girl."

His friends looked at him with an air of boredom. For a half hour now Eduardo Uribe had been doing his best to abort any attempt at talking.

Raúl rubbed the back of his hand over his fleshy lips. "If you don't make that imbecile shut up, I swear to God that I'll smash his face in for him."

Two days before, in a private room on San Marcoa Street, Uribe had gotten him drunk: Raúl and three women. They were celebrating the arrival of Raúl's check. Under the influence of the wine, Raúl began to pick up chairs and tables, then he undressed one of the women, who were running around the room laughing and screaming, and he ended up by holding one on each arm, like a furious Hercules, walking around the table. Uribe never had loved him so much as at that moment. His gigantic torso stood out in all its vigor: Raúl was laughing, Raúl was kissing, Raúl was loving. Two policemen, hearing the uproar, finally intervened, took them all to jail, and arrested them. Since then Raúl had not been speaking to Uribe.

"Ooo, I'm so scared! I'm so scared!" said Uribe. "If you only knew. He's getting more butch every day."

"And you, more fruity. If, instead of running around

drinking all the time you'd take a little more care of yourself, you wouldn't get into trouble."

Uribe turned to his comrades and made a gesture with his hands. "I wish you could have seen him, dead with fright, saying yes to everything the police asked him."

The rain was falling steadily into the flowered washbowl. Agustín had opened a bottle of gin: that afternoon his apathy was greater than usual, and he was trying to set himself up a little.

"They didn't say anything else?" he asked Raúl.

"No. Nothing else. At least not that I remember."

"It's all very strange," said Ana. "I can't imagine how they could have found out."

"They can't have found out anything," Luis Páez intervened. "If we didn't even know the name Francisco Guarner until just a few hours ago, how could they know it?"

"Telepathy," said Cortézar ironically.

"They've heard bells and they don't know where. But they want to give the impression of being well informed."

"I think," said Raúl, "that they're afraid we'll go ahead."

"Yes," said Cortézar, "we've all done enough talking, and they're the first to realize it. Now it's time for action, and we must behave accordingly."

"We have the means at the tip of our fingers. I think we're all ready."

"The thing is: Gerardo and his friends are a bunch of cowards. I have always been certain they never would dare see anything through."

"A few days ago," Agustín began, "I said that anyone who was not ready should back out then. It won't be held against him in the least."

His look traveled around the room. Everybody's eyes were fixed on him: it was like a mute plebescite in which everybody was doing his best to maintain the greatest resoluteness possible.

Little Luis Páez fixed his gaze on David with ill-concealed curiosity.

"If anybody has any objections, I think this is the best time to say so."

Cortézar cleared his throat. "The way I see it, the important thing is to determine just how we're going to pull it off. You've all spoken of Francisco Guarner and of how to approach him. But we haven't foreseen any of the consequences."

"Guarner receives every morning," explained Ana. "It would be the easiest thing in the world to get an interview. Any one of us can pass for a reporter. In the apartment there are only the maid and a secretary. The concierge is somewhat nosey, but you can avoid her by just hurrying past. The only difficulty is to leave the apartment without being seen; with the car running and ready to start, I defy anyone to catch up with us after ten minutes."

"Wouldn't it be better if two went instead of one?" David asked. "While one of us was liquidating Guarner, the other could be watching the rest of the house."

Agustín shook his head: "No. No accomplices. A single person alone arouses less suspicion. He who kills kills alone: he assumes the whole burden."

Large drops of rain which deadened the echo of his words splashed against the window panes. Frenzied birds took refuge in the openings under the eaves. The dripping of the rain went on, getting louder: plop, plop.

"In that case," said Cortézar, "circumstances are in our favor. We have nothing to reproach ourselves for."

"Gerardo and the Canaries know everything," said David. "Maybe we're singing 'victory' too soon."

"Gerardo's a fool," Raúl replied.

"Maybe so, but it's a bad beginning," David persisted.

"Do you think they'd be capable of saying something?"

"They wouldn't dream of it."

"The important thing," put in Agustín, "is to keep our heads. Once we're out in the street, we'll be in the clear."

Ana considered the discussion useless. She took it for granted that, as soon as the news of the crime spread, the whole country was going to be up in arms. Confronted with the corpse of the old politician, everybody would lose their *sang-froid*. Talk would stop once and for all. Every man would seek to justify himself.

Raúl interrupted him with a vigorous gesture.

"I think that before anything else we ought to determine the method of attack and who is going to be the one to do it."

Eduardo Uribe's voice rose up again, shrill and false, as if his throat were made of cloth. "The truth is that Raúl is dying to be the one who fires the little shot."

With his hat thrown back, his swollen lips under his thick mustache, and his shirt unbuttoned, Rivera was the image of scorn.

"Shit!" he said.

Agustín had left the open bottle of gin on the floor. He picked it up by the neck and thrust it to his lips.

"Nobody has discussed that point as yet."

Agustín played with his chin before answering. Naturally, he said to himself, the choice will be made by drawing lots, at the next leper session. That way we'll all have sufficient time to think, and we'll be able to make of it something like a floral preparation for death. He smiled. The idea isn't mine, of course, it's Tánger's. But it has, in its own way, a certain charm.

He stopped a moment to pour himself a drink. Before drinking, he held the glass between his fingers and turned it around with his other hand.

"All we have to do," he said, "is put a number of slips of paper between the pages of a book, as many as there are of us taking part in the drawing, seeing to it that the ends sticking out are all even. Actually one of them will be shorter than the rest. The one who pulls it is elected."

"You must have read that in some pirate stories," said Cortézar.

Agustín burst out laughing. "Yes, I have several of them under the table. Lola is very fond of them."

He showed them some with half-torn covers and titles such as: *The Hindu Enchanter, Death Has the Wings of a Butterfly.*

"Admit that you like them, too," said Luis Páez.

Agustín made a face: "I love them."

Cortézar parodied his languid voice, and everybody laughed.

"Who's going to put the slips in the book?"

Uribe caught the question on the fly.

"An innocent hand," he said.

All eyes turned toward him: he had just finished his game of solitaire and couldn't sit still.

"A small, soft, and well-formed hand."

"I presume you're not referring to your own," said Raúl.

Uribe's eyes glowed: "My heart is pure!"

He rolled up the sleeve of his coat to the elbow and raised his hand in the air affectedly.

"In the Middle Ages they always chose children to perform those tasks," he said. "And they also organized great crusades. It was a very beautiful thing. The priests traveled over the countryside recruiting little shepherds. 'To conquer the infidels,' they said, 'arms are not needed. The spectacle of these innocent children will be enough.' They got together more than a hundred thousand: a winged army of angels. When they reached the Mediterranean, the priests gave the order to advance. 'Before these innocents, as before Moses, the waters will open up wide.' The children obeyed and were drowned by the thousands. The few that remained were taken on battered ships and suffered the lash of storms until they arrived in Turkey, where they were sold as slaves."

When he finished, he made a great bow, like a magician. "Thank you, thank you!"

Ana got up: Tánger's jokes and the response he got annoyed her.

"Okay, then," she said. "In that case, it seems to me that everything is clear. Next Wednesday, I understand, you have your leper session. If before that time you think we should have another meeting, we can have it."

She had noticed through the window that the rain was stopping. Only a few straggling drops dripped in beads from the eaves and sounded on the slate projections.

There was a moment of silence.

"So," she said, "the best thing we can do now is leave. It's stopped raining; we better take advantage of it."

One after another, they left. Little Luis Páez was the last to leave. Before going, he took Agustín by the sleeve.

"Did you notice?"

He was pointing to the door through which the group had just disappeared.

"No. I don't know what you're talking about."

Little Luis's green eyes shone brightly. "David was white as wax."

He noticed that Agustín scratched his chin, as if the incident bothered him.

"It's curious. Do you think he was scared?"

Luis hesitated: that word, applied to one of the group, constituted a very serious accusation.

"It's hard to say," he said.

Curling his lips, Agustín cut him short: "In that case, all he has to do is say so and that will be the end of it."

Luis toyed with his cigarette.

"I don't think that he wants to leave us, either. But the fact that he should hesitate surprises me."

He stopped a few seconds, and then added: "In your place, I would try to help him regain his courage. I've noticed he has a lot of confidence in you, and anything you said could be a big help. Anyway, see what can be done."

They tried to call to him from the stairway. Agustín shrugged his shoulders. "I'll tell you something: don't worry about it."

Luis thanked him with a smile.

"You can tell me all about it some day."

Then he, too, hurried down the stairs.

                    *   *   *

His comrades were waiting for him in the doorway. It had begun to rain again, and only Cortézar had a raincoat. He offered it to Ana, who refused it with a shake of the head. "No, thanks."

They disappeared quickly down the street: Ana with Cortézar, the others in the opposite direction.

On the corner of Conde Duque David ran into Luis Páez. The boy had turned up his coat collar, and when he saw David a gentle smile lighted up his face.

"I was looking for you," he said.

They walked along close to the walls of the houses, close to where the water, dripping from the eaves, made monotonous bubbles.

"Listen," said Luis, "I don't want to interfere, but I have been noticing that for some time now you have been showing a great deal of interest in my sister."

Taking advantage of the position that the rain imposed upon them, Luis could observe him closely. David bit his lips. The hand in which he held his cigarette trembled.

"I don't know what you mean."

Luis took him by the arm. "We've been friends for a long time now, and there's no reason to hide anything from each other. I wanted to talk to you about my sister, but if it bothers you, drop it."

David's almond-shaped eyes contemplated him warily. "I did not say that it did, Luis. But the thing is—" he forced a smile, "you're the second one today that has approached me on the subject."

"I don't understand."

"I don't understand what's going on, either."

They walked along in silence for a little way.

"Raúl, too, came over to talk to me about it."

"Raúl? What did he say?"

"He spoke to me about Gloria."

Luis looked at him as if amazed. "What on earth for?"

David gulped. "It was in the bar this morning just after he had had a talk with the Canaries. He told me about it over the phone this afternoon, before we all got together. Maybe he thought that you wouldn't like it."

Luis realized that the initiative was slipping from his hands.

"May I know what he said to you?"

"Nothing special. He warned me that I should be careful."

"Of what?"

"Of Gloria."

Luis Páez scratched his head. "Now I'm the one who doesn't understand, really."

David tried to smile but did not succeed. "Your sister goes out with Jaime Betancourt. But, of course, you know that."

"Used to go out, you mean," said Luis.

"I understand they've released Betancourt."

"Is that all?"

"They told me not to meddle in things that were none of my business."

Little Luis spat on the ground. "Fools," he said.

They crossed the street almost at a run. They were going toward San Bernardo Street, where David was taking the subway, and he let Luis accompany him.

"Don't pay any attention to what they say. They don't know what they're doing."

"They told me that your sister went to meet Betancourt this morning." There was bitterness in David's words.

Luis shrugged his shoulders. "Women are all imbeciles. They draw up to the fire that throws the most heat. But there's no reason for you to be discouraged. Look: this is precisely what I wanted to talk to you about."

David did not say anything. A drop of rain rolled down the side of his nose, like a tear. He wiped his face with his handkerchief.

"Have you gone out with my sister often?"

"Yes."

"Lately?"

"Two or three times."

Luis stroked his chin. "That's funny. However, she's more interested in you than in anyone else."

"Don't you believe it. When I went out with her, Betancourt was in jail."

"So what?"

"Nothing. But that was the only reason why I was able to interest her at all."

Luis shook his head. "You're wrong. Gloria isn't so dumb as she may seem."

"I don't get you."

"It's very simple. What attracts her to Jaime is the fact that he's a revolutionary and that he's been in jail. She takes him for a hero, no less."

"And what has that got to do with me?"

"Just this: that so far you haven't proved yourself to her."

He walked in silence for a few moments and then went on in a lower voice: "It seems absurd, but that's the way it is."

David hesitated, afraid that Luis might be trying to lead him into something which he couldn't quite make out, and he was on the defensive.

"If that's the way it is, there's nothing I can do to convince her."

Luis tried to hide his impatience. "You're drowning in a teacup."

He noticed that David was turning to him questioningly, and he went on: "I spent part of yesterday afternoon with Gloria; we talked about all sorts of things, and from what she told me I gathered that it was you who interested her most."

"On the contrary, I think she's just stringing me along."

"No woman likes to give in."

He took David's arm again.

"Sometimes you seem awfully dumb. No girl snares a man just to give herself the pleasure of scorning him."

"I think she does."

The conversation was taking a dangerous turn, and Luis was the first to realize it. "As you can well imagine, I couldn't care less what Gloria does. I've told you all this just for your own sake. It annoys me that you should be the one to be made a fool of."

"Okay. Shoot."

Luis passed his hand over his mouth: his lips were very dry. "Yesterday we talked about you. Well, she said that she considered you more attractive and much more intelligent than Jaime. Only she said that he was braver. I told her that you, too, were a revolutionist."

Although it was almost dark now, Luis noticed that David was blushing: what he was saying seemed to be moving David deeply.

"I suppose so," he answered.

"No. You don't suppose anything. She thought that you wouldn't take part with us if the occasion arose. That's why I decided to warn you."

David understood now: he felt himself blushing to the roots of his hair. "In other words, a kind of test. Right?"

"Oh, come now. I didn't say that with any intention of offending. You know perfectly well that I have always considered you one of the gang."

David lowered his head. "No. You have nothing to apologize for. Besides, it's quite natural that you all should feel this way."

"I don't know what you mean."

"You have all been thinking of me as something of a coward. But you're the only one who has the honesty to say so."

"Don't be foolish," said Luis. "You know perfectly well that neither I nor anybody else has ever thought that."

"Look here, Luis. We'd better drop it. Don't think I'm blind."

"I've only told you the private opinion of my sister,

which none of us shares in any way whatsoever. She thinks you incapable of—"

David was going to reply but he stopped himself in time. To go on discussing the matter seemed stupid. They had reached the entrance of the subway at the bottom of San Bernardo Street, and they stood there, unable to make up their minds to say anything further.

"I've been idiotic, forgive me," Luis said.

David forced a smile. "There's nothing to forgive you for, Luis. You only said what you thought, and you know that I like frankness."

The smile, too forced, remained fixed on David's face, as though drawn by a strange stroke of the brush as an afterthought. Then he wiped his mouth with the back of his hand, and his face became very serious again—as if the smile had never existed.

"You're holding a grudge," said Luis.

"Nonsense."

The crowd, large at that hour, was pushing them along the passageway. A few yards from them a huge clock urged the people on with the nervous movements of its hands. Everything conspired against that dark moment, from which both of them wished to escape and yet which both prolonged.

"I'll come see you tomorrow. We can talk more calmly then," Luis offered.

"Just as you wish."

They shook hands.

$$\text{* * III * *}$$

S eated in the darkest corner of the studio, he was busy
making his usual mixtures. On the table where Agustín kept his water colors and gouaches, he had set up a full
arsenal of drinks. Tánger uncorked the bottles one by one,
compared their colors, and held them up toward the light
to appreciate their shadings and to pour a drop in each
glass.

"Oh, magic! To surrender oneself completely to alchemy! To fabricate cocktails!"

He remembered how when he was a child, in the garden of his family's country home, with the help of a bunch
of kids of whom he was the undisputed leader, he used to
collect as many ingredients as he could get his hands on.
He liked to mix them in a flask, make compounds, denature
them. He hoped that something new would emerge: the
miracle he had been waiting for—ever since the moment
he was born.

At the age of fifteen he had discovered the bartender's
art: liquors, syphon, ice, rinds of fruits, wild cherry brandy.
He invented recipes, made mixtures of colors, which he
invariably threw down the sink without tasting. No, that
wasn't it, either. The secret eluded him. He gave up, out of
boredom.

Having taken little sips of this and that, he was already
drunk as a lord. When his friends walked in, they ad-

dressed him in their usual affectionate little names. It was always the same: Eduardo Uribe got drunk, and the next day they patted him on the back. That was his destiny: as if the entire world with all its temptations conspired to keep him from studying.

A disturbing idea kept goading his brain, insistently. "Something has happened." It was absurd. He did not remember anything. The idea, however, was there, waggish, defiant. "Let's go places." He had gotten drunk with some friends, and he smiled as he remembered. Suddenly he saw everything clearly. "I was carrying a little barrel of gin, hung around my neck, and I was giving a drink to the thirsty."

He had spent the afternoon in the bars of Lavapiés, surrounded by old female gorillas and his little friends. The cigarette-vendor, a Galician woman of about fifty with a smiling face and gray hair, had kissed him on the head, calling him: "My love." In return, he gave her a drink of gin. He remembered having quenched the thirst of another woman, who was doubly fat because of all the skirts she wore one on top of the other, and who wore a flower in her hair over her ear. In the same bar he had been accosted by a man to whom he also gave a drink. In his corduroy trousers, his striped shirt, and his dark beret, the man looked like a distrustful lizard, or a black bird, and he had given Uribe his card.

Searching about in the numerous pockets of his jacket, Uribe found the card hidden away in one of the small ones. The man's name was Francisco Gómez, and he was a cabinet-maker. As Uribe read, a smile of triumph came over his entire face: I bring them light, color, and happiness, he thought. I am like one of those cloth flowers they put on the tables in cheap restaurants.

The furnishings of their homes, he knew from experi-

ence, were suffering from want of color. The dwellings of
such people, just like their lives, were gray, harsh. The
women planted geraniums and morning-glories on the balconies and put loud slipcovers over their furniture, for
they too, in their way, were looking for magic.

"Creatures such as we must always disguise reality. We
should wear masks and put wings on our shoulders. We are
Icaruses, fallen angels, relics of a dead splendor."

He went on rambling aloud, waving the card he had in
his hand; his trembling lips opened a little into a light line
of a smile.

"Were you saying something?"

A blonde, with solid breasts and wide hips, had stopped
in front of him: she had been one of Agustín's models for
a while, and, like most of the girls there, posed for the
sketching classes at the academy.

"When I was three years old, my parents signed a contract with a movie company. I played the part of a little
abandoned boy who was suffering from hunger and cold,
and whom the rest of the characters dressed and undressed, weaned and gave suck to. I think ten million
women wept seeing the picture. Now," he added in a
soft voice, "I wish only to fall into oblivion. I amuse myself in petty trades: I made drinks, I make verses. . . ."

The model left him with a stupid smile; as she walked
away, she gave the impression, from behind, of being much
heavier than she was: her curves stood out in relief all
over.

Another girl had also come up to him to pester him.
Uribe anticipated her questions.

"The answer is Ton-Kiki. Run along."

He remembered that years ago, disguised in an enormous wig and a pirate's beard, he had begged for alms at
the door of his own house. His mother had not recognized

him. She had wanted to send him away. "Perhaps some other time, my friend." Uribe had assumed a tragic look. "The stomach does not wait!" He had dropped to his knees. His mother had suddenly exclaimed: "Son!" and he had fallen into her arms: "Mother!" Then the two of them had turned around to acknowledge the applause of their public, who all the time had been witnessing the scene in tears from behind the fence. It had been positively sublime.

Realizing that he was digressing, he felt more drunk than ever. He was still holding the card in his hand, and he put it away. He took out another card instead: a picture of himself, dressed as a sailor, with a striped shirt, a straw hat, and a little cane.

Behind him, standing, Raúl seemed to be protecting him, arms resting on his shoulders. Hurriedly, Tánger put the picture back into his pocket thinking: "I'm getting off the track again."

He had gone directly from Lavapiés to a dingy little bar, where he had had a few more drinks. Someone had torn off the little barrel he carried—later he had found the chain that belonged to it. And that was where it must have been that they beat him up. He consulted his watch: twenty minutes to nine. Two hours remained a total blank, two hours in which he had no knowledge of what had happened nor of how he had gotten beat up. "For a long while now I have been doing unexpected things in places I know not of. Maybe I offered the traffic policemen a drink and then wiped their brows with my handkerchief." Yes, that must have been it. What's more, *he was sure*. Pretty soon now, they would be coming in en masse to thank him for it. They would offer him a bouquet of flowers. He smiled.

He gave himself over to the delights of alchemy with renewed ardor. He mixed the brown with the white, the yellow with the green: cognac, gin, manzanilla, a few drops

of menthe. He made out the inscription of a label: "Increase your prestige among your friends by serving
them . . ." He uncorked a squatty bottle: Ron de Mar-
tinica. "I need a *blue* drink." The violet brandy he kept in
a separate box, so he got up and crossed the room to get
it: "Hello, Tánger! Drunk as usual!" "Drunk again!" "Hungover, eh?" "Tánger. Tánger." His friends. He acknowl-
edged them with a smile. Someone slapped his behind: an
old gorilla-girl. He sat down again.

"Thanks." "Somebody, I have no idea who, is withering
away, is forming his body out of the dark." He had read
these words someplace, not long ago, and now they came
to his lips. He did not know why. How strange it was.
Strange things were happening that night. He consulted
the cards. If the first card is black, the puzzle will be
solved. He always knew the color of the first card: it was
always black. "I'm saved." He looked around him. Since
the day before Lola had been making preparations for the
leper session. Uribe was helping her: he arrived in the
studio carrying a whole load of stuff for the party. Now
the room was stocked with all sorts of things. Between
the wooden beams hung serpentines, Chinese lanterns, paper shades, colored ribbons: the whirlwind of fantasy that
accompanied him wherever he went.

Perched on top of a platform, he had given himself up
for a long while to the task of decorating the studio. His
magic hand had transformed it entirely. Between the pink
paper hangings the humid stains of the wall exhibited their
ulcers, open and repugnant. Canvases were piled up, one
on top of the other; sketches, favorite themes of Agustín
which Uribe liked: little ballerinas with dragonfly wings
on their shoulders; big, heavy women with little elves and
ants running all over their bodies; gigolos with thick mus-
taches, close-cropped and parted in the middle, enormous

hands, and black handkerchiefs around their necks.

He had taken out of the boxes a whole collection of daggers, all shapes and sizes: undulating, sinuous, ambiguous, like those which appeared in his dreams. Bunches of grapes hung pinned to the lampshades, and in the corner was a burlap bundle concealing a paradise of lights and colors, the secrets of which only he knew: paper trumpets, little hats, masks.

He smiled, satisfied. It was all his work, and he was there. They looked at him. All people did was look at him. He wanted to greet them: "Maybe in a little while what I am longing for will happen." Someone could whisper the formula into his ear, the secret. He wanted to remember what had happened that afternoon between five and seven, and he did *not* want to. Something stronger than himself urged him on: Two hours, one hundred and twenty minutes, seven thousand and two hundred seconds. Cloudy memories came to the surface of his memory. He put his hand to his face: *they had beaten him up between five and seven o'clock*. It was illogical. He seized the glass with the mixture and drank it down in one gulp.

"I simply must be amused."

*   *   *

The studio was gradually filling up. Lola, who was playing hostess, accompanied the new arrivals to the main room, where Cortézar was winding up the phonograph, and she told them to make themselves at home: "Here everybody does just whatever he pleases. The important thing is to be happy."

In the corner Uribe was preparing his concoctions; a few couples were dancing.

"And Agustín?"

"He's still in bed."

"Can we go in and see him?"

"Of course!"

In the hallway that led to the entrance Raúl Rivera was having a cigarette with some friends. The atmosphere was hot, and Raúl was in shirt sleeves. They were discussing a blonde girl who had just greeted them and with whom Raúl claimed to have had sexual relations.

"I tell you, that's the one. I met her on Atocha Street last year."

"What's she doing with that fat guy, then?"

"Must be her fiancé."

"Did you invite them?"

"Didn't I just say I don't know her name?"

"Then why has she come?"

"I haven't the slightest idea."

"Maybe she's a friend of Agustín's."

Lola came up to them with a tray of drinks. Her eyes were sparkling, her lips moist; she was drunk.

"You boars! You ought to be ashamed of yourselves staying out here, with so many good-looking girls inside."

"We're talking."

"Well, at least have a drink."

She handed them the drinks with a shaking hand.

Raúl smelled his before tasting it.

"Wow! A whole perfume shop!"

"One of Tánger's concoctions," said Lola.

"It would be!"

He returned it with a look of profound repugnance on his face. Lola laughed. A group of girls had just appeared in the door. The tallest, blond and slender, was wearing a tight-fitting close-knit sweater. She went up to Raúl.

"Hi ya, big boy."

"Hi, ugly!"

"Has it been going on for a long time?"

"Going on?"

"The music."

Raúl Rivera passed his hand over his mustache. "Do you mean to say there's music?"

She laughed: she had beautiful white teeth.

"You mean to say you don't hear it?"

"Well, I'll be—"

He feigned his surprise very well.

"You're all drunk. All men are alike. Drink, drink, drink, all the time. Can't you ever do anything else?"

Raúl buried his hairy hands in his pockets and balanced himself on his heels. He was smiling. "That all depends upon what you mean by 'something else.'"

The girl made a face. "Idiot!"

"Come on, let's go in."

Lola led them into the room. In the doorway she ran into Ana, who was wearing a dark suit that needed pressing, with a man's leather jacket that was too big for her slung over her shoulder.

"Bored?" Lola asked her.

Ana had noticed that when Lola spoke to her, the painter changed the intonation of her voice.

"Not at all," she answered, making an effort to be pleasant.

"Seeing you with your jacket on, I thought maybe you were leaving."

"I was cold."

"Really?"

Ana felt the contact of Lola's moist fingers on her hand and could not help shuddering a little.

"Won't you come and have a drink with me?"

"Of course."

She let herself be dragged toward the table where Eduardo Uribe was preparing his concoctions.

"I wish we could be friends," said Lola. "How about it?"

"If you wish."

They toasted. From his seat Uribe watched with luminous eyes, and then pointed at them.

"I see you."

"Shut up. You don't understand these things."

Uribe brought his index finger to his lips.

"The word is Ton-Kiki. Don't tell anybody."

Again Ana felt the contact of her fingers.

"Come, dear. I want you to say hello to Agustín."

They went into his room. Agustín Mendoza was still in his pajamas, lying on his back, enjoying his pipe with a distracted air, and when the two girls came in he slid over a little to make room for them.

"It's getting late," said Lola. "You ought to be dressed."

"I'm too lazy."

"That's just like you. Here's Ana, and you act as though you've never seen her before."

"Hello, Ana," said Agustín icily.

Lola's voice was monotonous, complaining. "Do you think that's a nice way to behave?"

"I'm going out like this."

"You're not decent."

"I'll put a robe on."

Lola sighed deeply and leaned toward Ana. "*You* tell him; maybe he'll pay more attention to you than to me. I need only tell him to do something, and he immediately decides to do the opposite."

"I? What do you want me to tell him?"

Lola's pleading attitude was becoming unbearable.

"I heard everything," said Agustín.

Changing his position, he stretched and yawned coarsely.

"I wasn't whispering," replied Lola. "I only want you

to behave reasonably. You've filled the studio with guests, and you have to tend to them."

"I don't know what I have to do with all this," exclaimed Ana.

Lola's alcoholic breath was repulsive, and Ana felt trapped between the two of them, feeling they were making her witness a previously rehearsed scene. She made a move to get up, but Lola forced her to stay.

"Please," she said. "Wait just a moment."

Agustín unbuttoned the top of his pajamas and began to scratch his hairy chest. He yawned again.

"Lola is very theatrical. She requires an audience for her scenes. One person is not enough. Besides, I don't know if you noticed, she's quite drunk."

Ana again felt the fumes of her breath as Lola said: "What did I tell you? He amuses himself all day long insulting me. It's not enough for him to be a useless bum. He also lies."

Agustín brought his finger to his temple and made a rotating movement.

"Recriminations do not become you, my sweet. They make you look old."

He got up off the bed and wrapped himself up in his robe.

"Ah, I almost forgot. I invited that Galician fellow that you like so much. I think you're wasting your time with me."

"You're a liar!"

She, too, had gotten up, and pulled Ana toward her.

"Don't pay any attention to him," she begged. "He's lying."

As Ana freed herself from the pressure of her fingers, she felt herself all prickly inside, like a cactus.

"Let me leave. I have nothing to do with any of this."

She left the room, but Lola caught up with her right outside the door.

"You've got to listen to me," she said.

She put her arm around Ana's waist and led her along, across the studio, filled with couples, and into a dingy little room at the end of the hall.

"You must hear me out," she said to Ana. "I have the right to be heard."

From his corner Uribe stuck his tongue out at them. The alcohol had gone to his head again, and once more he was beginning to see it all clearly. He felt himself aerial, floating. People called out to him and smiled at him. They patted him on the back. "Very nice, very nice," he told himself. "A great boy," and it seemed that the guests were nodding their heads in approval. "My presence is demanded all over." A brilliant halo enveloped him: it was as if he were sliding on a soapy floor.

"Tánger."

"Hello, you old bastard!"

"I want to talk to you."

"Don't you want a little drink?"

"Later. After we talk."

Whenever Luis Páez approached him it always was the same: Luis ordered and Uribe obeyed. Luis knew his weakness and used it to his own advantage. He would say to him: "I need thirty douros."

Uribe had money, but he never had more than he actually needed. Money lent to Luis was money lost. Nevertheless, he did not refuse. The boy's expression was mocking and implacable, and he knew how to go directly to the point.

"I need the money, and you're going to give it to me. You're dying to give it to me."

And Uribe would give it to him. He himself did not

know why. Luis spent the money to satisfy his whims. Usually on women. He wasn't even grateful. On the contrary, the fact that Uribe gave in to his demands constituted for Luis a motive for scorn. But, when the moment arrived, Uribe could not refuse.

"I'm not going to hit you, don't worry."

Uribe laughed and turned his pockets inside out: "I haven't a penny on me."

Luis went to get a chair and sat down in front of him.

"It's about something very simple," he said. "An idea invented especially for you. A little prank."

Uribe's eyes sparkled. "Do you mean it?"

"I've never been more serious."

"Oh!"

Uribe's face showed an immense delight. He took hold of a little bottle with a trembling hand and took a long drink.

"Is it a *wicked* idea?"

"Of course."

"Oh, tell me what it is."

He leaned forward to hear the secret with an avid look on his face. He had arrived at that state in which the soul, drunk on itself, abandons itself boldly to the event. What Luis was proposing seemed to him a tangible condensation of the atmosphere of frivolity that was floating around him. Undoubtedly this was the surprise that he had been waiting for. Something wicked and small and insinuating. "Like a lizard," he thought, "like a strange bird." He hadn't been mistaken, then.

"It's very simple," said Luis. "Tonight, when the party's over, we'll all stay and discuss the job we're going to pull. Do you remember?"

Uribe nodded drowsily. "Yes."

"We're going to play cards."

"Yes."

"And you'll cheat."

"For *real?*"

In the center of his eyes his pupils acquired the round-ness of two marbles. They were blue and playful.

"Listen to me carefully," said Luis. "Pay attention to everything I tell you and try to engrave it on your memory. Don't make me repeat things. We're going to decide by drawing who is going to kill the man."

"What man?" asked Uribe.

Luis began to lose patience. "Shut up and listen. We're going to kill a big shot, an old guy."

Tánger put his hand to his mouth: he was feeling happy. "He's old, you say?"

"Yes."

"I like the idea of killing an old man."

"We've done enough talking about it. This very night we're going to decide who'll be the one to bump him off. Agustín said something about doing it by drawing slips of paper. But at the last minute we've decided to do it with cards, playing poker. You'll deal out the cards, and the one that gets the worst hand will be it."

Uribe's face showed undivided attention. What Luis was saying seemed to him to have been suggested by him-self, as if the two of them had the same brain.

"Yes."

"All right. You know how to cheat. You showed me a lot of card tricks once. You took them out from under your sleeve and made them disappear."

"*And fly and skip about in the air and appear wherever I wish, and . . .*"

"Splendid. Now we're making sense. We'll play poker, and you'll deal out the cards."

"With tricks?"

"Without any tricks. Don't be so impatient. Only, when it's David's turn, you'll give him the bad hand."

Luis stopped a few seconds to watch the effect of his words. In Tánger's pale face the eyes shone like embers. Tánger put his hand to his mouth.

"Oh!"

"You'll find a way of doing it so that nobody notices. You'll have to give him different cards so that he doesn't even get a pair. In that way it will be he who does the shooting."

Uribe looked at him in ecstasy. All this was new, unforeseen, and he felt wrapped in a bright cloud. Once more they were turning to him. Therefore, *nothing had happened*. An eager desire seized him to carry on like mad, to exhibit his secrets to them. "I am a white dove."

"Calm down," said Luis. "We won't be playing for hours yet, and it is absolutely necessary that you remember exactly what I have told you. Above all, keep your mouth shut. This is just between you and me."

"And David?"

"He doesn't know anything about it."

"All this is very evil, isn't it?"

Luis paid no attention to him.

"Hell, it doesn't make any difference. It's all the same whether he does it or someone else does."

"You're doing this because he's a coward, aren't you?"

"That's right."

"And nothing will happen to him?"

"Why should anything happen to him? We're going to be there, aren't we?"

"Yes, of course."

"It's just a scare."

"Sure."

They were silent for a little while. Then Luis poured himself a drink.

"Will you remember what I've told you?"

"Of course. You'll wink at me while we're playing, and I—"

"I'll not wink at you, nor will I do anything else so stupid: I'm speaking to you in all seriousness, you idiot."

Uribe looked at him apologetically. "Oh, I'm sorry. I just said that. Of course I'll remember. I'll do everything. But don't look at me like that. You make me sad. You make me feel old. I like you more when you smile."

"All right. I'll smile then."

"No, not like that. There! Oh well. I know what I mean."

He brought his hand to his head. "I'm very drunk."

He turned toward one of the women, who was pouring herself a glass of crème de menthe, and began to make faces at her. He twisted his mouth, rolled his eyes, panted.

"I suppose I can drink a little," he said to Luis.

"As long as you're fairly sober within a couple of hours, you can do whatever you want. Don't forget, now. No one is to know a word of this."

"All right. I'll be as silent as the grave."

*　*　*

Someone had given a push to the light bulb over their heads. Protected by the flat shade, the swinging light highlighted fragmentarily the faces of the guests: the faces stood out with suddenness, whitewashed; glasses, backs of chairs, naked arms, gestures, postures sprang forth. The wave respected nobody. David felt himself swaying on a swing that little by little was losing its speed. He watched the light: round, with delicate filaments extended radially, it looked like a spider swinging from the end of his thread. Protests were heard from all over: those who were drunk felt as though they were at sea, the earth beneath their feet failing them.

"That's enough! Quit it! I'm dizzy!"

"Who did that?"

"Tánger—who else?"

David turned toward the corner following the accusing finger: Eduardo Uribe was seated on top of the improvised bar, with his hands crossed over his chest, surrounded by a group of women admirers.

"That's not true," said one of them. "Tánger is right here, being a very good boy and telling us stories."

Uribe rewarded her with a caress.

"Thanks, darling."

Someone stopped the swinging of the light, straightened the shade, and put back the decorations that had fallen.

"High time!" exclaimed a voice.

An unknown girl made room for David in the group that was listening to Uribe. She handed him a glass of gin and brought her finger to her lips.

"Look at him. He's in good form tonight."

Uribe had noticed David's arrival and looked disappointed.

"The stars are not favorable to you today, poet. Mars and Venus are making love, squatting, right in front of your very beard."

The same girl intervened, obviously impatient.

"Go on, Tánger."

Uribe paid no attention to her: he spoke only to David, mysteriously.

"Prepare yourself. Your hour has come."

David decided to play the game with him, and forced a smile.

"Okay. I'll bear that in mind."

The girls insisted. "Come on, Tánger."

"What's said is said."

"Said? What did you say?"

"The essential."

He wiped his lips with his handkerchief.

"Above all, no condescension."

He left the group, and David took him by the arm.

"Where are the rest? I just arrived a moment ago, and I've seen only you and Raúl."

"Agustín is in his room. He hasn't gotten up yet since morning."

"And Ana?"

"Lola took her with her. They've been conspiring in there somewhere for over an hour."

David went to Agustín's room. He found him dressed, but still lying down. The light that slipped in through the door cut him transversally across the bed. The rest of the room was dark.

David watched him empty his pipe in the chamber pot —a gesture he had started for the sole purpose of irritating Lola, which had now become a habit.

"What's the matter with you?" David said.

"Nothing. I'm bored, that's all."

He made room for him on the bed. The lights were out, and David noticed the presence of another person, a woman.

"You know Celia, don't you?"

David shook his head. He had just made a discovery: the woman was crying.

"I came to talk to you."

Agustín stretched himself on the bed again, in such a way that the light did not shine in his face.

"Go ahead."

"Alone."

Agustín made a movement with his hand.

"Beat it, will you? I'll call you later."

The girl got up and left the room slowly. David did not get to see her face.

"Well, we're alone."

David bit his fingernails before speaking. As always when he faced Agustín, he felt inwardly disarmed.

"The news has just reached me that one day not so long ago you all discussed among yourselves whether or not I should be allowed to participate in the job. Apparently there were various personal opinions, and I only wanted to tell you that it's all the same to me. I'm used to such things and all the more so since I got to know all of you. But you must remember this. When the thought occurred to you, you might have told me about it. I wouldn't have reproached you at all. But since you did accept me, if now you have changed your mind about me, or if there is someone who is against me, I have the right to be told. I am just as much involved in the affair as you are, and I deserve to be treated on an equal basis. If I said 'yes,' there's no reason for doubting my word now, and I demand an explanation. Anyone against me ought to tell me so to my face, without beating about the bush. If he proves that I'm no good, I'll be the first to accept it."

He spoke in a calm voice, but the trembling of his hands betrayed his true feelings. His heart beat fast. He turned sideways avoiding Agustín's look.

"You're wrong," he heard him say. "Nobody has dared to doubt your word. Whoever told you that was not telling the truth." .

David was waiting for that answer and clenched his teeth. Luis's confidential talk had left no room for doubt. But he did not wish to give up so easily.

"I have it from a good source, Agustín," he replied, "and believe me: I do not hold it against you. I believe that everyone has a perfect right to hold whatever opinion he pleases about the next guy. All I ask for is the chance to defend myself."

"Listen to me, David. When I proposed this, I gave you —you and all the rest—complete freedom. It was all the same to me whether you said yes or no. What the hell! I would have done it just the same alone; or with Ana, as she wanted it. I only wanted to give you all the opportunity. Since we were all in it together from the beginning, it makes sense that we finish in the same way. Don't you think so?"

He spoke in his lush, thick voice, which David had not heard for a long time. He remembered the day they had met in Barcelona. He had gone with a friend of his to the Liceo Café, and there he met Agustín Mendoza, surrounded by painters, poets, and anarchists. That was four years ago, and his friendship had been for him the most important change in his life. Since that meeting David had ceased being the studious fellow, the pride of his family, the one everybody held up as an example, to become a good-for-nothing, a failure, a mediocre poet. When Agustín went to Madrid David had followed him. And now he was amazed to think that, in the same circumstances, he would have done the same thing now. It was strange.

"In Barcelona on another occasion," said Agustín, "you made a similar scene, and I called you stupid. It was a summer evening, I remember it very well. I walked with you all the way to Pedralbes, where you were living with your grandmother. I told you then: 'You've got to be courageous if you want to face yourself, and I think you are; I would be very sorry if you were to disappoint me.' Or words to that effect. Even then you had that damned tendency toward mental masturbation, and I wanted you to stop it. Your problem was and is a question of confidence. If you don't have confidence in yourself, there's no point in your trying to do anything."

He spoke to him as though he were speaking to a little boy, just as he had done four years ago, and David felt like breaking down and crying. He realized that nothing else mattered to him: only the fleeting moment as he saw himself reflected full length.

The old tennis court, where his mother had had his picture taken years before, was covered at the time with weeds and bramble: for years nobody had played on it. The court was no longer red. Only a few reddish mounds that remained near the woodshed testified to a time when the net divided the court into two, and his aunts exhibited the delicate swishing of their skirts during the game. The wind had spread the seeds of the bordering bushes, and a myriad of shoots had burst through the former pink surface. At the end of the court in a circular cement tank floated wisps of green beards, which his brothers used to pull with a reed spear; and swarms of dragonflies careened around like tiny helicopters, rocked by the disheveling afternoon breeze.

Under the medlar trees there are three rockers: Agustín's, Juana's, and his own. While he is speaking, a bumble bee buzzes around the drinks and the wind disperses the penetrating odor of the rosebays. Juana is between the two of them, more beautiful than ever, and David's one desire is that Agustín look at her with the same eyes with which he himself does, and that Agustín find her as beautiful as he himself finds her: her arms are ivory white, and one can visualize her budding breasts beginning to insinuate themselves under her blouse. Ordinarily she talks incessantly; but now she doesn't say a word. He is afraid that

Agustín might not appreciate her, and he makes an effort to help her appear at her best, but suddenly he realizes that a current of affection has been established between them without his intervention, and this discovery fills him, he does not know why, with sadness.

Two days before, hidden in a corner of the garden where the foliage was thickest, Juana and he had smoked a package of cigarettes, which David pretended to have stolen out of his father's pocket, and which actually he had bought at a tobacco shop. They sat facing each other so that their knees touched, and Juana, as usual, made fun of his awkwardness. She knew how to exhale through the nose, and she played the trick on him of "making it come out of her eyes." When she laughed, her breasts trembled gently, and David suddenly felt the savage desire to press his fingers into her skin, to pull her toward himself, and to kiss her. Juana was slender, small, and white: she hated to have people put their hands on her, and she cringed from any demonstration of affection. When her girlfriends kissed her, she turned her head to one side with a look of disgust, and she spoke with horror of her school friends, dressed in black, like dwarfed nuns, with damp hands and ruddy complexions. To put his hand on her knee cost him a horrible effort, and his heart went to his mouth. Juana had looked at him with rancor in her pale blue eyes, and suddenly, with unexpected meanness, she touched the lighted cigarette to the back of his hand. David was on the point of drawing it back with a cry, but his fingers remained fast to the soft skin, while his eyes filled with tears. Juana finally withdrew the cigarette: "Your pride, David, your damned pride! You'd throw yourself out of the window if I asked you to."

Now, he was telling Agustín what had taken place,

showing him the burn on his hand—and David saw them laughing at him.

He was jealous of one and of the other at the same time: Juana listened to Agustín's stories as though enchanted. Agustín spoke exclusively for Juana. And suddenly all their qualities became hateful to him: he wanted Agustín to be mediocre and Juana to be less beautiful. When he had arranged their meeting, he had obeyed the suicidal impulse of destroying everything he loved. He knew that Agustín had a way with women and that Juana admired, above everything else, boldness. They were made for each other, and David had annihilated himself by introducing them to each other. God, oh God! He felt his blood pulsing in his brain; he saw Juana laugh: her teeth were like those of a young animal. Agustín, too, laughed; and he watched them with shining eyes. And suddenly, under the pretext of showing them some old furniture, he took them to the woodshed, and there he left them, locked in.

I do hope they do it. Oh, yes; I hope they do it. Before his face the bougainvillaeas dangled their army of little purple bells and yellow clappers. Dancing oleanders bent over the fence rail and brushed his hair as he ran toward the house. Pale, small shrubs unfolded their flowering masses to the dying afternoon. The air had become filled with cries of birds, and the gravel of the garden path crunched under his footsteps. Pity, pity. "If abyss means profundity, shall we not say that the heart of man is an abyss? Man can express his thoughts by means of words, but what soul will let itself be penetrated, what heart let itself be seen? Who knows what is transpiring within the heart? What power it has within, what it does within, what it thinks within, what schemes it hatches within? Don't you know that the profundity of man is such that it escapes the very man in whom it is?" Agustín had taken him by the arm and made him look at him straight in the eye: "You're a child, David. You torture yourself in the most absurd way, for things that have no importance. Why didn't you tell me that you loved her? Why? Why?"

There was a pause, during which the noise of the music suddenly became shrill: someone had opened a door somewhere.

"Well, I've told you all I came to tell you," David whispered.

"So, what do you want me to do? Tell you yes, that we don't trust you? I would be lying if I said so."

David did not answer. He had extended his two hands into the zone of the light, and was contemplating them absorbedly.

"Look here. Get all that nonsense out of your head. Let your imagination alone. Don't torture yourself."

Agustín took his pipe out of his pocket and filled it. David held his lighter toward him, and the flame ran over his face like a grease stain.

"It's curious," Agustín said suddenly. "It seems only yesterday that we were meeting in the café on the Ramblas. We talked about assault as if it were something utopian, impossible. How old were you then?"

"Nineteen. I had just come back from France."

"And I had just finished my baccalaureate a few months before, remember? When I think of what we were then and what we are now I am amazed at myself. Don't you feel something like that, too?"

"Yes. We have lived very fast, without ever looking behind. Sometimes I wonder what has happened to us," said David. "I have the impression that we have died; that now we are somebody else."

"The fact is that nothing binds us to the past," Agustín

interrupted. "Nor even to the future. We live from day to day."

"Often when I get up I ask myself what I'll do today, and I don't know what to answer. I have the feeling that I'm looking for an answer, and, as a matter of fact, I don't even know the question."

"Perhaps we'll know before long," answered Agustín. "And others will say it in our name."

"We've lost the best years," murmured David. "The game will have been over forever."

"That's just the point: To get it over with."

Agustín gritted his teeth and added: "One day or another, the end will have to come."

David was on the point of asking: "Are you sure that this is not the last manifestation of our game?" He himself was firmly convinced, but he did not dare; he was afraid that Agustín might consider it a sign of weakness.

And the brusque contact with his hand had produced a shudder in him.

"And it is better that it be today, don't you think?"

*   *   *

The light hung from the center of the ceiling, enveloped in a fluted paper shade, rough to the touch. At a sign from Agustín, David turned it off again. The gesture of turning it on had been purely mechanical. The reflex, perhaps, of an impish child.

"Be still," he said.

David obeyed him, looking at him curiously. They had been friends for a long time, and Agustín had never spoken to him like that. He felt filled with uneasiness and tenderness at the same time.

"You have known me a long time," Agustín continued. "I have told you how spoiled I was as a child. It wasn't my fault. My parents loved me too much, and they never dared refuse me anything. I was the only object in life for them; a kind of gift, or surprise, or grace. Three years before I was born my mother had given birth to a little brother, stillborn. My mother had to be sent to a sanatorium. The doctor had said that probably they would never have another child, and when I was, nevertheless, born, everybody received me with cries of joy and much applause.

"They probably still have hundreds of photographs of me at home: the day of my christening, my first steps, in a little sailor suit, by the sea, on the beach, and in the country. My mere existence gave them a kind of wild happiness. They were always taking me to the garden to take my picture. In time my face came to adapt itself to this comedy: all day long, it seemed to wait, patiently, with studied poses, for the click of the camera.

"Long before you knew me I considered myself a privileged character. Any praise, no matter how extravagant, seemed to me the result of careful and accurate thinking. Surrounded by people who smiled at me and flattered me, I floated about like a drunken insect, with the suggestive wings of a butterfly, and although I was coquettish enough to, I pretended not to notice the admiration that I aroused, in reality I lived as in a dream, filled with satisfaction, adorned with medals of a pretended humility, and smiling at everybody as though I were a bashful, timid child.

"Even as a child (it almost makes me blush to admit it), my tastes were already very special, but instead of what usually happens in such cases, my parents took great pains to encourage them. Because of their own artistic bent, they refused to consider it a tragedy that I should devote myself to drawing and to taking piano lessons from an old, half-crazy teacher.

"My father used to paint during the hours he had free from his work; and it was his ambition that I should be a painter. He continually regaled me with boxes of paints, canvases, and palettes. Many an afternoon he allowed me to go with him to his studio, where, seated on a stool, I followed the progress of his brush. He liked to consult me about colors, and when he finished, he would ask me quite seriously for my opinion. On other occasions he would encourage me to draw. He would ask me to make him a still life, a portrait, a water color. For hours I remained absorbed in my work, entirely satisfied. Sometimes, if he liked the picture, he would take it home and show it to my mother. All this may seem absurd, especially if you take into account that I was barely fourteen years old, but it all formed a part of the educational theory by which he was bringing me up.

"As for my mother, she had gotten the idea into her head that I was a great actor: on my sixteenth birthday she gave me a chest filled with costumes, beards, wigs, and masks. In the rear of the house there was a kind of stage where amateur artists would play in benefit performances organized by my mother. There I learned to recite Rimbaud's 'Le Bateau Ivre,' all dressed up in one of my costumes. One day she decided to bring my father, who did not suspect a thing. I recited the poem in its entirety, with all the emotion I was capable of, and when I finished, I discovered that my parents were both weeping. From then on, it was decided that I was to be an actor.

"I immediately began my studies in the school of dramatic art, where I had to undergo a very rigid discipline: forced to learn by heart abominable texts. But I took advantage of that experience to recite at home the works that I loved: the doubts of Macbeth, poems of Blake. I was burning with all sorts of ambitious projects that I knew would cause astonishment and admiration. And in my imagination I thought I could hear a chorus of fantastic applause, distant and diffuse, like a confused humming.

"The continuous tribute that I received from my parents made me swell with pride. As I said, my mere presence was enough to give them happiness. In me they saw the unexpected, the miraculous. As a consequence, I was exempt from any law. Everything contributed to making me feel that I was different. I listened to people talk with obvious awe about my talent. Many times when they thought I was asleep, they talked about the plans that they were hatching for me, plans that I followed with closed eyes, while my heart beat rapidly within my breast. Without realizing it, I was storing up vanity, pretended humility, false love, complacency: all that which is generally called good sentiments. My soul was an absurd mixture of contradictory virtues poorly matched. And secretly I felt an asphyxiating sensation of ill-being.

"My mother said later that she already knew at that time that I was condemned, and that my beauty, alas, was the beauty of the devil. I can't say the same for myself: I didn't know anything. I did not harbor against my parents any resentment, and their fawning, pawing devotion rather flattered me. My aim was to please: I wanted to respond to the hopes pinned on me. It was later, years later that I realized my narrowness and my oppression. I was wearing one of the costumes which they had just given me; under its great folds I felt a completely different being, and just a bit insolent. Dressed as a Negro, I recited 'Une Saison en l'Enfer' before the wardrobe mirror in my room. When I reached the invocation of the ancestors, I made the poet's anger my own; I felt detached from myself and I forgot where I was.

"I admit without humility that I recited the lines quite

well, and I identified myself easily with the subject. Some of the phrases seemed to spring spontaneously from within me. I was surprised, almost, to see them written down, such was the identity that bound us. The words of the poet had put me in touch with hatred, and its call awakened an ancient echo in my blood.

"As I was saying, my parents dazzled me with the spectacle of their devotion. They courted me, they praised me, they smiled upon me. And suddenly their subservience began to seem distasteful to me. I had never encountered any resistence in our relationship: only acquiescence. I always got what I wanted. Any decision reached by me acquired in their eyes an extraordinary value. They outdid themselves for me alone, and granted me a freedom of choice that no other boy of my age enjoyed. But by giving me the liberty to do what I wished, they were sacrificing themselves for my sake; on the other hand, through their very sacrifice they were actually making me beholden to them. The skein was extremely subtle, and it was not easy to disentangle. Behind the noble words I saw the bribe of love and the cowardice of sacrifice rear their heads. All right, I said to myself, I shall not be the one to surrender.

"My mother, especially, loved me with a tenderness that was truly tyrannical. The dream of her life had been to have a son like me, rebellious, impulsive, and proud; and in my first steps toward liberty I counted on her willing support. I did not bother informing my father, who was less intelligent than she, of the change: he lived locked up in his world, which my mother guarded and which was sufficient to make him happy, but not her. She realized that a personality like my father's was not enough to fulfill her. Tranquillity did not satisfy her. She had a need of company which nothing would satisfy, and she had to have the nearness of a being on which to rest the immense emptiness of her soul.

"I made her the confidante of my first escapades, and my father did not suspect anything, shut in as he was in his little world of glass. We formed between us a kind of society, from which my father was excluded and whose purpose was the revelation of our most intimate secrets. I kept her informed of my first amorous adventures, told her about my nights out, never omitting a single detail. At times my frankness went to inconceivable extremes. But my mother never said anything. She just gave me the money I needed, carefully keeping everything hidden from my father. The fact that I trusted her so much seemed to make her happy. In a way, it was for her a rather elegant manner of being unfaithful to my father.

"Those confidences, at first limited to the realm of my sexual experiences, grew later into my desire for freedom. Little by little I felt a hatred develop in me of everything around me. I was beginning to realize that another's love creates in us a multitude of ties that limit and coerce us. 'Love is soft, sticky, and pawing,' I told her. 'It weakens us and ends up by dominating us.' My mother listened to me without blinking an eyelash, as if nothing I said affected her. Perhaps she imagined that it did not apply to her: that I was talking in the abstract. When I had finished, she urged me to keep my silence: 'That is all very well; but don't ever tell that to anyone. A thought, once repeated, loses its value, evaporates. This must remain between the two of us.'

"Her obstinate love knew no limits: it wrapped itself around me like clothes that are too tight. My confessions, no matter how shameless, gave her one reason more for loving me. She never tried to stop them. She simply accepted them, as she accepted everything mine, without realizing that it was precisely her acceptance which was separating us most. In time I came to encompass her in my hatred, and my words had no other object than to torture her.

"I told her again and again to the point of satiety that my love had disintegrated, that I was looking for the opportune moment to leave her side. I even reproached her for the education I had received, the fruits of which she was feeling: 'There you are, that is what you have brought on yourself. Perhaps if you had been hard, everything would have been different. But now it is too late.' My mother listened to me, her face contracted with pain. All she could do was to bow her head submissively, and to my insults she responded obstinately: 'You are good, but you insist upon hiding it.'

"These conversations, always the same, ended up by tiring me. I found them useless and degrading. 'I don't know what pleasure you can get out of them,' I said to her. 'One would think you enjoy torturing yourself.'

"And my mother, refusing to answer, looked at me with relentless, pursuing eyes. 'Please,' she murmured, 'please; I beg of you.'

"My father, on the other hand, lived deceived to the very end. When he began to understand, it was too late: my mother's zealous vigilance had done its work. It took him suddenly, without giving him time to recover; hence, his defeat was the more deadly. He found himself faced with a consummate fact: the tumbling down of all his castles. And in his stupor he did not even have the strength to say a single word to me.

"I remember that around that time I decided to play a filthy trick on my mother. My father often had models around who posed for him. Most of them were pretty and attractive. There was one in particular, small and insinuating, who fascinated me a good deal. Her body, as harmonious as a statue's, seemed molded out of rubber. I called my father's attention to her, knowing his occasional weakness for women, and I encouraged him to take her on as his mistress. One afternoon at my instigation he made love to her in his studio, and that same evening I hastened to tell my mother all about it. 'Don't be angry with him,' I said to her. 'The whole thing was my doing.' I saw her turn pale, white with anger, but she didn't say a word. Only later when I was going to bed she came to my room, her eyes swollen from crying.

" 'You're a beast, Agustín. I would not do a thing like that even to the person I hated most in the world.'

"Her answer made me understand that nothing would ever change her, and on the following day I told them of my intention to leave for Paris. I did it with the utmost brevity, without asking them for their consent. Naturally, they hastened to make it possible. They went immediately to buy my tickets. They overwhelmed me with their preparations. They understood absolutely nothing about my motives, and they hoped to soften me with their affection.

"They knew perfectly well that all their hopes for my future had just come to an end. It was enough to look at them to understand that they felt themselves frustrated and miserable. They asked me if I would write to them, and I answered no. Then they asked my permission to write to me. I replied that they could do so if they got any pleasure out of it, and that as far as I was concerned I saw no reason why they should not. They drove me to the station and during the ride they did not find a word to say. It seems to me now that they already knew that I would not ever go back to them.

"However, they tried not to give up hope. They imagined that Paris, Lisbon, Madrid would mean only stages, and that in the end reality would call me back again to Barcelona. They offered me sufficient money to establish a dramatic-arts school there. Nowhere, they said, could I find such opportunities to get ahead. They promised to let me live the type of life that I wanted to. Oh, they proved themselves absurdly magnanimous. They sacrificed themselves for me up to the very end.

"When I arrived in Paris, about five years ago, I rented a studio, where I began immediately to daub lots of canvases. I knew well enough that I was no painter of genius, but I did hope to make myself a place in the theater. However, I ran up against the insurmountable obstacle of my accent. Nothing ever came of the tryouts I had. My voice did not interest anyone. Then I began to work in a series of incredible places, the kind of jobs with which American millionaires always start off their careers: newspaper boy, waiter, elevator boy, dishwasher. On the way back to the studio I would go marketing. I had rented an electric plate, and every night I cooked a few strips of bacon and a large pot of coffee.

"I had nothing else to eat, and during the day I felt the walls of my stomach contract as if they were made of rubber. Also, at night in bed I suffered from the cold, and to try to get warm I used to put a pan of water on to boil, and from time to time I'd dip my hands in it. One day during that time I received a letter from my mother with a blank check in it. I was stretched out on the divan (a horrible one with scarlet flowers which I shall never forget), alone with my hunger and the cold. That blank check filled me with fury. Almost instantly I wrote my answer, a single word—which you can imagine—and I ran out and deposited it in the nearest mailbox.

"A fine rain was falling, and I felt a few drops of it run down my neck; I was wrapped up in hatred, hunger, and cold, encased in an impermeable film. I knew that I had just liberated myself forever, since my only gratuitous act, yes the only one, lay in the refusal of the money. The hatred that was choking in my throat gave me back my identity. To have given in to my mother would have been the equivalent of accepting her moral code. My ability to refuse the money rescued me, and I believed myself freed at last.

"And in spite of it—how can I tell you, David—I feel dead. Or what amounts to the same thing: I am bored. For hours at a time I do nothing but cough and yawn and smoke innumerable cigarettes. I have to invent alibis to prove to myself that I exist. Alibis for what, against whom?" In the heavy atmosphere of the room, his questions seemed to float, thin out, and hang in the air. "Oh, I know they say I'm a fool. They tell me that I can still go back. And yet—" his voice had become harsh, and David's heart was beating violently, "and yet, I do not want to go back. I must burn my bridges. Cut off the only way out. You understand?"

"Yes." David was breathless. "The coming of age."

"Kill! Kill!"

* * *

In front of the tarnished mirror of the dressing-room, with a candelabrum on either side of his face, Eduardo Uribe gave himself over to his favorite madness: his love of dressing up, the longing to escape from himself.

The room was submerged in a semi-darkness, and the mirror gave back in duplicate the wavy silhouette of the flames and the twisted arms of the candelabrum that the girl was holding at his right.

"Ah, to transform oneself; to surrender oneself to the

dizziness of masks." His dry lips adhered to the lips of the Uribe of the mirror, his eyes searched for the contact of the eyes of the mask. He had taken his tubes of paint out of the wardrobe and tried out the colors on the cover of the portfolio.

"One ought to cover mirrors and destroy all glasses. I couldn't resist the temptation of falling in love with myself."

Carefully he distributed the colors over his face; the green, the orange, the ocher on the cheeks; over the eyebrows a thick line of indigo blue; on the eyelids a touch of violet. The lips were black.

"How do you like it?"

The girl put the candelabrum down on the table and dipped the brush in an orange bowl. She did not know what to say. The disquieting character whose back was turned toward her, and whom she could see only through the mirror, filled her with terror.

"You look very beautiful," she began.

But she stopped in astonishment. Uribe mussed up his hair with his two hands, curling the ends upwards. The shadow that he projected was that of a landscape of tasseled corn swept by the wind. Suddenly, without saying a word, he began to dye the strands red.

The girl let out a shriek. "Now you look just like the devil."

Tánger gave her the pleasure of contemplating him for a few seconds. The clever distribution of the shades accentuated the outline of his features; the sharp nose, the dry lips, all his premature lines. Satisfied with the examination, he felt himself in a talkative vein.

"In Panama," he said, "the disguises are almost rituals. Young men walk through the streets half naked, their sunburned bodies covered with paint. Some give themselves painful tatoos, and stick tufts of feathers with hot tar over their bodies.

"Six years ago I traveled through America with my parents, and passed a week in Balboa. It was during carnival time, and a great crowd invaded the sidewalks: men marvelously disguised as women; suspicious bodies with caressing looks, like silk. I went toward the wharf, and I could hardly get through. A rain of flour and confetti fell through the foliage of the serpentines, lanterns, and street lamps. Negroes drank bottles of pure alcohol, and people danced and kissed right out in the street.

"And there I saw a man dressed up in a domino, with the purest and most finished disguise I have ever seen. He had shaved off half his mustache, half his beard, one eyebrow, and the hair on one side of his head, and he had smeared it all with whitewash. The other half: beard, mustache, hair, eyebrow was rigorously black. His body was symmetrically squared from head to foot, and so were the shorts covering his private parts. Oh, it was terrifying to see him like that, white and black with the black iris in the white part of the face and the white cornea in the black part, rolling his eyes ceaselessly—as though he had one of those masks where the color of the eyes changes when little pieces of cardboard are moved behind the empty sockets.

"There was also a crowd of . . . a little whore with little ribbons tied on to her teats . . . but no, I'm drunk. That belongs to another story."

The girl looked at him, her eyes filled with astonishment.

"Oh, go on. Tell it!"

The clown had returned. "Useless, my little one. The

secret doesn't belong to me. I promised that I would not talk, and I won't talk."

The girl did not say anything, but Uribe turned to her again: "*Index prohibitum.* No use insisting."

And to the alias in the mirror: "Oh, you're drunk!"

He looked at himself attentively: topped by the stiff crest, his face was a perfect combination of the seven colors of the spectrum.

"I should like to spin at such a speed that I would see everything *white.*"

Before giving himself his final approval, he added one more touch: over the fresh paint he distributed little tufts of fuzz. The girl started for the door.

"No, not yet."

He stopped to tie his silk cape. As usual at the moment before one of his transformations, an undefinable anguish took hold of him. Would he escape from himself? Would he succeed this time in being different?

He had often enjoyed the subtle charm of self-mystification. His love for disguises also was a part of that need for escape. Each landscape conferred upon him a new personality; to each stranger, a different personality. He took advantage of chance encounters to deform himself; before those he did not know, he was like a blank book: on its pages he could write whatever he chose.

He invented a thousand and one personalities for himself. He was exasperated by his own inability to escape the judgments that his faults merited, and his timidity led him to evasion by confessing everything. The greater the necessity for hiding it, the more urgent his confession became. His sincerity was, in a word, a pitiful lie.

The idea that others might talk about him terrified him, and anticipating their comments, he behaved and dressed in such a way that necessarily attracted attention: he propagated rumors and false stories about himself. But it seemed to him that now it was not the others who discovered him, but rather that it was he who was revealing the others, since he had anticipated their suspicions and since what he sought was their surprise.

Now, with his terrifying Indian warpaint, Uribe made a sensational entrance. He had raised his arms so that the girl's shawl hung from his arms like sleeves, and he waved them in the air like a bat.

In the penumbra of the studio the couples were dancing very close together. Nobody noticed Uribe until he arrived at the middle of the room: then they could not help registering terror.

"Oh! Oh!" Ah!'s and Oh!'s, little shrieks.

"Oh! It's Tánger."

The record had finished, and nobody remembered to turn off the phonograph: the needle went round and round, dull and hoarse.

"Good heavens!"

"Incredible!"

"How did you manage to do it?"

"I didn't recognize you!"

"You look perfectly horrible!"

Uribe felt very happy hearing their voices. He imparted blessings.

"My children . . ."

The proximity of the faces that surrounded him increased his madness, as though by refraction. They offered him a little pitcher of wine, and he drank it down in one gulp. He went toward some of the women as if he were about to kiss them, and a violent protest arose.

"No, Tánger. . . . Not that."

"You're full of paint. You'll get us all dirty."

The dizzying sensation at the unknown seized him again; the necessity to improvise.

"I want to go out on the balcony and fly with my false wings. I want to go out into the street and frighten the office clerks with my cries. I want to steal the frost from the rooftops and make a gift of it to the blind doves."

He had fulfilled his purpose. His head was spinning. But his fear was not leaving him. During two hours something had taken place.

"Come, come with me."

He was afraid to stay alone. In his drunkenness and in his cries he was haunted again by the need to vindicate himself, to find out what had happened that afternoon.

He knew that if they left him alone he would tell all: the desire was stronger than he was. He remembered Luis. "I have to be silent." He brought his hand to his forehead. He did not want to look.

"My little brothers."

He had noticed a blond insignificant-looking young man whose face, he did not know just why, was familiar to him. And he felt his strength leaving him: he was giving up: he was going to confess. "Oh, no. Oh, no, no . . ."

"Boy! Yes, you, you, you . . . the one who's looking at me; boy, you who are looking at me."

He gave his words a mocking tone; he was imitating the way some of his old teachers used to speak.

"You mean me?"

"Yes, come here."

He took him to the dressing-room: in front of the mirror and the lighted candelabrum.

He swallowed hard. Again he recognized it: the defeat of the intelligence; the soft and indecisive dizziness that invaded his entrails. "Very well, let us begin."

He had taken out a purple bottle, and while he drank,

he realized at that very moment that it was already inevitable. He would confess precisely in front of this boy; before him and before no other.

The boy looked at him, still completely taken by surprise.

"I think I know you. Your disguise—"

Uribe cut him off with a gesture. "It's a trick! Everything is a trick. So are my trousers. They were given to me just as an adornment."

Rubbing his hands across his face, he made the paint run from his lips, and it was beginning to stain his neck.

"I hate everything that is true," he said. "I thrive on lies. I put disguises on things: serpentines, tinsel. I love the fleeting."

The boy looked at him stupefied: "You— Who are you?"

Uribe looked at him sternly. "That you will know shortly, you naughty little boy. But first you must learn to obey me and hold onto that happy little tongue of yours, eh? Now, follow me. We shall leave without being seen. On the landing of the stairway there is an abandoned room where we can talk in private."

He picked up one of the candelabra and started toward the door.

"Where are you taking me?"

The boy was standing still behind him. Uribe turned on him furiously.

"That is of neither interest nor concern to you. If you've left one of those horrible little whores who are running around in there, you can just tell her that you will be back shortly. Don't worry: I'm not going to do anything to you. My needs are not physical."

He opened the door of the dressing-room and pointed out the way to him. While the boy obeyed, the expression on Uribe's face suffered a change. Now, it was the clown that was predominating again.

"Let's go out. In the street little empty archangels are infringing on the traffic laws by driving around on the left."

He turned toward the mirror and murmured: "I'm mad!"

Calm reigned in the little room; only the flames of the high candlestick wavered and twisted around the white ribbon of the wick.

* * *

Uribe held a glass of violet-colored liquor between his hands and raised it to his lips before speaking.

"It's called '*Parfait Amour,*' " he said.

His young friend squirmed in a small wicker chair. Uribe from his armchair measured him, dominated him, overwhelmed him.

"That means 'Perfect Love,' I believe."

"Exactly," replied Uribe. "Love in blank. Love inviolate. You're a very clever boy."

He drank a sip and offered it to the boy.

"Here, taste it. You look like a pretty clean fellow, so maybe it won't nauseate me to have you drink from the same glass."

The boy gave a nervous little laugh. The drink that Tánger offered him repulsed him, but he did not dare refuse it. He swallowed a little of it and said: "It's very good. Thank you."

Uribe began to lose his disguise. The paint had run from one corner of his face to the other, and between the black lips his teeth protruded, incisive and shiny white.

The only light in the room was the three-branch candelabrum, whose flames danced frenetically. Uribe repressed a shiver.

"There's a draft," he said. "Will you see if the window is shut?"

The boy got up hastily. Uribe had locked the door after entering the room off the stairway and put the key in his pocket. He did not know just how all this was going to end.

The boy adjusted the window, and immediately the flames stopped dancing and clung so close to the twisted wick that they were reduced to minute tongues of fire.

"How dark!" he said. "And how quiet it is!"

He had sat down in the wicker chair again, and was looking apprehensively at Uribe's painted face. Something in Uribe's gestures and in his voice reminded the boy of something, he knew not what.

Tánger paid no attention to him. With an abstracted air, he soaked a handkerchief in a little bottle of turpentine and wiped his face carefully.

"Did you like the disguise?" he asked him after a while. The boy gave a slight nod.

"It's very good," he murmured. "You shouldn't take it off."

"I've always liked disguises," said Uribe. "When I was a little boy I used to collect them by the dozen. My father was an impresario, and I used to act in theaters and circuses. Sometimes I did very indecent numbers. But usually I danced. And every year I yearned for the arrival of carnival. I like to see people dress up and go walking through the streets with masks. Haven't you ever tried to dress up as a woman, or a redskin, or as a pirate?"

"No."

"Well, you ought to. When we lived in Tangiers I went

around with a group of newsboys. They taught me how to dress up. I had jellabas, camel-hair burnooses, and haiks. I collected musical instruments, too: the bender, the flute, the tebel, the guermbrik, the deranga, and castanets. The boys dressed up in animal skins and wore butterfly cocoons around their ankles. Everything was very beautiful then."

He had taken out a little mirror from his pocket, and looking into it, he plucked the paint out of his eyebrows. The presence of the boy tranquilized him. He felt himself caught between the desire to keep quiet and the wish to confide in him.

"That must have been a long way from here," he heard the boy say.

"Yes. In Africa."

"In Africa? Have you been there?"

"I have been in five parts of the world and to the North Pole and the South Pole," replied Uribe, "but my native city is Tangiers."

He rubbed the handkerchief over his lips, and stopped a second to catch his breath.

"My parents had an important diplomatic position there. They were great admirers of the Count Coudonhovo Ka lergi, and when I was seven years old they made me learn Esperanto. At that time I knew French, English, German, Italian, and Greek and Latin, but they insisted upon my learning Esperanto. Do you want me to speak some for you?"

"I wouldn't understand it," said the boy.

"Bah! Do you think we understand each other when we speak the same language? Do you think there is any real communication between two human beings? Or are we merely loudspeakers, transmitting different programs simultaneously?"

The questions floated on the air and dissolved into the

sordid walls of the little room, intermixing with the languishing echo of the dance music.

"I think that—" began the young fellow.

"I think that no one has asked you what you think."

He gave up trying to remove his make-up and looked at himself in the mirror, discouraged. He saw himself old, tired. The obtuse presence of the boy calmed him and infuriated him at the same time. Two hours remained a blank. An emptiness. A hollow. He brought his hand to his forehead. He wished he were drunker than he really was. He could not manage to escape. The disguises were ineffectual.

He touched with the cushion of his finger the place where, that afternoon, someone had hit him. In the candlelight, once the trace of the paint was gone, the mark still showed: dark, the color of liver. "Now, let's see," he said, "there were the two gorillas; I was seated with them. I was making love to them." But this wasn't it—it was in the washroom that they had hit him. They had taken him in there, almost dragged him in.

His hands seized the glass desperately: it was empty. Immediately he reached for the bottle. It, too, was empty. He turned to the boy, gasping.

"Listen," he said to him, "you're a clever boy: see if you can give me an explanation. Listen to me. Don't miss a single detail."

The boy looked at him terrified. Now that Uribe was stripped of the thick layer of paint, the boy had, at last, discovered who he was. His voice, his gestures had seemed, from the very beginning, recognizable, almost familiar. That very afternoon in a bar on Echegaray Street, Uribe had been thrown out bodily—for reasons that tied in perfectly with the boy's own recent suspicions of Uribe.

He felt a cold sweat run down his face. He remembered

that Uribe had locked the door and had put the key in his pocket. Terrible stories came to his mind, old warnings of schoolmates: *"Sometimes they're dangerous. They even attack."* He had let himself fall stupidly into the trap, and he was ashamed of himself.

"This afternoon," Uribe went on, "I had a dreadful experience. Somebody beat me up. They say we like to be beaten up, but that's not true. It's horrible to have somebody lay his hand on you. One time a whore slapped me in the face. It was ghastly—"

The confession, like an undefinable nausea, scaled his throat. He understood that he was about to let go, and he decided to save himself by putting on an act.

"It's like when they beat you at school. When I was twelve years old they hit me on the back of the hand with a ruler. I remember one old teacher who used to dye his hair white, who went so far as skinning my knuckles. At that time, I was a sickly, thin child; I lived in continual dread."

He picked up the bottle of liquor mechanically. He had launched into another fabricated story and needed to re-enforce himself. When the boy noticed the movement, he got up.

"If you want, I'll go and get some more. I'll be back in a second."

He had spoken with too much anxiety, and he was the first to realize it. He told himself to keep calm.

"No one has given you permission to get up from that chair," said Tánger.

He vaguely felt the boy's fear, and the sensation did not displease him. He decided to take advantage of it.

"The picture changed as soon as I got out of school. I was scarcely sixteen years old, and I fell in love with a girl at a picnic. We had met by chance, while trying to decipher a hieroglyph of Thebes, and a bond of affection formed between us immediately. Alicia was blond, slender, and agile. She had the quality of a gazelle. Each one of her movements in itself had an irresistible charm, and her body was so made that it constantly demanded caressing.

"She liked to walk through the park dressed as Cleopatra, and I accompanied her, filled with joy, overwhelming her with kisses on the hand, the hair, on the back of the neck, and on the lips. I compared her to the sea, to the sky, to the ships, and to the clouds. I abstracted her from all precise forms, as if she herself were the essence of all forms, and when I kissed her hand and embraced her, it seemed as if I were kissing and embracing the whole of nature—excuse me—"

He bent over toward the other side and vomited. The young fellow looked at him with eyes bulging out of their sockets. A horrible idea had entered his mind: "He's crazy. I'm dealing with an insane man." He ran his tongue over his lips. He trembled. Uribe continued spitting for a few moments and finally wiped his mouth with his handkerchief.

"Alicia," he went on in a tranquil voice, "had awakened the latent poet in me, and when I was with her I felt happy and enriched. I gave her birds and fruit, I adorned her with wild flowers. We often went together to a ruined temple, and there I would ask her to dance an orphic hymn for me. Her movements outlined themselves against the blue of the sea and the gold of the sand, like one of those bas-reliefs that can be seen at the museum in Naples.

"One day when I won the lottery I bought her a tiny deer, and from that day on Alicia, the deer, and I formed an inseparable trio. We were also followed by two buffoons and a dwarf that my father had under contract.

"We asked that life continue that way, in the pleasure

of the present, without ties to bind us to the past or concern for the future life. Everything was simple, and, therefore, magical. And although our respective dynasties had conjured up envy, hatred, and venom against us, their opposition, instead of annoying us, added to our happiness.

"Those months were the happiest of my life, and during that time I came to forget everything. Nothing other than Alicia existed for me, and with Alicia the sky, the sea, the flowers, and the birds. At her side I began to feel myself a boy and to enjoy the freedom which I had never tasted as a child.

"When it rained we would wade in the puddles and sing songs; we took refuge under the branches of the trees and played at giving each other as many kisses as there were raindrops falling. We imagined that the world existed only for us and that we were the only inhabitants of the world. And it made us happy to greet the slaves who worked in the fields, throw kisses at them, and make them share in our happiness.

"We lived in an eternal spring where nothing mattered outside of ourselves. In this return to childhood there was something infinitely pure and clean. Without any previous understanding we had tacitly agreed not to speak of the future, and it was precisely because of this freedom from care that our love rang so pure. Alicia was my fairy and I was her archangel. She let herself be loved with simplicity, and when she lowered her eyelids for me to kiss, my happiness was beyond words. Do you understand?"

The young fellow's face showed complete lack of comprehension. His lips were taut, and he studied absorbedly the light of the candelabrum, where one of the wicks was on the point of going out. He was afraid of remaining alone with Uribe.

"I understand," he muttered.

"You lie," replied Tánger, "you understand absolutely nothing. You have come here to spy on me, and you're getting all ready to tell everything I have told you."

Uribe had noticed the terror of the boy, who looked at him appalled, and he decided to make use of him to save himself.

"I know you, you dirty little thing, you and the stool pigeons like you. Do you think I am so stupid? Maybe you know how I punish types like you."

The boy continued to sit motionless in his wicker chair. He looked at Uribe with glassy eyes, trembling.

"Really, I— I swear that—"

Uribe took the empty glass and smashed it on the floor. He felt inspired, strong. His demon was whispering in his ear.

"Enough!"

He took the candelabrum in his left hand and went toward the door. The shadows, delirious, terrified, receded along the walls. He opened the door, went out, and locked the door behind him.

From the landing he heard the boy's footsteps nearing the door, and he shrugged his shoulders.

"Let me out! Let me out! I can't see a thing in here. Open! Open up!"

He crossed the landing of the stairway and went into the studio. The effort that he had just made had left him exhausted, drained. The only thing he felt now was desire to sleep. To rest his head on some soft object.

From the hall he glanced around at the different people dancing and drinking. Raúl, Mendoza, Ana were swarming about, not suspecting what had just gone on. He wanted to be in a quiet place where the voices of drunken people might not reach him. He poured himself a gin and drank it down in one swallow. He was himself again. They had recognized him in spite of his disguise. Everybody had called him "Tánger."

In the distance he heard his prisoner pounding on the door; he sunk his hand that was clinging to the key deeper into his pocket. "Let him rot there! Let them all rot! I don't give a damn!" To forget. He would have liked a drug that would grant the sleeper the faculty of not remembering the past.

His stomach weighed on him heavily, as if he had filled it with mercury. His brain was a dance of confused, changing ideas. He remained motionless with his lip drooping, swollen by the vertical light of the lamp. Everything in the place was repugnant to him; the voices and the cries, the lanterns, the hats, the costumes.

The young boy knocked harder and harder on the door. The stairway was alive with people. Noises, voices could be heard coming closer and closer. A very fat, middle-aged woman came into the studio and began to scream like a banshee. Uribe felt guilty.

"I'm the one. It's my fault!"

He handed the key to Ana. The woman, her hands on her hips, was shouting her head off.

"Pigs! Worse than pigs! Making such a racket at this hour. And in such a respectable house, too!"

Raúl Rivera in shirt sleeves, his arms crossed, stood in front of her impudently.

"The door is at the end of the hall, just in case you don't know."

The woman almost wept with rage. She was sorry she was not a man, rather than a weak, defenseless widow, and she wanted to slap his face. Raúl held back her arm.

"Take it easy, lady, and above all keep calm. Just go quietly, will you? Like a nice little girl."

The party was coming to an end. Embarrassed, most of the girls began putting on their coats. Only Raúl, who had sent the intruder away—though she continued to make a row in the hallway, knocking on the concierge's door—and was now dancing with a dark-haired girl, seemed not in the least concerned about what had happened.

The prisoner, who had just been set free, pointed wildly at Tánger, covering him with insults, making accusations. A fat-cheeked girl pulled at his sleeve and tried to make him be quiet, while everyone else celebrated the incident with applause and laughter.

Uribe felt a terrible weakness in his knees and a desire to vomit. He wanted to sleep, close his eyes, be lulled like a baby. He was acting more drunk than he really was, and he knew it. Once again he was play-acting. He went up to Raúl, staggering.

"I want to sleep," he begged. "Take me home, Raúl. I couldn't make it alone."

He pretended that the words wouldn't come out. The vapors of the alcohol beclouded the lucidity of his thoughts, but did not succeed in hiding his lie.

"The truth is, Tánger," said Raúl's little brunette, "you're drunk as a lord."

"If you want a nursemaid to rock you to sleep," said Raúl, "go buy yourself one at the market."

They were dancing very close to each other, like two young animals, and they withdrew from Uribe, laughing.

Uribe was about to follow them when he felt someone pulling at his sleeve. He turned around. It was Luis Páez.

"My dear artist," Uribe said. "You are a witness to the disrespect of which I have just been the object. The challenge is to the death. To the death and without pistols."

Without paying the least attention to him, Luis took

him to the lavatory. Uribe let himself be dragged along. He raved on: "Heaven is witness to my innocence."

Luis slipped the bolt of the washroom door, and corralled Uribe against the wall. He took him by the lapels with both hands and shook him like a rag doll.

"The trick," Uribe managed to stammer out, "I had forgotten. I—"

Luis slapped his face with the back of his hand. The blow, a good one, left the mark of Luis's knuckles for quite a while. Uribe felt as though he had been stoned. He felt his knees wobbling, and he held on to the towel rack, his lips inert. He stood at Luis's side, humiliated and confused, crying like a baby.

"You stupid bastard! Is this the way you keep your word? You big fairy! You good-for-nothing fairy!"

Brutally Luis forced him to straighten up, and pulling him by the lapels, shook him again. Luis's lips were tightly pressed, and his eyes shone with hardness.

"You're going to do what I tell you, whether you want to or not, do you hear? I know only too well how to make you and your kind dance. Or do you want me to hit you again?"

He raised his hand threateningly. Tánger's eyes showed immense panic, and he could not utter a word. Luis curled his lip derisively and spat on the floor.

"No. It's not worth the trouble. It would give you a pleasure you don't deserve. You guys like that sort of thing."

He let go of him suddenly, and Uribe crumpled down like a puppet. Luis heard him groan and then vomit.

With an air of indifference, he crossed the room from one end to the other, puffing ceaselessly on a cigarette he had just lighted.

*   *   *

They gathered around the table that had served as a bar, while Ana removed the bottles and glasses. The guests had all left some time ago. Under the muddy light of the electric bulb the little group looked like a scene taken from a movie.

They were surrounded by the vestiges of the leper session: glasses, colored masks, crushed cigarette butts. Someone had pulled off the greenish lampshade from the light and the cloth bunches of grapes, but the paper hangings and Tánger's fantastic decorating still remained. The night rain oozed between the cracks in the cement and intermittently dripped down onto the metal cuspidor. Uribe shuffled the cards: he made small packs which he passed alternately from one hand to the other and mixed again and again, letting them slide together, his thumbs raised. Under the vertical rays of the electric light bulb, his face took on a sickly, livid hue. He had turned up his coat collar around his neck, way up to his ears, and, in spite of that, he was shivering.

"Are you feeling sick?" Ana had asked.

"Hungover."

The others, seated in a circle, looked at him listlessly. They were all sleepy. The evening was like all the others. They had not succeeded in convincing themselves that they were really deciding something very important. They drank in silence, bored.

"When do we begin?" asked Ana.

"Whenever you like."

They played from left to right, with forty-eight cards, without the joker. Eduardo Uribe dealt first three cards and then two to each of the players.

Cortézar kept the first three face down, waiting for the other two. Only then did he dare to look at them. They said it was bad luck to do otherwise. But he was the only one to remember it. He repressed a nervous yawn and looked at Agustín Mendoza.

Agustín had taken his pipe out of his pocket and was watching his companions with perfect calm. You could tell the character of each one of them, he thought, by the way they play. Poker is the X ray of the human soul. Raúl, for example, had looked at his cards for a split second, and his face revealed nothing. Sometimes he would stay with a pair of tens; and when he showed, he inevitably won. His luck in the game was so proverbial that, before getting into any game, he had to be coaxed. David, on the other hand, did not know how to assert himself; he never bet unless he was sure of winning. Luis always smoked out the plays. Cortézar was at least consistent: he trusted to luck, had ups and downs. As to Ana, Agustín had never played with her before.

He watched David studying his hand. His face was rigid, as though starched, and Agustín deduced that luck had not been favorable to him. He shrugged his shoulders. The game depended only on chance; the one who had the worst hand lost. And, in spite of that, David's face gave him away.

The cards had been dealt, and each one looked at his hand. Raúl, only, pretended to be indifferent. He leaned back, with his knees against the table, in the attitude of a mere spectator.

Agustín asked for three cards, which Uribe dealt him from the pack, placing underneath it the cards that he gave back to him. Cortézar exchanged two.

When it came to Raúl's turn, he merely said: "I'm okay, thanks."

Raúl said it with humility, as though excusing himself. He noticed that when Luis picked his cards up, he looked

displeased and glanced Raúl's way. The bottles that Ana
had piled up on the wooden table in the corner projected
gigantic, deformed shadows against the wall.

Luis, in turn, looked at Tánger: Luis did not yet dare to
consult the faces of his companions, and he tried to catch
Tánger's eye. A half-hour earlier, in the washroom, he had
struck Uribe brutally until he had made him cry. Then he
had rubbed Uribe's forehead with cologne and dried his
tears with a handkerchief. He had even patted his shoulder a little. The memory of it made him want to burst out
laughing.

David asked for three cards. Between his hands he was
holding a glass of manzanilla, which he would bring
mechanically to his lips every so often; he was trying to
behave in a very natural manner, and he was hardly succeeding.

He picked up the cards and put them down on the
table before looking at them. He looked unabashed, chal-
lenging. He knew the answer in advance, and was calmly
abandoning himself to his fate. The choice, for some obscure reason, seemed to him the logical consequence of a
series of facts for which he was responsible. He felt only
a little discomfort in his ear, and he drank the glass of
manzanilla, vaguely hoping that perhaps it would dispel
the sensation.

His new cards were all different, and of different suits.
Before he looked at them David had heard the voices of
the rest of the players, announcing their threes-of-a-kind,
their straights, and their flushes. Then he found out that
he still had only a pair of nines. "It had to be this way,"
he thought.

And with a bitter smile, he waited for the moment in
which the rest would believe themselves obliged to console him.

✳ ✳✳ IV ✳✳ ✳

Archangels' wings vibrating like harps, days light as feathers, as snowflakes: it was many years ago that David had seen a pistol for the first time, and never, until now, had he been conscious of the coldness of its metal; the butt seemed to be waiting for the clasp of the hand the finger, the soft contact of the trigger. Sacred talisman, taboo object, it would be necessary to cover it with lace, make up to it for the loss of its precious essence. When Augustín had given it to him, he explained how it worked in a few words. "All you have to do is hold it like this, you aim through here, this is the safety catch." Words, neat formulas within the grasp of any apprentice. But, what about the other? Dear God, what about the other?

"It's like splashing the waters with your fist and throwing the nets out to the sea. *Everything flows, runs away, we remain forever strange.*" The mirror returned him a white, bloodless image, lips strained tight as old scars. The pistol was black in his hands; the index would clutch over the metal, the bullet would sink softly. He, David, the assassin. David boy, good David, friend David, David condemned with the soul of a coward. He turned out the light and then turned it on again, without the pistol now. He must become familiar with death, he needed to know the old man, know what color his eyes were, love him before he committed the crime. "For each one kills the thing he loves, by each let this be heard, some do it with a bitter look, some with a flattering word, the coward does it with a kiss, the brave man with a sword." How much he must have suffered, the one who had written that; he had reached the last zone, the zone where questions transform themselves into slipknots and fasten themselves voraciously around our throats.

The joyous notes of a folk song came up from the floor below. Leaning on the window sill, David thought he could see lewd women being swished along by the bell-like sweep of their skirts, tracing whirlpools of colors, bodies that hurled their forms into the air, gestures like flashes of lightning, like sparks. He passed his hand over his forehead: a little boy perspiring. The black pistol, there, waiting to open the way to a myriad of beings who lay in ambush for the banquet of death, bursting in their own decay. A Bible lay open on the table: "Jehovah, Lord, God of the strong"; they were condemning him; there, too, they condemned him. The high-pitched voice of an announcer came to his ears. So it wasn't a phonograph, not even a player-piano. Doña Raquel had her radio turned on, and nimble heels drummed on the top of an old piano. "Lord, Lord of the weak," he thought. Milky cobwebs over his eyes: he was crying. The wind shook the clothes that were hanging up to dry on the neighboring rooftop and whistled in his ears like the noises of a conch shell. David closed the window: the music was hurting him. He wanted to see Tánger dressed as a musician, showing some of his tricks; taking out cards from the back of his ears, making Chinese shadows on the walls with his hands. Now he was far away. They had left him alone before the black object that awaited the hollow of his hand, the sudden decision of the finger. He sat down at the table and opened his diary at random.

*   *   *

"My childhood, which had seemed to me something very simple, suddenly seems, now that I try to take it all in, enormously complicated. The memory I have of it is blurred and fragmentary, and the more I dwell upon detailed incidents, the more worthy I consider it of being remembered.

"I was a lukewarm, colorless child, with low vitality and very precarious health, which constantly tormented my parents. I come from a distinguished and socially prominent family of which I am the end of the line. Everything contributed, therefore, toward making me an heir to no matter what—memories, name, or fortunes—and the fact that I had brothers did not lessen in the least my own responsibility. In my parents' days Barcelona was as highly populated as it is now. It had just gotten rid of its walls, and, like someone who has just taken off a suit that is too small for him, it stretched out happily over the plain. The wealth was in the hands of a few families, and my grandfather's fortune was considered among the greatest. He had made it in the West Indies, and, like all Indians of his time, he lived, in a magnificent Moorish-style chalet, on a comfortable income from his sugar mill in Matanzas.

"I never met him, but I know through hearsay that he was a real character. I have kept, however, a memory of what he looked like from a photograph—an immense picture with a black background which presided over the family gatherings in the dining-room: a terrible and rude face that kept me awake at night. My grandmother, his wife, was a plump little woman with a face covered with warts, like dried-up sprouts. To her I owe my taste for reading and solitude. A long time before she had lost one of her sons while he was asleep, and the fear that history might repeat itself impelled her to awaken me every time she saw me asleep. "Sleep is the image of death," she would say by way of excuse. And even now it seems I can see her smile, her forehead covered with microscopic drops of perspiration. My parents are two good people with nothing unusual about them, whose personalities perish completely in the blending of their respective vagueness. They are blurred and diffuse, without a drop of good red blood in their veins; and no matter how much I brood about them, I am always surprised to find how far apart people can feel, in spite of blood ties, for I have nothing whatsoever in common with them.

"Shortly before I was born, my maternal grandfather's fortune had dwindled to almost nothing. He had been an enterprising man, and obviously an outstanding one, but he never took the trouble to provide for his sons. His domineering nature made him decide to keep them away from the business. He was used to playing hard, and their presence doubtless would have been a nuisance to him. As he was a reckless speculator whose affairs were always terribly involved, the inheritance that he left at the time of his death, although large in amount, was equally large in complications and headaches. My uncles were not prepared to carry the weight that fell on their shoulders, and on the advice of all the members of the family, they liquidated the hacienda in Cuba.

"In spite of this, however, my childhood was spent amidst the greatest of ease and comfort, studded with tutors and friars. Our fortune was still considerable so I always knew the fullness of satisfied desires. My father's main preoccupation, fond as he was of neat formulas, was to see that he made a good businessman of me. The lesson he had received from his father had not been in vain. Quite frequently he would take the car and drive me, along with one or another of my brothers, to the factory, with the idea that we should from early childhood get used to and take an interest in the business. There I came in contact with a strange world of half-naked children, with whom I felt an impulse to play, but who remained at my side, black and distrustful, like dark lizards. To my amazement I learned that they always went hungry, and that they even longed for dishes which at home I ate only through force. This gave them, in my eyes, an enormous prestige, and beside them I felt mediocre, timid, and mean.

"I have often thought that the money our parents save up for us does little more than increase our weakness. As a child, I was made to attend as a patron the christening of the workers' children. It was a social measure, and I do not reproach the family for it. Perhaps if I had been in their place, I would have done the same thing; although I think that between our generations there is some difference: we are not, like them, so convinced of our rights, and if the time came to defend our rights, we would do so perhaps out of selfishness, but not as a matter of principle.

"As I said before, they used to give me big bags of candy, which I distributed among the children, like a happy messenger from another world. I felt that I should beg to be forgiven for my position. I felt vaguely that I was among the chosen, as though someone had made a lottery, and my number had been the winner. And even now, when I leave a round of tips, I do not do it so much out of generosity as out of timidity and the desire for a pardon. I very soon realized that the world did not end with the walls of my house, and the version of it that my parents offered me was not enough to satisfy my curiosity.

"The image that I hold of myself is dirty, blurred, and asphyxiating. My parents showered upon me an absurd amount of care that knew no limitations. Each year at school I yearned for the arrival of summer, when we moved to our country house. It was an old building that had belonged to my great-grandparents, and I was much happier there than in the rigid cloister of the schoolroom. For most of the day my time was my own, and during the long afternoons I amused myself wandering through the rooms filled with useless objects. There were trunks stuffed with books, colored lampshades, torn screens, and little saints' niches studded with shells and flowers; and I felt there like a guest in some fantastic country.

"To the educational system of my parents, I preferred the one that Don Angel allowed, a ridiculous tutor who gave us Latin lessons in the mornings during the summer. Don Angel was heavy and red; his movements were gauche, his gestures grotesque, and he always wore gold-rimmed glasses on the bridge of his voluminous nose. His dress was picturesque and slovenly, his shirts extravagantly colored. Member of a once well-to-do family whose small income obliged him to earn his own living teaching the children of the rich, Don Angel had won over my father with his lucid Latin phraseology. When he spoke, he sprinkled his conversation with a substantial mixture of quotations that he reproduced in the original. I often suspected that he himself did not always know what he was saying, but so impressive was his mien when he gave forth with the Latin that my father affirmed very seriously that he had 'convinced' him.

"Don Angel spent the greater part of the day stretched out on the sofa doing crossword puzzles, at which he was singularly adept because of his useless encyclopedic knowledge. While he made me recite declensions, he would stuff snuff up his hairy nose and sneeze with obvious enjoyment. He had taken it upon himself to make of me and of my brothers models of the well-educated young man, and he tried to awaken in me a taste for the refined and the exquisite. He surrounded me with Greek and Latin poets, 'appropriately translated.' And it was on his insistence that my parents forbade me to read pirate stories. According to Don Angel, the young soul became savage and easily deformed if one went in for that kind of reading, and no amount of zeal was too much if contagion was to be avoided.

"Conscious of the social position of my father, he tried to make me understand the duties and obligations that my father's status imposed on me: 'You are of the chosen,' he would say to me, 'and you should behave as such. One does not cast pearls before swine.' He advised me to cultivate the right people and spoke with repugnance of those who did not even own a piece of land to die on. He liked to call a spade a spade, and his hatred of poverty betrayed both his desire to belong to the privileged class and his lack of compassion for suffering; and while he complacently condoned my giving a costly present to a boy of my own class, he would become furious if I gave alms to a poor boy: 'They are dirty, horrible, and covered with sores. They are beneath your consideration.'

"Although I spent most of the day playing with my brothers, the tenant-farmers' children running around the fields attracted me with their shouting. They were younger than I was but they played freely with nobody watching them. They wore little shirts and shorts that barely reached their knees, and they always went barefoot. Through timidity, I had never gone near them, and when we stumbled upon each other accidentally, I could not even manage to say hello.

"I remember one September afternoon when they were emptying the ponds. My father had put gold fish in them, and as the level of the water lowered I saw the fish dart like arrows, squirming and wriggling. In the parts of the ponds where there was less water, they stayed crowded together in little pools from which they vainly tried to escape; the way they desperately lashed their tails about, it seemed that they knew their end was near. I was looking at them, filled with anguish, because I realized I was helpless to save them, when a group of boys drew near the pond and asked me what was going on.

"I showed them the writhing fish, and they went down the ladder, buried their feet in the mud, and proceeded to put the fish in pails of water, which they handed up to me. I felt immediately happy. The sight of the fish, wriggling in the pails, drunk with the joy of life, filled me with a real joy. When I put my hand in, I felt them slipping between my fingers, and before I knew it, I caught myself singing out loud.

"I was completely absorbed in this activity when I heard a terrible shout at my back. The presence of Don Angel with his congested face and disheveled hair made me shudder with fear. I felt the pail slipping from my hands; a few fish fell on the sand, palpitating, their golden backs spattered with mud. But Don Angel did not even give me time to pick them up. Filled with anger, he dragged me away by the arm toward the house.

"That day and those that followed his scornful attitude made me feel the magnitude of my crime: I had dishonored and demeaned myself, perhaps irreparably, by exposing myself to those dirty and unworthy people. He spoke with real horror of the tenant-farmers' children, 'naked and slimy like water worms,' and he swore he would stifle forever my plebeian instincts. Unfortunately for him, he wasn't able to do so; he died the following month, in the middle of the Latin lesson. Suddenly he had become still and rigid, before he was even able to finish snuffing up the tobacco that lay in the palm of his hand. After this happened my parents left for Europe, and we went to live at the home of our rich great-aunt.

"Doña Lucía, as we all called her, was a devout and capricious woman who lived alone, surrounded by her medicines, her canaries, and her saints. Her house was situated in the hilly section, near the Pedralbes monastery. The rooms were immense and inhospitable, filled with overstuffed furniture and heavy draperies; but Gabriel and I, we preferred the attic to the rest of the house. There all the objects were piled one on top of another without rhyme or reason: the broken-down armchairs next to the dusty mirrors, the endtables with chests of drawers. We wandered around in a perpetual state of delight, fascinated one moment by the torn coverings, the next by the complicated mechanism of a broken clock which had stopped running years ago. The old country beds had a naked look, exposing the rusty spirals of their springs. We looked at the plans of former estates, and at a parchment with special benedictions from the pontiff to the fortunate descendants of my great-grandfather. Sometimes my aunt would take us by the hand and point out to us the exact origin of each object.

"At the time I did not suspect the contradictory nature that lay hidden within the breast of that old woman. Her personality was a curious mixture of tenderness and refined cruelty. On the one hand, the words that she uttered assumed a sweet and flattering tone. She wanted us to be good and quiet, innocent as new-born babes. This attitude of hers was reflected even in her devotions. The images of her saints were fat-cheeked and pink, dressed in soft, bright-colored clothes. She imagined heaven as a gigantic kindergarten, filled with big, fat angels, and when she spoke of Jesus, she referred to his childhood and his swaddling clothes.

"On the other hand, my aunt was a child, and her egotism pushed her to inconceivable extremes. Inordinately stingy, she was absolutely incapable of giving. She spent most of the day ensconced in her lounge, her breviary between her hands, on a gallery that faced a near-by monastery. Her greatest amusement consisted in observing the recess period of the monks, for whom she made up affectionate nicknames and with whom, one after another, she fell in love.

"The monks' toilet was located in a small out-building, the path of which ran right below my aunt's observation post. Doña Lucía was very curious, and she had amused herself by computing a statistical average of those who went to the toilet during the afternoon recess; and at times she could be heard sorrowfully lamenting about the digestive troubles of one or another of the monks. One day I found her in a most unusual state of excitement: she, who had always been content to lie stretched out on her chaise longue, this time had not been able to stay still a moment longer. She ran from one side to the other like a little bird, her hair disheveled and her face red. She was seized by hiccups mixed with laughter, and she stayed by the window the whole afternoon. Later I learned that she had sent to the monastery a box of laxative candy, the effects of which she could certainly vouch for, as she kept her eyes fixed on the path of the monks. Curiosity and boredom can push one to doing many extraordinary things, and my aunt demonstrated that she was capable of almost anything.

"When the new school year began my parents sent me to a very expensive private school. There, influenced by everybody else, I plunged into the cult of charity and kindness. My companions were soft, delicate, and spiritually unctuous. I can visualize them just as they are now, their faces fatter than ever, leaning languidly over some bar in some club, saying: 'Bartender, fix me up with something that will surprise me, will you?' I learned in that boarding-school how to study through emulation. The Fathers tried to instill in me what they called 'a healthy desire for com-petition,' and, as a matter of fact, they succeeded in en-slaving me. In the missions collections that were taken up for clothes for the poor children, they wrote on the black-board the name of the winner and the amount he had given; underneath, came the rest of the names, in strict order according to the amount of the donation. Whenever a change in the classification occurred, it was like a change in football standings: with a benevolent smile, the teacher would scratch out the name of the young gentleman who had just been dethroned and put up the name of the new leader. And the one who finally triumphed personally dis-tributed the toys to the poor children, was photographed with them, smiling at them, petting them, and imitating all the attitudes that ministers are wont to assume on such occasions.

"They also organized some childish contests, with the help of the Fathers, in which our knowledge and our ca-pacity for nervous resistance were put to test. For a whole hour we would riddle one another with questions, while the teacher presided over the contest from his plush armchair. My greatest ambition was to be the first in everything. A morbid need for applause spurred me on. I struggled for the best scores with all my might, and although I some-times feigned indifference to fame and glory and pre-tended to be immune to praise, in reality my heart over-flowed with happiness each time that the principal, in the monthly distribution of prizes, announced: 'David has broken the record in the missions collection. This means he has sacrificed the most. He is also first in good behavior, and his grades are the highest in the class.' Applause resounded from everybody, and I smiled with false modesty, in keeping with my role of model boy.

"At a time when boys my age spent most of the day playing, I was absorbed in my work and duties. All obstacles seemed slight to me, as long as I could continue to hold first place. I spent hours and hours learning the test questions by heart, but I was wily enough to disguise this effort with a supposed natural talent for learning anything by merely glancing over it. My teachers fell into the trap; they spoke repeatedly of my gifts, with singular respect. They used me as a guinea pig for their recitals, and although that meant many, many hours' extra work, I was more than satisfied with the complacent smile of the teacher when he said: 'Oh, for you it is nothing at all.'

"I wanted to live up to all their hopes; I feared I might disappoint them. The possibility of losing first place kept me awake nights. The teachers realized this, and they used it as a weapon against me. 'You should be thankful,' they said, 'for not being a boy like the rest of them; for having been born rich and privileged; for your extraordinary talent.' And they would warn me: 'You almost didn't make first place. Watch out. Don't rest on your laurels, lest next month they are taken away from you.' And the happiness that I felt when I got the prize dissolved before the fear that they might take it away from me the following month. In this way I obstinately continued to wear my crown of laurel, and, featured on the cover of the school magazine, I looked like some imaginary emperor: simple, good, and friendly.

"I had become accustomed to praise. I have sometimes thought that if my companions had applauded my evil deeds instead, I could easily have been the perfect model of the bad student. It all sprang from an obscure need to apologize for something, and it is only in that light that

I came to understand myself as I am now. The notion that
people had placed their hopes in me dominated my whole
childhood, and this idea was still with me when I entered
the university. Only the meeting with Agustín, which occurred months later, succeeded in arousing me from my
lethargy."

He stopped, breathing hard. His head was heavy. In re-
reading his diary he had obeyed the same impulse which,
now, was making him close it, as if the reading of it had
cleared up something for him. A strange uneasiness made
him light one cigarette after the other, and he kept running his hand through his unruly hair. He took a drink
from the pitcher, and realized that he had another kind of
thirst. "Drink?" He had never done it. However . . . To
his mind came the story of the factory girl who, after
spending the best years of her life in a mill, had given herself to the first man whom she came across in the street,
to revenge herself for her fate. He, too, felt the need to go
down in the street to mix with people, to forget the class to
which he belonged. *To be a cell in a torrent of cells, wan-
der through the moribund streets of upturned pavements,
to be a drop of water whose death leaves no void.* He
touched his hand to his lips; they were very dry. It seemed
to him he was forgetting something, and he tried to remember what it was. He gave up: an itching sensation ran
through his whole body. He had three free days left until
Saturday. He closed the diary and buried it in the drawer.
Then he put his top coat on and went out into the street.

*   *   *

For the day will come when the Lord will separate the
strong from the weak, the wheat from the chaff, and make
in his tent "a feast of fat things, a feast of wine on the
lees, of fat things full of marrow, of wine on the lees well

refined." He is lying on his stomach on the floor, and his grandmother is behind him pushing herself with her foot; the rocker is made of black wood with a straw back. On the wall there is an oleograph of his aunt and uncle, and on the shelf the photograph of Grandfather in his sea-captain's uniform. "It was in Santiago," she says, "he was all alone, and he killed five hundred Yankees." "Oh," I say, "I'll bet there are hardly any Yankees left alive." "Two or three," says Eduardo. He is holding a ladyfinger, and from time to time he nibbles on it with his rat-like teeth. "Do you want some cocoa?" she says. "I want gin," I say. "I'm thirsty." The woman serves some. "Continue," she says. "How handsome the grandfather was!" "Yes, very handsome." "Why did he kill so many Yankees?" "They wanted to steal his lands from him. He was Spanish." "I am Spanish, too," says Eduardo. "We are all Spaniards," says the grandmother. "And I?" says Paula. "You, too, my dear." "And I," says Paco. "Also, also . . ." I open the album, and she says: "That's me forty years ago; the man at my side is your grandfather." And I say: "Why did he die?" "It was God's will," she says. "He always takes the best." She gives herself another shove with her foot and continues reading the book. "Is it the same one as yesterday?" I ask her. "Yes, the Holy Bible." "Why the same one always?" I say. "Because it is God's word." I open it at random, and I look at the pictures. "Who are those people?" "The Egyptians." "What's happening to them?" "God is punishing them." "Why is He punishing them?" "Because they are bad." "And those little children?" "They are also bad." "What have they done?" She says that we should be obedient and always remember that God is watching us. "And Grandfather?" I say. "He, too, is looking down at us." "Then the dead . . ." I say. "Everything is appearances:

we are amphorae, molds of substances, relics of a dead past."

What is he saying? Oh, I don't know! He is muttering. It's the shock.

The air has become all sand. My eyes burn and the blades of the fans move in space. I want to drink, and I pick up the glass again. "No, my friend, you've had enough." "Enough?" I say. "But I have only had—" "Fourteen," says he. And he begins to count them with the pencil that he takes from behind his ear. "Fourteen, no more no less. That's not counting those you had when you came in. Besides, you look bad." "That shouldn't be any concern of yours," I say. "Each one looks after his own and does not worry about . . ." "See, didn't I tell you? You can't even stand up straight." I mean no, that everything is appearances: "They have never considered me one of their own," I say. "It's as if there had been a barrier. There are those who kill and those who let themselves be killed. Don't you understand?" The man laughs and says: "Of course! You've got a great talent for oratory. Why don't you run for office?" Everybody laughs, and they invite me to continue. "I wanted the test: the chance to show them that I was one of them, that I also accept the rules of the game." They look at me with their coltish faces, lapping up my words like a sweet and sticky gooseberry jam. "Go ahead, explain yourself, you're a student, aren't you?" I look him straight in the eye: "You are not he." "Of course I am not he," he says, "I am I." He is fat and wears thick glasses. "I study law," I say. "Do you want to be a lawyer?" "Yes," I say. "Bravo," he says. "You want to be a lawyer, and you are studying to be one."

I am thirsty.

"Today should be a great day for me," I say. "Is it your

birthday, by any chance?" says he. "No, it isn't my birthday." "Then, why is it a great day for you?" "Because I
have the opportunity that I have always wanted." "Ah?
Yes?" he says. "And what opportunity is that?" I want to
tell him that there are very few people who dispose of a
rich stock of ideas, and fewer still who will take the trouble to live them, and that they belong to that chosen
species who play the leading roles in all adventures, who
live for us the loves of their novels, the dangers of the
movies, and the free existence which everybody covets.
And we, we put in their hands the taste for living and for
loving and for doing that which we would desire, and
perhaps, without their sacrifice, we would not even succeed in imagining . . . "You sing very badly," he says.
"I know it. I have always had a very bad voice." "Besides
you're drunk." "That's possible," I say. "They have thrown
me out of three bars already." "You're really tying one
on; don't you want to rest a little?" There is a wooden
bench under the light, and we sit down there, the two
of us. "Have you quarreled with the girlfriend?" he asks.
"I don't have any girlfriend," I say. "I had one, but that
was a long time ago." "You did right, and I congratulate
you. I wasn't so clever, and now I have her the whole
blessed day long in the house making a nuisance of herself. She says that if she had not married me she would
have been a great artist, and right now she would be
riding around Madrid in an automobile. Doesn't that
strike you as funny?" I laugh to please him and he puts
a hand on my shoulder. "You're a nice fellow, and you
should take it easy on the drinking." He makes an obscure
sign to me, which I do not understand, and says: "The
one thing kills the other." "It always happens that way,"
I say to him. "It's the law of life. If one does not kill, he
must expect that . . ." "I know a fellow who can't do it

anymore, unless he's artificially stimulated," he says, "all because of alcohol." "As a matter of fact, I hardly drink." "Ha! Ha!" says he, "you're very funny." I let myself be slapped affectionately on the back, and I look at him in the face: his eyes are shining like liquid, and he has a Mongul mustache. "On the other hand, I still keep my virility," he says, "the same as when I was your age. And that in spite of the fact that I like to drink, too." "I got drunk without realizing it," I say. "I had a headache, and I thought that it would calm me down." "Today I am completely sober, and do you know how many drinks I have had?" "Five," I say. "Nine." He takes my arm and helps me get up. "There's a house near by that's perfectly reliable. If you invite me, we can go there." "I invite you," I say. "You are very nice," he says. He puts his arm around my waist and helps me to walk straight. In the doorway there is a drawing of a fat-cheeked boy who is floating over a pale landscape of meringue clouds with the aid of only the two wings growing out of his ears. "Look!" I say. "He hasn't any body." "Go on," he says, "that's Cupid." He takes me to the hall and helps me up the stairs. "If you want me to, I'll carry you up," he says. "Thanks. You are very kind, but I'll try to make it alone." "Let me at least help you by the arm." "Don't bother," I say. "We have to behave decently. This is a respectable house." He pushes open the door, which leads to the back parlor. "Hello, Ricardo," says the woman. "Who is that boy?" "He's a friend." "Well, well, looks like he's just a little drunk." "I didn't really mean to be," I say. "As a matter of fact I should have stayed at home and rested." "You can rest here," she says. "I'll have you meet some of the girls." She goes to get them and comes back into the room. "Hello, Ricardo, hi, good evening," they say. "And who's this?" "It is I." "It's a friend." "Hello," I say. "He has a nice face," they say. He squeezes my arm above the elbow and presents me to them: "This boy likes to do things up well." "Drinks all around," I say. "You've had enough, young fellow," says the old woman. "Just one drink," I say. "All right," she says with a sigh. The blonde sits down beside me. "Hello, Dreamy Eyes!" "Hello," I say. "You didn't catch cold outside, did you?"

I am hot. My head is on fire.

She uncorks a bottle: "Drink a little of this." I drink it. It sticks in my stomach. "I'm feeling sick." "Didn't I tell you? The best thing for you to do is to lie down and tell me all about it." "Yes," I say to her, "as a matter of fact, I do need some rest." Ricardo embraces me: "Here's luck!" "Let's go, Dreamy Eyes, I'll fix your bed up for you." "What about the bottle?" I say. "We won't need it," she says.

"What are you doing?" "I'm going. I've got work to do." "At this hour?" "I realize now that I drank only to give myself strength, and it's a cowardly act." "Dreamy Eyes, Dreamy Eyes," she says. She doesn't move, just looks at me with disgust. "Don't you love me even a little bit?" I start putting my clothes on, and don't say anything to her. "Not even a little bit?" she says. I look at myself in the mirror. "I need a comb." She smooths my hair down and ties my tie. "When will you come back?" "Tomorrow." "You're a little liar." "Well, now—so soon?" "He says he has work to do." "Good-by," I say. They kiss me. She accompanies me to the street door. "Take it easy. Don't fall now." "I'm all right," I say. It is raining. Standing still, I stretch out my arms. I let the rain drench my face. "Are you all right?" "Yes, I'm all right, thank you." "Looks like you enjoy getting wet." "I was distracted," I say. "Come,

step inside this doorway, at least, so you won't get wet."
The lower part of my body is like rubber, and I let myself
be led. "Here's a bar, right here." The barman looks at
me and bursts out laughing. "Oh, it's you again?" "I don't
know you," I say. "I don't know what you mean." "Well, I
know you. You drank a whole bottle of gin." "I don't remember," I say. "Well, you have a bad memory. I thought
you had gone to bed." "I don't feel well," I say. "Naturally," he says, "if you insist on drinking so much you'll
soon go and join your grandfather." "And how do you
know who my grandfather is?" "You just told me about
him," he says. "That's true," I say, "I had forgotten." My
head goes around like a merry-go-round, and my stomach
is bloated like a balloon. "I am guilty of great cowardice,"
I say, "and I deserve the most profound scorn." "Come off
it, don't be like that. It isn't as bad as all that. Everybody
has a bad day once in a while, even the best of us." "I did
it because I am afraid," I say. He gives me his hand so that
I won't fall. "Why don't you go to the washroom? Come
on, I'll hold you up." "Thanks, I can go alone."

*My God, how did it happen? I don't know: I found him
there on the stairway, white as a corpse.*

I go out into the street. Taxi. "Hell, no; I won't take
you." "You won't take me?" "You're drunk." "I'll pay you
double." "Okay," he says. "Straight ahead, I'll show you
the way." "Be sure you don't vomit." "Don't worry, I've
already done that." "Sometimes it comes back," he says,
"and the upholstery in this car is new." I feel of it, just
to be congenial. "It's very good stuff," I say, "it would
really be a shame."

Bathe his temples with alcohol. Poor fellow!

Someone shakes my head, and a dizziness comes over
me. "If I had had more confidence in myself I wouldn't
have gotten drunk," I say. "That's what they always say

the morning after the night before," he answers me. I take my head in my hands. "If you find yourself getting sick, just tell me," he says. "I'm just thinking, thanks." I shut my eyes again, and he says to me: "Is this it?" "Yes, Number 17." Oh, God, what happened to me?

Look, he's moving. Keep on rubbing him.

The concierge has seen me and asks: "How pale you are! Are you sick?" "It's nothing at all, thanks. Just the heat." "The heat? You must mean the cold." "Yes, the cold," I say. I begin to climb the stairs, and they escape me. One, two, three, four, five. I fall. Five, six, seven, eight. "If Agustín knew," I say. "Oh, if he only knew."

David, David, do you hear me?

My head feels like lead. I look at the rainbow for a few moments. A slight contraction throws me into darkness. I try to gradually open my eyelids: purple, red, orange, the close white explosion. I go through the whole thing again with my hand, and the shadows thicken again. A violet-colored presentiment becomes suddenly yellow. I take my hand away.

Good Lord, David, what a scare you gave us, we thought you were dead.

❖   ❖   ❖

They called him to the telephone an hour before supper, and it was an old friend who just happened to be passing through Madrid. David went down to Doña Raquel's apartment, just below his own, to receive the call. The friend was bringing him some fresh laundry that his mother had sent. David told him that he was going to be out of town for a little while, and that he could leave the package any convenient place. He realized only upon hanging up that he had spoken as though he were never going to have any use for the clothes; and he could not help shivering.

He had not been downstairs more than a few minutes, and, returning to his apartment, he closed the door and locked it. He was starting toward his room when he saw the figure of Gloria Páez.

She was standing next to the desk so that the lamp lighted up the lower portion of her body while the upper half was in shadow. Blinded by the light, David scarcely recognized her.

"Don't be alarmed. It's only me."

He had stepped back imperceptibly, and for a moment it seemed to him he was still dreaming.

"I saw the light from the stairway, and the door was open. There wasn't anybody here."

Going toward her, he could study her more calmly. She seemed to be paler than usual, and her hand, which for an instant he held in his, burned with the contact.

"I had just gone downstairs for a moment," he stammered. "I . . . I did not know."

He felt uneasy, as if her visit broke the rules of the imaginary and very personal game he was playing. Suddenly, with a shock, he realized he knew what she was going to say. And he felt a great pity for her: almost the desire to apologize to her. She put her gloves on top of the table and glanced around the room.

"It's cold in here. I don't know how you can live here in the winter time."

She said it in a voice he did not know, which produced a strange uneasiness in him.

"I've got some coffee on the hot plate. I'll see if it's ready."

He stepped aside, much relieved to escape her gaze. He

was afraid he could not bear it if he had to stand in front of her a moment longer. The effects of his passing out the night before had not left him, and he felt extremely weak. A tooth-edged crown of little blue flames licked the coffee pot gently. David lifted up the top: it was boiling already. He took the strainer and filled the two cups.

"I don't have any sugar," he said apologetically.

"It doesn't make any difference. Thanks."

He saw as she raised the cup to her lips that her hand was shaking. As for himself, he was afraid of spilling his coffee and put it down on the table.

Gloria was wearing a subtle perfume which gradually invaded the whole room, as if someone had scattered bouquets of magnolias around. When she had come before, she had looked around inquisitively, asking questions and smiling. Today she remained standing, strained, not daring to break the silence.

"I heard you had a fainting-spell yesterday, and I wanted to know how you were—"

She stopped a few seconds and contemplated her hands under the lamplight.

"It took me a long time to make up my mind to come, and believe me it was not easy." She consulted her watch. "I have only a few minutes, but I don't want to leave without having a talk with you." She was going to say that Jaime was waiting for her downstairs, but she refrained. "There has been a misunderstanding between us, and I must straighten it out."

Even before Gloria said anything, David felt a great calm come over him: it seemed that everything was smooth and simple, and that he had been waiting for this visit for years. Smiling, he encouraged her to go on.

"When I came to see you the first time, I did it with no deliberate plan. Luis had asked me to, and I did not ask him for any explanation. I had taken a liking to you last summer, and I had no ulterior motives. Besides, I did not know that you were in love with me. I did not want to make you suffer or see you hurt. I wanted to do my brother a favor, and as you and I were friends . . ."

David nodded his head slowly.

"Don't let it bother you," he said, "it doesn't matter."

She looked at him in astonishment because his voice betrayed no resentment. It was, on the contrary, placid, and for the first time since Gloria had known him he was not trembling.

"I didn't know what all of you were up to, nor that Luis had told you that I wanted you to join the gang. I have never wanted that of you. I—"

Again he interrupted her. "I know it. I knew it already when he told me, and when you came to see me."

"Then?"

He thought he saw her lips quiver a little, and he whispered softly, as though embarrassed.

"Sometimes it is sweet to be deceived."

A shadow of a smile distended his pale lips.

"I did not mind, I assure you. I would do the same thing again, even if I knew you were making fun of me." He put his hand on his chest, as if the simple gesture would sum up all that he was thinking.

Now he was able to drink his coffee, and he did so calmly and deliberately, his eyes never leaving hers.

"Besides, I would have accepted without you. At least I make myself think so. As far as Luis is concerned . . . you really ought to thank him on my behalf, if he put the idea in your head. I was passing through a rather bad period when you came. I needed you."

He said it with extreme simplicity, and he himself was surprised at the accuracy with which his words responded to his thoughts. The tick-tock of the minute hand of the clock could be heard. Soon they would be closing the street door, and Gloria would have to leave.

"You have no reason to apologize, honestly. My mother taught me a long time ago to be grateful for happiness, without worrying about the motives behind it."

He realized that time was conspiring against this moment of peace, making him feel strangely free. They would have to separate in a very short time, and David thought only of making the time left as agreeable as possible.

"Oh, come now. Buck up. You're not going to cry now. Come, come. It's of no importance."

With tears in her eyes, Gloria seemed to him strangely diminished, and a phrase of Tánger's came to his lips: "We love only that which can hurt us." With a corner of his handkerchief he began to wipe away her tears.

"Now it turns out that you, too, are weak. . . ."

He had said it without irony, but it had the effect of a slap in the face to her.

"You— You—" she said.

He was afraid of saying good-by like that. He made a desperate effort to calm her.

"Look. Everybody's going to notice that you've been crying. You're a child. I've told you it's of no importance."

He raised her chin and looked into her face.

"Like that! Like good friends. It's late. I had better take you home. Believe me: you need not feel sorry for me; it would be absurd that I should arouse your pity."

"I—" she said.

David averted her glance.

"I have been hoping for an opportunity like this for a long time, Gloria. Don't think I don't know what all of you think of me; and although I do not show it, I suffer a good deal. As you already know, I fainted yesterday; and I think it was from fear. Fear that I might not be able to go through with it. I even dream about it. Something is threatening Agustín, and I intervene and receive the bullet. I let myself be hurt, be killed, I don't know what. And yet, I'm not suffering. A great sense of calmness seems to have invaded me."

And Gloria recalled what her brother had said to her some months ago: "David is the kind that in a duel would let himself be killed."

She wanted to say something and could not. She contented herself with kissing him lightly on the lips. Then she fled down the stairs.

David remained in the empty room, hesitating and lost.

V

Señor Guarner was eating breakfast in the Empire dining-room of his residence, absorbed in his morning newspaper, when they announced that a young man was waiting to see him.

The day before the secretary had left him an orderly list of the day's callers: an assistant secretary of the Cabinet; the president of the Mallorcan Society; Gerardo Segura, newspaperman.

Señor Guarner put aside the speech of the *señor Ministro* to the members of the Cattle and Grain Commission and went to his study, where he received callers.

The reporter was sitting in front of the table, with a black leather briefcase on his knees.

"Señor Segura?"

He got up—a boy who seemed to be only a little over twenty, with golden hair and blue eyes that opened with sudden innocence, bright and blinking. When Guarner put out his hand, the young man hesitated to take it.

"How do you do?"

"He's bashful," Guarner thought; and, imagining that his habit of looking straight into the eyes of the person to whom he spoke might bother the boy, he tried not to look directly at him. He leaned back in an armchair close by and, with a gesture, indicated to the young man that he should take a seat, too.

"What can I do for you? Do feel free to speak."

The boy sat down awkwardly, giving the impression of being confused and embarrassed at the same time. Guarner looked at the boy's hands: they were white, delicate, and sensitive, with the slender fingers of a man who has never done hard work.

Looks like a rich boy, Guarner thought to himself, probably comes from a distinguished family, in spite of the fact that he's dressed rather carelessly.

"I'm a reporter on *El Alcázar*—" he began. He had finally broken the ice after much effort; but he had interrupted himself before he got half way through.

Guarner smiled at him, noticing that the boy's lack of ease made him at once attractive and strange.

"A good job for a fellow your age. Have you been at it a long time?"

The young man hesitated. "No, just a few weeks."

He looked so abandoned that one felt like helping him and the voice, although hesitating, was an extremely pleasant one.

"The hardest part is, without a doubt, the apprenticeship," Guarner went on. "Until you're really familiar with a trade, it is somewhat annoying. Even if you have the calling. Later on it's an entirely different matter. I, myself, when I began my parliamentary career, and I am speaking now of the days of Canalejas and of Maura, had my times of discouragement; but afterwards one forgets those bad moments."

The telephone rang, and he noticed that the boy gave a start. It was curious; one would have said that he was afraid. Guarner talked for a minute or so and then hung up.

"I have just been talking with a countryman of yours, a Sevillian, and a very good friend of mine. His name is Ramírez, Secretary of Fine Arts. But probably you don't know him. He hasn't lived in Sevilla for fifteen years."

The young man did not have an Andalusian accent, however. Thinking he read suspicion in Guarner's eyes, the boy
hastened to say: "As a matter of fact, I am not a Sevillian.
My family is from Barcelona."

Guarner smiled, as if this fact brought them closer together. "Catalonian? My grandparents were born there.
Actually, I'm half Catalonian myself. My mother's maiden
name was Font: very Catalonian, to be sure."

He brought his chair up closer to the boy's, wanting to
seem even more cordial. Their knees, now, were almost
touching.

"Incidentally, I visited your city three weeks ago, when
I attended the Co-operative Convention. I have some
good friends there, and they insisted so much. I found it
more beautiful than ever. It is certainly surprising how
it grows from one year to the other."

"Oh, yes; it seems to me I read something about that
convention in the papers."

"Very likely. The press gave the doings a great deal of
space. You may remember my speech?"

The young man shook his head negatively. Guarner
thought he was nervous and offered him a cigarette.

"No, thanks."

The older man lighted one, and continued: "The speech
contained some quotations from Maragall, which I had
practiced reading in their language, thinking that it was
going to please them, but I guess my pronunciation was
quite bad. Those who were seated toward the back could
not even understand me."

A light smile came over him. "Too bad we don't have
enough time to learn all the things we'd like to learn."

The young man did not answer. He remained sitting
erect in the chair, the briefcase still on his knees. Every

once in a while he brought his right hand to his coat pocket, but he withdrew it immediately, with a convulsive shudder.

Despairing of getting an answer, Guarner broached the main subject again: "Well, I imagine you have come to get a story on the secondary-school project. Some newspapermen came to see me yesterday afternoon already: Seguí, Javier Balaños, do you know them?"

No, he did not know them. The man's eyes persecuted him for moments at a time, relentlessly.

"They asked me to clarify a few obscure points in the program. If you wish, I can give you a copy. That will save us both a lot of trouble."

The boy's voice came out hoarse from the depth of his throat. "If you will—"

Guarner turned his back to him: on the table, on top of the mountains of papers that he never could get in order, he had left a typewritten copy. He began to look for it. *"His eyes!"* A suspicion had just entered his mind, but he refused to believe it. It was too absurd.

"I know I put it here somewhere, but with all these papers it's going to be difficult to put my hands on it."

The boy did not answer him. Guarner could hear him panting now, and he had great difficulty refraining from turning to look at him, but he managed to control himself.

"Finally! Here it is. I think that's it . . . yes."

He turned around; the boy had stood up, and was staring at him with a wild look in his eyes. His blue eyes blinked as though hurt by glare, and his right hand was clutching something hidden in the pocket of his jacket. In spite of himself, Guarner stepped back.

"Is there anything wrong?"

He got no answer. The boy was looking straight at him with such intensity that Guarner turned away for a moment. Filled with pity, he bridged the distance that separated them.

"Are you feeling ill?"

He took him by the arm—the one that was not holding the gun in the pocket—and tried to guide him toward the sofa.

But the muscles of his body were tense, and his arm was taut. In spite of the effort, Guarner could not make him move. He stood stiff and motionless, obstinately erect, like a plaster statue, against the light.

Then Guarner took him by the lapels and shook him hard. Leaning so close that he could feel the young man's breath on his face, he saw the hand in the pocket and the dark object the fingers were grasping. A great sadness came over him.

"My boy," he murmured.

The tension in the boy's muscles relaxed little by little, and then his eyelids blinked, released from the same tension, while the little muscles on the surface of his skin twitched. His features distended and broke into tiny wrinkles. And for a moment Guarner felt that he was embracing a man as old as he.

Meekly, he let Guarner lead him to a seat. The light hit him squarely in the face, again, and his skin absorbed it like a sponge.

"Come, now; take it easy; it was nothing at all."

He accepted the glass of water that Guarner had on top of the table, and drank it in little sips, mechanically.

"Do you feel better? Do you want me to bring you something?"

Without knowing why, Guarner felt impotent in front of this young man; guilty for still being alive. It was strange. He was not afraid at all, and he felt calmer than ever. As for the boy, he was not paying any attention to him: his thoughts were doubtless far away. He let Guarner put his hand over his and let him wipe away the saliva from the corners of his mouth with a handkerchief.

"Come on, son. Calm yourself."

At last he seemed to be listening to Guarner. His eyes were resting on the older man's—shining—whether out of panic or not, it was hard to tell. He tried to get up, but his knees refused to support him. He was still very weak.

"You— You—" he began.

He was shocked to discover that the butt of the pistol was sticking out of his pocket, and tried to hide it, but he read in Guarner's eyes that he, too, knew it.

Then he noticed the caress of the old man's hand, and withdrew his own violently.

"Let me alone," he said.

This time he managed to stand up; his disheveled hair hung down over his forehead, and his eyes sparkled like pieces of glass in the sun. He was crying. Guarner wanted to draw closer to him: he had never before valued his own life so little, nor had it ever before seemed to weigh so heavily on him.

"My poor boy—" But he was stopped by the expression on the face before him, so wrought with rage.

"Shut up! You have no right to call me that!"

His right hand, independent, moving, perhaps, of its own will searched nervously for the revolver. Guarner did not move.

"Coward! You're not even capable of defending yourself by calling the police. You prefer to let yourself be killed. Even in that— Dirty pity!" and he turned and left the room.

Guarner was shattered. The violence of the boy's words had shaken him so that he was scarcely able to realize what had been happening. He ran after him.

"Please. Don't go away like that. You are in no condition to go out in the street—"

The sharp slamming of the door cut his sentence in half; the boy had left.

When the maid came in, attracted by the noise of their voices, she found the old man with his hands to his face, crying like a child.

* * *

The club coupé Luis Páez had rented was parked on the corner with the motor running, ready for the getaway. From their station in the middle of the block, Raúl and Cortézar kept their eyes on the door through which their comrade was to come and on the rear end of the car, which at the moment they were watching. Their job was a reconnaissance job, and only in the case of extreme danger were they to intervene and help the escape.

They had been waiting for half an hour, and the sidewalk was littered with cigarette butts. Raúl walked up and down with his hat thrown back, smoking incessantly. Cortézar, behind him, just looked attentively at the window display in an optical shop. The shop next to it sold ladies' underwear, and one of the clerks, standing in the doorway, followed absorbedly the movement of the street: couples, isolated passers-by hurrying along under the ashen gray sky.

At the other end of the block a pair of *guardias* had stopped by a wooden bench. One of them, enormous and solid, had a large black mustache and was well over six feet tall. The other one, shorter and weaker-looking, ran his tongue along some cigarette paper and then bent over to get a light from the big guy, who cupped his hands around the flame.

"Do you suppose they're going to stand there forever," whispered Cortézar.

Raúl said nothing. Cortézar had spoken in a whisper, although there was nobody passing by, and this cowardly attitude irritated Raúl. He was on the point of saying something cutting, but he refrained. He looked at his watch; the second hand was advancing with hateful slowness, taking an incredibly long time to complete one circle, and when it had done so, it signified merely that one minute had passed. It was exasperating.

"If light travels at three hundred thousand kilometers per second and a minute has sixty seconds, during a minute it will have traveled, let's see now . . . three hundred per second. Whew! I never did know how to solve such problems."

The *guardias*, smoking beside the wooden bench, were now talking with a young woman out for a walk with her little boy, whom they were all contemplating lovingly.

"Apparently," said Cortézar, "they don't intend to move on."

If David were discovered as he tried to leave, the presence of the *guardias* could jeopardize everything; they would be obliged to shoot.

"Yes, they're going to continue standing there all day."

"They're smoking a cigarette, the bastards."

"They're tired!"

"Look, the big fellow is patting the little boy on the head."

"That's all we need: 'Hello, cute little boy, how are you? I am a *guardia!* Look how tall I am!' He imitated a high, falsetto voice.

"Soon they'll be sitting down with the mother," said Cortézar. "Just you wait and see."

"Look at her. Smiling: 'Oh, just like a little boy! Pay no attention to him; he always likes to play with *guardias*.'"

"'Are those real pistols?' 'Bang! Bang! Little boy dead.'"

"Now the big guy's swinging him between his legs. How adorable! The *guardia* spreads his legs so that the little boy can duck under them. What a clever little boy! 'Bang, bang.' 'Once more.'"

"Just look at Mama: 'I am a young mother. Twenty-two years old. Last Saturday we took him to the movies, and he was so enthusiastic. Every time he sees a *guardia* he wants to kill him.'"

"'Ha, ha! I'm dead! The little boy has killed me. Bang.'"

"'Look how the little boy laughs, how cute!'"

"The little shit!"

"The little bastard!"

Glowering, they continued to watch them, while the mother smiled and the *guardia* lifted the boy up in his arms.

"If he doesn't watch out, we'll be the ones to shoot him," said Raúl.

"We'll take care of the little angel."

"They would blame the *guardia* for it."

"Let the *guardia* go screw himself."

"Can't you just imagine the mother: 'Murder, murder! They've killed my son. Help, help! *Guardias*.'"

"'We are the *guardias*, Señora, and you don't have to yell at us like that; we're not deaf. Besides, we haven't killed anybody. That filthy brat of yours died all by himself.'"

"And she: 'So, my son is a filthy brat, is he? I'll show you who's a brat! Take that, and that, and that!'"

"'Oh, stop, stop! You're hurting us!'"

They broke into laughter, nervous and impatient. Noticing their gaiety, a woman just passing by turned around and looked at them. *David*. They consulted their watches again: twenty-five minutes to twelve.

"He's been up there over a half-hour already," said Cortézar. "I can't understand what takes him so long."

"Maybe the old man has a visitor. Don't be so impatient."

"For all that's left of his life. . . . Well, I guess he's lived his life, anyway, don't you?"

Raúl held back a nervous yawn. The hand in his pocket gripped his pistol mechanically.

"Old people are a bunch of egotists. If they're not killed early in life, there's no way of getting rid of them."

"The country is run by the old goats. They're exploiting us."

"We should make them work for us."

"Yes, with a pick and shovel."

"If we liquidated them, their heirs would be most grateful to us."

" 'Look here, Señora. We have accelerated the death of your dear old grandfather. Wouldn't you like to make us a little gift?' "

" 'But, of course! Whatever you wish. The truth is, you have done us a great favor. The old boy was getting to be quite a nuisance.' "

" 'Besides, he smelled pretty bad. All old men, before they die, stink.' "

They stopped their act for a few seconds.

"Look," exclaimed Raúl, pointing in the direction of the *guardias*, "they've left."

"I can scarcely believe it."

"They've gone some place else to make a noise."

"They smelled danger, if you ask me."

"We would have taken care of them, all right!"

"The cowards! They've left."

"With their tails between their legs."

They had nothing to say to each other, but they felt compelled to keep on talking, as if they were preparing an alibi for themselves: a running away, an escape valve.

"Look, the concierge is out there sweeping again. How many times a day do you suppose she does that?"

"I wouldn't know. There are people who can't sit still. They have to be working all the time."

"She acts like she's got St. Vitus's Dance, poor soul."

A clock in the neighborhood struck the three-quarter hour; it must have been fast. They had only twenty minutes to twelve. Cortézar couldn't stand it any longer and turned to Raúl.

"You don't think something peculiar has happened to him, do you? He should have been down long ago."

"Listen. Wait here a moment. I'm going to speak to Agustín."

He walked away, trying to be casual. When he reached the house where Guarner lived, he risked a quick glance around: there was nobody in sight.

The trees along the street sent up their naked branches against a leaden, gray sky. The last leaves of autumn were dancing between the feet of the passers-by, or stood out in relief at the tops of the trees.

"What the hell can he be doing up there so long?" Cortézar asked Luis Páez. Luis, seated at the wheel, shrugged his shoulders indifferently.

"I've had the motor running for half an hour."

In the back seat Agustín Mendoza refilled his pipe; Ana was nervously biting her fingernails. There was a moment of silence.

"You don't think something might have happened to him?" Cortézar asked.

Luis turned around and looked at him. "Happen to him?

What do you want to happen to him? A fainting-spell? Or that the old guy took a pot shot at him? If anything had happened, there'd be a commotion around the entrance by this time. And take a look, the concierge is still out there sweeping the sidewalk."

Cortézar merely skipped Agustín's remark. "I was never of the opinion that David should be the one to do it. He has always seemed to me the one least fitted for the job, of all of us."

"Then why did you consent to it?" asked Luis. "All David had to say was that he wasn't interested, and we'd have been spared all this."

Agustín brought his pipe to his lips. "You're all talking as though, instead of David's killing the guy, the old man had got David. That's a bit wild, I think."

"I'm going to have to turn the motor off," said Luis. "If I keep it running, I'll not answer for what might happen later."

"Turn it off then."

"That's what I'm going to do."

He pressed one of the buttons on the dashboard, and the coupé stopped shaking.

"Have you checked the gas?"

"We've got enough to take us as far as Alicante."

"I don't think we have to go that far," joked Cortézar. He turned to Ana and said: "What do you think?"

Agustín waved his hand. "Don't ask her anything. She's in ecstasy. She has just confessed to me that through this criminal act she hopes to redeem her soul."

Ana did not bother answering. The realization of her plans was completely different from what she had imagined. Her participation was slight, nil, so far as the police would be concerned. Ever since she had made the pact with Agustín, she had been obsessed with the idea that she had embarked on a venture that no longer interested her. Agustín's behavior now irritated her profoundly, and she could hardly control herself.

"She feels herself left out of it," she heard him say. "She thinks that we haven't understood the act's magnificent possibilities."

In spite of her hatred, Ana could not help admiring the singular talent that he displayed in analyzing her: Agustín was one of those men clever at picking out the *raison d'être* of other people, at baring to the light the secret mechanism of their thoughts.

"She says she left the anarchists because they did not understand her. They were a bunch of brutes. They did not realize that she had a soul, too. And you know how delicate the feminine soul is! Do I make myself understood or don't I?"

"You don't," Luis said, "and the best thing you can do is shut up."

Agustín paid no attention to him. "Women are extraordinary, believe me. As long as you recognize their right to have a soul, you can do whatever you wish with them. Of course, the most important thing must be the soul. And there are so few who realize this."

"Careful," said Cortézar.

David had just come out of the doorway and was looking around with a baffled expression. Luis started the car and opened the front door. Everybody's heart was beating violently.

"The stupid bastard!" exclaimed Agustín. "He turned the wrong way."

David, instead of going toward the waiting car, had started walking in the opposite direction. He had left the briefcase in Guarner's apartment, and was carrying a dark object in his right hand.

"Let's go," said Luis. "We'll pick him up on the other street."

The coupé, taking off with a jerk, started up full speed ahead along Diego de León Street. Cortézar stayed on the sidewalk in order to give warning.

Raúl, meanwhile, had rushed after David. He approached him excitedly: the street was half deserted, and he had to take the risk.

"What happened?"

David said nothing. He was still carrying the pistol in his hand; Raúl looked back: the doorway was empty, nobody was following them. He caught him by the sleeve and began to shake him.

"Did you kill him? Tell me, did you kill him?"

He couldn't make him talk, and he had to struggle to try to force the pistol out of his hand. The street was almost empty, but some women passing by turned around to look at them. David walked along as though in a trance.

"You imbecile!" whispered Raúl. "Please, will you let go of it?"

He struck him angrily on the chest, and David doubled up, panting like a hunted animal, and finally released his grip.

The pistol fell to the ground: Raúl kicked it down the mouth of a near-by sewer.

"Let me have it, let me have it," David stammered.

Raúl heard some footsteps behind him, and he lifted the safety catch of his own revolver. Taking advantage of the short pause, he turned around to take a look: it was Cortézar. But already some people who had seen Raúl struggling with David were turning around and staring at them again, whispering to one another.

"Come on, hurry up!"

He took David by the arm and made him turn the

corner. He was sweating. Dozens of people had seen them on the street; maybe they were already running to get the *guardias*. They were going to be caught in the most stupid way. He felt a violent anger against David, and he pressed his arm furiously.

"You fool! You fool!"

All of his pent-up hatred made him curse as he had never done before. Hundreds of glances seemed to be singling him out. His whole back was a sea of oscillating needles that penetrated his skin with a frenetic rhythm. He felt like screaming, like biting. Then, noticing that his knees were not obeying him and that his legs were going ahead faster than he wanted them to, he knew that he had become a prey to panic.

Cortézar was following them from a distance, cautiously, trying to keep a discreet pace behind. As they approached the corner, he glanced anxiously around looking for the car. It was not there. And he felt his anguish increase.

David, letting himself be dragged along by the arm, was muttering incomprehensible words. They had reached the other corner, where they stopped to rest. Their behavior might awaken suspicion; in the middle of the block Raúl saw a *guardia* in uniform. On Maldonado Street, no one was following them. There was an empty cab at the curb, and he put David in it.

"Wait a second," Raúl said. "I'm going to tell Cortézar."

He turned the corner, on the run, and made a sign to Cortézar to come. The street was empty.

"Quick. I've got him there, in a taxi."

Cortézar was pale, and his eyes glowed like embers.

"Did he kill him?" he said.

"No, he didn't kill him! Come on, hurry up!"

They ran to the corner, and stopped dead when they got there: the taxi had gone.

*   *   *

They got in the front seat, and the car sped away.

"All right! Nobody's following us now. Will you explain yourselves a little more calmly?"

It was Luis who was speaking: he was driving with a very professional air, and he arched his eyebrows mockingly. Raúl gave him a fiery look.

"What do you want me to explain?" he blurted. "Didn't I just tell you that he got away in the taxi, without any explanation?"

"You should have demanded one of him," Luis answered.

Raúl smiled bitterly. "Sure, on top of dragging him two blocks, surrounded by people who were watching us, I should have asked him for an explanation. Now it will even turn out that it's all my fault."

"No, no one said you were to blame," answered Luis. "But anyone else in your place wouldn't have let him escape in such an idiotic way, and we wouldn't find ourselves up the blind alley we're in; we'd at least know what to expect."

"I already explained to you that I left him settled in the taxi, and I went to get Cortézar. You guys," he added with a smirk, "weren't in sight."

"There was no reason for you to go and look for Cortézar. He's a big boy now: he wouldn't have gotten lost. If you found a taxi, the most logical thing would have been to get away as fast as you could. It seems to me that's just common sense."

"Common sense, shit! Didn't I tell you that when I put him in the taxi he was half conscious? I had to drag him two whole blocks, and how was I to know that he was going to beat it?"

"Nevertheless, I insist that you shouldn't have left him alone. Since the taxi was there—"

Raúl threw up his arms in despair. "Oh, go to hell!"

The look of superiority on Luis's face exasperated him: he knew that when he was struggling right out in the open street with David to get the gun away from him, he was risking his own neck, and Luis's criticism could only mean that Luis was totally unaware of what he had done.

"Cut the arguing, you two," said Agustín. "At this point it won't get you anywhere. No one could care less whether David left you holding the bag in the street."

"I still say he shouldn't have left David," said Luis obstinately.

He spoke with the deliberate purpose of being annoying. Everybody's nerves were on edge and it didn't take much to make them flare up.

Raúl loosened the knot of his tie and began to fan himself with a piece of cardboard which he had taken out of his coat pocket. He turned to Agustín and began to tell him once more what had happened, gesticulating wildly.

Whenever Raúl speaks, Luis said to himself, you don't know what he's talking about, but he ends up by being convincing somehow. But Luis was still determined to continue the attack.

"If only you had stayed with him in the taxi instead of going for Cortézar, you would have saved yourself all these explanations."

"What did I tell you?" Raúl exclaimed. "Now it turns out that it *is* all my fault."

As he spoke, he removed his jacket, which was inhibiting his gestures. His shirt sleeves were rolled up above his elbows, and his sweat formed damp circles under his armpits. He crossed his arms over his chest and resumed his bitter smirk.

"I didn't say you were to blame," said Luis. "But you

shouldn't have let him go. Cortézar is old enough to take care of himself. He knows what he's doing."

"Shut up, once and for all," said Agustín. "No use in adding more fuel to the fire."

Luis let go of the wheel for a moment. "I'm not. I was only saying that if he'd stayed with David, instead of going after Cortézar—"

"Yes, and then we wouldn't find ourselves in the situation we're in now, and Cortézar is old enough to know what he's doing. You've already told us all that."

"Then—"

"You better pay more attention to your driving. Unless you're planning to run somebody over."

"Who knows? Maybe I am," said Luis.

He put a cigarette between his lips and stepped on the accelerator. There was a moment of silence, during which all of them seemed to be taking in the magnitude of their failure.

"I told you guys," said Cortézar suddenly. "I always thought that David was the last one for the job. Any of us could have done it, except David. It was stupid of us to have accepted him in the first place."

Luis turned around abruptly, as if somebody had pinched him.

"Then why did he agree to it? We didn't force him; he was the one to let himself in for it, voluntarily."

"We shouldn't have made him one of us in the first place. He always was a coward. A good kid, I grant you. But a coward. It was no secret. You all knew it. As long as we didn't admit Uribe, we shouldn't have accepted him, either."

"All this is very fine," replied Luis, "but you should have said it a long time ago. When Agustín said that David had to be told, no one had the slightest objection. I was the only one who expressed any doubt, and for a moment I thought I was going to get slugged."

Raúl fingered his mustache and looked at him challengingly. "If you're referring to me, speak more clearly. I don't like these indirect digs."

Luis sneered: "I'm not referring to anybody in particular," he said, "but if you think I'm referring to you, you must have some reason for thinking so."

The endless, sterile, discussion threatened to go on and on, until Agustín cut it off with a wave of the hand.

"Luis is right. I was the one who suggested that we should tell David. I've known him for many years, and he's a good friend of mine. It seemed to me that it was my duty to tell him. He had collaborated with us on the magazine, and I didn't want to humiliate him unnecessarily. When I put it up to him, I thought I was offering him an opportunity. Better yet, his opportunity. If he had succeeded, David would at this very moment be one of us. He'd have had his baptism of fire, of blood. If he has failed, the fault is his: he'll have to face the consequences."

"Consequences? What consequences?"

"That's my affair. I'm the one who is to blame, and it's up to me to make things right."

The car was speeding up Abascal Street in the direction of the new University City buildings.

"In any case," said Cortézar, "if he had to take part, we shouldn't have let him be anything more than a mere accomplice. If he'd stayed outside in the street, things would be different now."

"We all had an equal chance," Luis answered. "It was not we who chose him; it was Fate."

They were at it again; Cortézar gave him a light.

"Do you think they caught him in the act?"

Raúl stopped fanning himself for a few seconds. "How

should I know! When he came out of the house he was holding the pistol in his hand. The first thing I asked him was if he had killed him, and he said no."

"However," observed Agustín, "there was no shouting or yelling, and nobody came to the windows; if there had been, there was time enough to arouse the whole neighborhood."

Raúl's answer was cut short: Luis had taken a sharp curve too fast, and the wheels skidded, shrieking stridently.

"No, nobody followed us," Raúl said.

"Then—"

"Maybe they didn't dare to even put their noses out of the window."

"The police are probably in the apartment by now," said Cortézar.

"They must have telephoned for them."

The idea that the police might possibly be on their tail filled them with excitement. Luis increased the speed of the car imperceptibly.

"No doubt there'll be a story of the attempt in the evening papers," said Cortézar.

"Who knows? Sometimes they keep it quiet so as not to stir up the public."

"As long as David has had enough sense not to go home in the taxi—"

"Hell—to try to identify him would be like looking for a needle," said Luis.

"Besides, they won't have time."

It was Agustín who had spoken: Luis turned around to look at him.

"What do you mean by that?"

Agustín's face expressed perfect calm, but his big, blue eyes, bloodshot, shifted nervously. Luis could not help shivering.

"Nothing. I didn't mean a thing."

Again there was a pause. Luis looked at his friend's face through the rear-view mirror and felt his heart beat faster and faster.

"We'll have to get the newspapers," said Cortézar. "I'll bet anything the old man has informed the police."

He turned toward Ana, who had not opened her mouth once since she had gotten into the car, and looked at her in amazement. Her face was rigidly stiff, like pasteboard, and a slight squint accented the almost mineral hardness of her pupils. He saw her move her lips.

"It's disgraceful. . . ."

"What was that?" asked Cortézar.

She did not budge, nor bother to answer him. She was talking to herself—moving her lips again.

"It's so disgraceful. . . ."

Seated in the back of the car, a silent witness to the conversation, which reached her ears in snatches, without meaning, reduced to a confused humming, she had suddenly understood *everything*. Her dreams haunted her, cutting her to the quick; the newspaper headlines, the insults, the threats; she took a look around her. "I am surrounded by a bunch of kids who tried to behave like men." Maybe it would even come out in the papers: a ridiculous attempt of little importance, three lines, nothing; the bourgeois were going to have a good laugh over it. She could not control herself, and she hid her head in her hands. The chatter went on around her.

*   *   *

They had agreed to meet at four o'clock in the afternoon, and they took leave of one another there in the street. Agustín hailed a taxi at the first stand: he had to go to see a friend of his, and he was afraid he would be late. When he arrived he told the driver to wait, and he went up the stairs two at a time.

"Señor Castro, please."

The employee, a platinum blonde, looked at him inquisitively. Agustín, with his muffler wrapped around his neck, did not look like the firm's usual type of client.

She finished the letter that she was typing, sighed audibly, and then stood up. A silk blouse outlined her pointed breasts, and as she walked through the dark corridor that led to the inner offices, Agustín noticed that she pushed her bust forward. Bored, impatient, he took a look around him. On the desk a horrible landscape of yellow and purple announced the commercial products of the firm. The bare walls were flayed and peeling. On a shelf a fan stood motionless: a horrible mechanical toy of dark petals.

"This way, please."

She conducted him to a small room with the word DIRECTOR on the door. Castro was seated at the desk, near the typewriter. He stood up as Agustín entered.

"What brings you here?"

They exchanged the usual formal words of greetings between old friends. Then Agustín went right to the point.

"A few months ago you spoke to me of a captain of gendarmes who helped his friends cross over into Portugal."

Castro arched his eyebrows, slightly astonished. "Yes."

"Could you give me his address?"

"Of course."

He took a card out of a folder and wrote his name on it plainly.

"Has something happened?" he asked.

Agustín smiled. "Oh, for the moment, nothing special, but it's possible—"

"I hope you haven't killed the Chief of State," he said jokingly.

"Don't worry. I'm much more modest than that."

"Well, with your theories—"

Three years before, in Barcelona, Agustín had gotten Castro out of a very serious jam, and since then Castro had remained absolutely faithful to him.

"I'll write a few lines for you, if you wish."

"Perhaps it would be better."

For a few seconds both of them remained silent. The only thing that could be heard was the scratching of the pen across the card. Agustín asked: "Do you have any idea of what one ought to pay in such cases?"

The thin trace of a smile outlined itself on the lips of his friend. "Don't worry about it. I'll take care of it."

"No, no, I don't want you to feel obliged because—"

"Don't even mention it. We're friends and we trust each other. I would tell you if . . ."

Agustín offered him a cigarette.

"I prefer my own brand, thanks."

He put the letter into an envelope and handed it to him.

"I didn't date it," he said.

"Thanks."

Again they were silent, and Agustín glanced around the room.

"You've got a nice place here," he said.

"Yes, I earn a good living."

"Getting fat, of course!"

Castro smiled. "You said it."

"And a very fetching secretary."

"Between the acts."

They spoke like two old friends who no longer have anything to say to each other, and whose friendship is nourished only on remembrances of things past.

"And you?"

"Right on top, as always."

"I envy you," said Castro.

"That's what a lot of people say."

Castro had stood up again and was accompanying Agustín through the corridor.

"I'll drop you a line from Portugal."

"I wish you could do things some other way."

"In any case, I'll write you."

They shook hands, and Agustín merely said thanks.

* * *

Cortézar left the newspapers on the table. He had gone down to buy them at the corner stand in the hope of finding some mention of the attempted murder, and by the look of disappointment on his face, his friends gathered that nothing had been printed.

"Not a word."

He said it with embarrassment, as if he were directly responsible, and he hastened to add: "Maybe they didn't get it in on time."

Over and above the embarrassment, moral and physical, Luis's words rang clearly.

"Time . . . there's been more than enough time; they never made up the paper before two o'clock."

Raúl made a move instinctively. "Let me look. Perhaps, at the last moment—"

"No, there's nothing there, either. I've already looked."

The newspaper remained folded on the table. There was a moment of silence.

"Perhaps," said Cortézar, "they want to keep it quiet for the moment."

Luis burst out laughing: his eyes were hard, as though

engraved in enamel and his laughter pierced the air disagreeably.

"Keep it quiet, you say? Don't make me laugh. The fact that some insignificant kid tries to kill a guy like that is no affair of state, believe me! On the other hand, as a story, it's not so bad. A nice little story! The old men will drool all over themselves talking about vice and corruption and all that rot. My dear papa loves to breakfast every morning on the little scandals like that. He looks at me over his paper: 'Here's something, Luis, this may interest you. Read it, read it.' And he rubs his hands looking at me out of the corner of his eye. Like on the days they publish statistics on venereal diseases: 'Look, just look at it, what devastation!' And he asks my opinion and fawns over me just like a dog. Since they don't dare speak to us in the first person, they borrow their opinions from the newspapers. Oh, I assure you, for them it would be a wonderful item."

"With this difference," said Raúl, "that if our names appeared, the story wouldn't strike them so funny."

"My father," said Luis, "would choke on his breakfasts for the rest of his life. Then, as usual, he would blame my mother."

"Then," murmured Cortézar, "I can't understand why the incident did not come out in the papers. If it's a good piece of news, all the more reason why they should print it."

He wanted to reverse the argument, but Luis cut him off: "Very simple. If the papers haven't mentioned it, it's because Guarner hasn't told them, and if Guarner hasn't opened his mouth, *it's because no attempt was made.*"

"I don't understand you. Try to speak a little more clearly."

"In two words: David fooled us with the pistol and the little street scene with Raúl. There was no attempted assault of any kind, I'm sure. David didn't take the pistol out of his pocket until he was out of the house."

"That's absurd," said Cortézar. "It makes no sense. If he didn't dare shoot the old man, why would he take the pistol out later?"

"Moreover," Raúl added, "you'd be the last one to know. You weren't even there when he came out. You didn't see the look on his face, as I did. I'm not defending him, what the hell, but something had happened to the kid. Just what, I know as much as you do. But he was completely gone, as though he were dead."

Luis had read his thoughts: he twirled his glass between his fingers and put it on the table upside down.

"What's happened to you, Raúl, is clearer than water. You figured you'd acted the big hero, and that stops you from admitting you really fouled up."

Like a rising vapor, the blood rushed to Raúl's face. But before he had time to react, Agustín broke in:

"Let's cut the senseless accusations. If Raúl fouled up, so did we all. That's the first point. Second, who knows yet whether we really did or not; until we find David, we don't know a thing."

"Exactly," said Cortézar, "until we talk with David, we don't know anything for sure. Whatever we decide before then will just be a waste of time."

"What time did you call him?"

"First at one o'clock and then again at four. He wasn't in, so I left a message."

"Then the only thing we can do is to wait for him. Unless he has left—"

"Left?" said Raúl. "Where do you think he would go?"

"How should I know! If he hasn't given any signs of life up to now, there must be some reason. He can't be riding around in a taxi all day long."

"Don't worry," said Agustín, "he'll come back."

He said it with such certainty that it rather surprised them.

"Besides," he added in a low voice, "it's a matter that concerns me alone. I am the one who has to balance the accounts."

His look, as he walked around the table, had a coldness, a depth that could not be accurately described by any color. There was a long silence.

"In principle," said Cortézar, "that does not seem to me such a bad idea. I was always against his coming in with us."

"I know it," said Agustín, "and for that reason, I free you from any responsibility whatsoever. It's my fault, and it's up to me to take the consequences."

Raúl stretched his hands out in front of him: enormous, pale hands, shadowed with down, made to knead, to crush something between them.

"I'd like to know what you call 'consequences,' " he said.

Something floated around in the atmosphere, something indefinite, hostile, that cut off Agustín's reply before it could be formed. The atmosphere was stifling, heavy, and stormy. Outside, the rain was about to break.

Agustín hesitated for a few moments and then said: "You guys think that it's all my fault and you're right. If David got into the group, he did so with my support. And if we're up a blind alley now, I'm responsible for that, too. Therefore, I consider it my right to deal with the problem as I see fit."

Agustín looked at them again with an arrogant air, and he himself was the first to be surprised that they should show any resistance. It was not clear opposition, but something troubling, reflected in a multitude of fragmentary elements: the movements of lips, of fingers, the grating sound of a fingernail scratching the surface of wood. . . .

"I wouldn't want anything bad to happen to David," said Raúl.

He had raised his head and was smoothing his mustache mechanically.

"No one said that something bad has to happen to him," replied Agustín. "I merely said that this is my business, and I am going to take care of it as I see fit."

Raúl looked at him obstinately. "And I merely said that David has always seemed to me a good guy."

The atmosphere had become rarefied. Cortézar felt obliged to intervene.

"You are both getting away from the point. Agustín says one thing and you say something else. You'll never understand each other like that."

He stopped for a moment. Outside it had started to rain pitchforks, too hard for it to last. The drops were coming down on the roof like volleys of buckshot; they drowned and diminished the sound of his words.

"A friend's a friend," said Raúl.

His moral code was very neat, reduced to a few standards to which he clung tenaciously.

"David is my best friend," said Agustín, "and I am the first to recognize his qualities. But we are not discussing that. I was simply telling you that I'm the only one qualified to demand an accounting from him."

"I think," said Raúl, throwing his hat back, "that we ought to question him first. I'm the one who saw him this morning, and I know something happened to the kid. I'm not defending him, but—"

"All right. We know all that. You've already told us. Besides, I intend to do just that. Before deciding anything I'll talk to him first. No one can be condemned without proof."

Raúl did not say anything: by the faces of the other two, he realized that Agustín's opinion would prevail. And he shrugged his shoulders.

"Do what you please. You decide. If you are a friend of his, you have an excellent chance to prove it. As far as I'm concerned, I've already said that I have nothing against him, and I still consider him a damn good friend."

It was a defeat in every sense of the word, and he felt irritated with himself for having given in so soon.

"We're all agreed," observed Agustín. "David is a great guy, but he's mixed up in something very much more serious. When he decided to take part, he not only risked his own neck, but ours, too. He committed himself to something, and he didn't keep his word. David's no longer a baby. If he hasn't done the job, he will have to justify himself; and if he doesn't justify himself, he'll have to accept whatever happens."

His reasoning was perfect: Raúl, though angry, had to admit it. He felt the desire to protect David from an imaginary danger, but he said only: "I know. But this is different. He is a comrade."

"Comrade or not, he has betrayed our confidence."

"And he's covered us with ridicule," said Cortézar. "For months now we've talked about this thing, and now, to have it turn out like this."

"Yes," said Raúl, "all this is true, but there is something else." He did not know what, and he was irritated at his ignorance.

"Looking at it calmly, it's almost better that the papers didn't say anything. If they were to print the story, it would make us blush with shame."

"Really, the only one who has been able to realize it is Ana."

David had no possible defense. He should have been

able to do it somehow, Raúl said to himself. But now he'd lost his chance. Raúl stood up and leaned against one of the window shutters; at the other end of the room where the roof fell obliquely almost touching the floor Eduardo Uribe was sleeping on a mat, his back turned to them.

He made a habit of presenting himself at his friends' house any old time, and stretching out anywhere until the charwoman came in and chased him out.

Raúl put his nose against the window; after the deluge of just a few moments before, there had come a perfect calm: the passers-by walked along the street without umbrellas, and the last straggling drops burst on the balcony ledge like soap bubbles.

Raúl began putting on his coat without a word, and, looking at his friends, he yawned.

"I haven't eaten yet," he said, "and I'm famished."

"I could do with some food, myself," said Cortézar.

"Come along with me, then. I know where we can get some good shellfish."

Agustín and Luis remained sitting.

"When are you coming back?"

Raúl made a face: "Whenever you need me: *Je suis à votre disposition.*"

"I'll call you tonight, then. You'll be eating supper at the *residencia,* I suppose?"

"Right," answered Raúl.

He bowed his giant body and went out after Cortézar.

Quiet had descended for a few moments on the room. Only the final breathing of the rain could be heard: the moans, sighs, and groans of the straggling raindrops. Agustín took his pipe out of his pocket.

"What do you think?" he said.

Luis made a movement of the lips. "I don't know what you're referring to."

"Raúl."

The wax match described a brief spiral in the air and landed on the carpet. It burned down slowly, until it remained twisted and motionless, like a white worm.

"I don't think he'll say anything," Luis whispered.

"That's what I hope."

He puffed on his pipe indifferently, staring down emptily into the carpet.

"Can I count on you?"

Luis was waiting for this question, and his heart beat rapidly. "Of course."

"I haven't telephoned David."

"No?"

"But he's home. I think he knows it already."

Luis tightened his lips, as if to give himself strength. He took a cigarette out of the pack and lighted it with a steady hand.

"When do we go?"

A column of smoke passed before his eyes, like a tattered scarf.

"This evening."

"Have you thought of something?"

"It's difficult. But we must do something. There will be no need of violence. He's beaten already."

"Do you think so?"

"I know him."

"And the rest?"

"We'll tell them that he was going to betray us."

Luis threw his freshly lit cigarette against the windowpane.

"You know, I had always thought it." His voice came out hoarse, in spite of himself.

"Thought it?"

"That it would end up like this."

"Are you afraid?" asked Agustín.

"I'll go as far as you go."

He felt a dark protest within him. Each part of his body showed its displeasure in its own way; cold, heat, thirst, discomfort, irritation, weariness. Luis poured himself a cognac defiantly.

"We can do it between seven and eight-thirty," said Agustín. "At that time the concierge goes to the neighborhood church for Rosary. It's the only way of avoiding her."

"It's much more complicated than—" He had begun to speak without realizing it, and stopped, afraid. Agustín had arched his eyebrows and was playing with his chin.

"You were saying?"

Luis passed his hand over his forehead. "Nothing. I didn't say anything."

Agustín's mocking smile spread across his face and ended fixed to his eyes. Luis felt a heavy anger rising to his head.

"Then there's no reason to talk," he heard him say. "I am not forcing you to do it."

Luis felt slightly dizzy, as though he'd had a few drinks, and he remembered David: "There are many ways of forcing one." He felt himself trapped in his own net.

"Leave the car on the corner, and try not to let anybody see you. In short, like this morning. We'll meet each other there at eight. I'll be in front of the bakery door."

"And the weapon?"

"Don't worry. I'll carry it. It's all my responsibility."

"Why don't we go together?"

"I have several things to do meanwhile. You just take charge of the car."

"Are you going to arrange everything alone?"

"Don't worry. Do what I tell you and have confidence."

As he poured himself a cognac into one of the glasses

and sipped it slowly, Luis watched him, fascinated. For some time now he had been feeling an itching at his back, as though someone were spying on him from behind. He turned around suddenly and discovered in the shadow the face of Tánger.

"Pretending to be asleep, eh?"

Eduardo Uribe's very presence was a reproach, reminding him too much of what had happened at the leper session, and he felt himself fill with rage. He went up to him with a rigid face. A salty film had formed over his eyes, and he advanced slowly.

"Can you tell me what you're doing in this corner?"

A storm was hovering over him, and Uribe began to tremble.

"I was just sleeping," he said humbly. "I couldn't sleep a wink last night, and I was sleepy. Agustín gave me permission to sleep here, on the floor. I swear I haven't heard a thing."

Luis grabbed him by the lapels and made him get up from the mat, but Agustín came between them.

"Let him alone," he ordered.

Uribe stretched out again on the mat and looked at them alternatively with frightened eyes.

"He was spying on us," said Luis.

"It makes no difference. He won't say anything."

Tánger smoothed out his coat with his hands, and then studied his hands with an offended look. He was very much frightened, but made a great effort to appear perfectly calm.

"I was just sleeping here," he said, "and I wasn't doing anybody any harm. I tried to help you. I brought some goodies for when you'd be coming home from the war."

He looked all around him with an absorbed air and then rolled over on the straw mattress.

"But I ate them all up," he said desolately. "Or the rats did. I don't know. I don't remember."

Luis looked at him, his fists clenched.

"The thing for you to do is to get the hell out of here. Get out!" He snapped his fingers, and Uribe got to his feet.

"I don't have to be told the same thing twice. When I'm not wanted one place, I go somewhere else."

He did a pirouette like a clown and from the door he shouted: "I'm a fugitive."

On the stairway he wiped his forehead. "That was a narrow escape." But he thought they were spying on him from the landing, and he continued his monologue in a low voice: "*I was at home tending to my little chores.*" He looked up. There was no one there.

He went out into the street. It had just stopped raining a little while ago, and now, as if the emanation that rose from the ground had gone upwards, a cool breeze swept the bellies of the clouds and disheveled the grass of the parkways lining the street. Lights were being turned on. From a distance the long rows of newly built houses seemed to lack a third dimension. The light oozed, like yellowish steam, through the windows of the houses, and little puddles of water spotted the sidewalks.

A terrible anguish had taken hold of Tánger. He reproached himself for not having intervened before, for having waited till the end. "I should have confessed," he thought. But his fear of Luis had been stronger. Even now, again, he was betraying his confidence. He remembered that Raúl had gone to a bar on Claudio Street, and he hoped to find him there. "He has to help me," he thought, "I'll tell him what I have done."

He ran against the wind, and it seemed as though the whole of nature was conspiring against him: the leaves of the trees, the dripping water, the falling rain struck him in the face, and as he ran on, he was struck by the notion that the street was running in the opposite direction while he remained in the same spot, like a swimmer against the current. Impossible thoughts besieged him: "Oh, if I were someone else, if I weren't— If I could begin another life—" He passed in front of a church and crossed himself. "They're going to kill David."

The wind was getting stronger. He opened his mouth and began to swallow great gulps of air. He had reached the bar on Claudio Street and took a look through the window: Raúl wasn't there. He asked the girl. No, he had left—she didn't know where. He went out again. Maybe he'd be in his *residencia*. He had to find him. He came upon the concierge as he went in. Good afternoon. Some dark men were waiting in the reception room with their hats on their knees. He slipped up the stairs and turned to stick his tongue out at them. The lights were on in Raúl's room, and he entered without knocking.

"Looking for Raúl?" Planas said to him. "I haven't seen hide nor hair of him almost all day."

Uribe looked at him in astonishment. Planas, as always, was studying. His face was recently shaved and talcumed. He spoke slowly, hardly opening his lips: Fru-fru-fru-fru. . . . Always the same. Hateful, thought Uribe, always studying. He sweats. He sprays you when he speaks.

". . . that when he comes I'll give him the message immediately, unless . . ."

He spoke like an old maid and he had the mannerisms of a virgin. Repulsive. How nauseating.

"How nauseating!"

"Did you say something?"

"I said: 'How nauseating!' "

He heard Planas laugh. Uribe picked up a piece of

paper and a pencil and wrote: "They are going to kill David this very evening." He left it on top of Raúl's pillow and felt much relieved: the secret had ceased being one.

He went out into the street. What a relief! Planas made him so sick. They say he studies all day. Horrors! He remembered David and felt his emotion taking hold of him again. Now I am the only one left. His whole life depends upon me. Tears swelled in his eyes, and he realized that he had never been so happy as at that moment. I'll save him and I'll save myself. He had reached the taxi stand, and he gave the driver David's address.

*　*　*

It was only when he opened his eyes that he became conscious of the fact that he had been asleep for a long while. He had heard the clock striking, increasing the strokes one by one, and between dreams he had been startled by the dull thud of the shutters' banging together against the window frame. Now the light on the ceiling formed a wavy semicircle which extended radially, just like a fan. The rest of the room was still submerged in semi-darkness.

David tried in vain to get up. His arms, his legs, his whole body responded to the call of his will in a very weak and distant way. A vague feeling of nausea came up from his stomach to his throat. His tongue was a strip of leather; his lips, two molds of rubber. Something, nonetheless, had remained awake as he lay like a bundle on the mattress; on awakening, he looked around him, without astonishment. He calculated the hour by the intensity of the light outside: his watch had stopped. Finally, after a great effort, he managed to get up.

A confusion of sounds rose from the street. The voices, the noises coagulated in the expectant silence of the room, like something necessarily demanded by his impatient senses. Ideas resisted him; he could not think of anything. He found himself under the complete domination of the senses, which—in view of the obvious incapacity of his brain to make order out of chaos—claimed freedom of action with the firm sureness of the established, the habitual, of that which is part of the body.

He tried to remember what had happened, and he could not. He wanted to find an explanation, a key to the events of the day, and he looked around him helplessly. The fragmentary vision of Guarner's face, of his silky beard, of his own fingers clenched around the trigger, all made up separate images that he was unable to connect. "I have failed," he thought, "I tried to shoot, but I couldn't." His thoughts came to him aloud; he could not help it. He repeated them again mechanically, and passed his hand over his forehead, soaked with sweat.

"I was gripping the revolver with all my strength, and still I could not. When I was a boy, I used to say to myself: 'If before reaching the first house I still haven't kissed Juana on the lips, I'm an idiot,' and in spite of it I did not kiss her, and I gave myself three more houses. And still I did not dare to kiss her, and no matter how much I was dying to, I had to insult myself again. With Guarner the same thing happened. I wanted to kiss Juana, and I did not have the guts. By this time she has probably married a man who knows how to dominate her. She understood all too well. If she had gone on with me, it would have been a failure. People like me are no good for marriage. Gloria, too, realized this. She says that Betancourt knows exactly what he wants, and that I merely go along in tow. She despises me. Perhaps she's right, and I'm not much of a man. In Papa's factory it was the same thing. Papa yelled his head off at his employees, and I blushed with embarrassment. I wanted to do something that, in his eyes, would separate me from him. I have always wanted to be forgiven for something, *I don't know what*. It is very strange this business of wanting something and not knowing what it is."

He realized that he was wandering, and he let himself fall back on the bed. How heavy his head was! How tired! An idea had just occurred to him, and he said it out loud: "I think all those foolish things because I am still dreaming them." Sleep, sleep, sleep, close your eyes. He opened them again and again to decipher, in the semi-darkness, the figures that the light projected across the bed. For hours, just as he was doing now, he had stayed in the room doing nothing, just yawning. While the rain beat on the windowpane he lay on his back in bed. He did not even sleep. He watched the slithering ribbons that the water formed on the pane, and when he had used up all his tobacco, he collected all the butts in the palm of his hand and rolled them up in a new paper. He looked over toward the window. On the night table, next to the mirror, lay a volume of poetry. He picked it up indolently, but the fatigue that distended his muscles kept him from keeping his eyelids open. The lines danced in front of his eyes: they were simply printed words without any meaning whatsoever, without beauty or rhythm. He let the book fall to the floor.

"It's strange that it had to happen to me precisely this morning. It could have happened any other day, and it would not have mattered at all. Sometimes it seemed as though the body anticipates one's desires. At school I was the model student, but I might equally have been the worst one. I don't have initiative like Agustín, nor do I react properly in a crisis. Everything seems obscure to me, and I say nothing. Or, at certain times, I get sick. It's as if someone were interrupting something of my own that I do not wish to share with anybody. If something bothers me, the body takes over for me and invents all kinds of rules; I am overcome with a vague but constant feeling of ill-being: I no longer have the strength to escape, but I set myself free in my own way, and the more my irritation increases, the more my discomfort. That's what Agustín calls the escape valve. Lots of people are cowardly, but they hide it better than I do. Their courage is a form of self-deceit. Only people like Luis know what they are doing. They can do without the affection of others and are able to reduce everything to a question of utility. If you give to me, I give. If you read to me, I read. And so on ad infinitum. Perhaps they're on the right track. They see I'm a coward, and, in all fairness, I have to admit that they are not wrong. They gave me an opportunity. I had a pistol and he was an old man. But I'm wandering again. . . ."

He remained still, half wrapped up in the bedclothes, without a thought to disturb him; he looked into the empty air, fixed his eyes on the arms of the ceiling-light fixture, on the greenish-gray tarnish that stained the tips of the bracket. Often, when the light began to grow dim, he had shared the death of everything visible: the mute defeat of geometry, absorbed in a shadow that dissolved outlines and confused objects. The darkness became more and more dense. A feeling of enervation gradually took hold of him as he lay stretched out on the bed; he felt as though his vital strength, abandoning him, were feeding, by osmosis, on the atmosphere of the room. In the room next door the faucet of the washbasin was dripping, and David followed its sound with painful attentiveness, as if the solution of some puzzle depended upon its continuing.

He closed his eyes and dreamed that he was in the politician's home. His office was, however, Agustín's studio, and Guarner was speaking to him half drunk. They were playing poker, and Uribe was cheating. Then, without knowing just how, he found himself with a pistol in his hand, and Juana at his side gave him three minutes in which to murder the old man: "One, two, three, if you don't do it before the third house, you're a coward." He advanced along a highway shaded by trees where a huge crowd, all consulting their wristwatches, were urging him on with shouts and applause. Juana had become Gloria, and the old man was no longer Guarner, but his own grandfather. David tried to defend himself: "Everything is unfair. You've cheated." And Gloria tried to make him understand that, at that moment, whether there had been cheating or not made no difference. This was his big chance and he could not let it escape him. Hurry! Hurry! The revolver was stuck, and, in spite of his efforts, he could not make it go off. Around him the shouting and the applause grew louder: images, disconnected flashes, like anagrams, from a magic lantern. Shouts. Voices. Hurry. Kill. Kill—

He woke up startled, his forehead bathed in sweat. He felt undone, feverish. His head was heavy. It had grown dark, and through the window of the patio he looked at the lights of the neighboring houses. It was curious to see them like luminous bubbles, miraculously suspended in the air, with their imprecise halo of yellow pollen. He remained stretched out on the bed, and the light tinted his face and his eyes with the color of manzanilla, making him look liverish. An ambiguous feeling of disquietude warned him of the seriousness of the moment, but he felt himself incapable of reacting. With his gaze fixed on the furnishings of the room, he quietly abandoned himself to his fate. He was sleepy: his eyes closed on him. Again the noise of the drops as they detached themselves from the faucet. In a stupor he raised to his lips the glass of milk that the concierge had brought up to him that morning, and he began to sip at it, although he was not thirsty. They were minutes of torpor, of heaviness, of stupefaction, and he realized it. "Something important is being decided," he thought. "Something has happened, and I don't know what it is." Images of the past came to his memory, childhood memories of his grandfather. It was strange. Now that he thought of it, he had the same face as Guarner. Maybe it was because both had beards. But he stopped immediately: any amount of reflection cost him too much effort. Unnerved as he was by fatigue, he clung to the present desperately as if his whole life were condensed in the brief passing of the seconds marked by the pulsing of blood through his temples.

The electric light bulbs from the patio projected into the room a cloudy, imprecise light. Everything seemed to be very dirty: the frameless mirror on the table, the dark cloth that covered the desk, the wallpaper. Suddenly his ears started to hurt him. At first, very little. Then, more and more differentiated, painful thrusts came, keeping time with the beating of his pulse. He brought the glass of milk to his lips again, and it suddenly seemed nauseating. The light was getting more and more muddy, and the more carefully he observed the walls and the contents of the room, the more he concluded that everything rested on a false foundation: it was an immense décor of papier-mâché.

The pain in his ears was becoming unbearable. He sat on the edge of the bed, and amused himself listening to the creaking of the springs. "When I was a boy," he thought, "I used to like to jump up and down on the old bedsprings." He looked at his watch: it showed a quarter to two. It had stopped. Reluctantly, he got up and began to pace the room from one end to the other. The light from the patio bothered him, and he closed the blinds. Then he pushed the window wide open, instead: there was a full moon, and he stood watching it for a few minutes. "It looks like a toy," he thought, "like one of those that Tánger hangs over his bed." He remembered the glass of milk again and was about to bring it to his lips but stopped. Again he felt the undefinable nausea of the milk and the desire to lie down and rest. After hesitating briefly he lay down again, and from the bed, drowsy now, he listened to the neighborhood church bells.

He had the sensation that something unknown was nearing him, and the longing to escape seized him. He felt that all he had to do was to open his hand, and some pitying soul would hand him a rope. "I must do something," he thought, "before it is too late." The atmosphere had become thick, asphyxiating. And, as if in response to his physical discomfort, he felt increasing within him the fears that were restraining him, the origin of which he could not determine. He wanted to move, and he remained inert. He moved in a climate of lassitude and dullness and could not say anything to himself but: "Something's going to happen, something's going to happen, something's going to happen."

He went to sleep again and woke up, and went back to sleep again. He dreamed out loud. Then he turned over in bed and closed his eyelids. An unbearable pressure to hurry persecuted him. His heart beat violently. There was something of great importance he could not remember at that moment—he was supposed to do something right away, in a hurry, and he did not know what it was. He looked about him. A voice whispered in his ear: "You still have time. You still have time." "Time for what?" he asked. But the voice did not answer, it only repeated the

THE YOUNG ASSASSINS 238

refrain, obstinately, monotonously: "You still have time."
He sat up in bed and inspected the room. There was nobody; everything was motionless, in the usual order.
"They've played a trick on me," he thought. "I have to
get out of here and unmask them." He tried to jump out
of bed but he let himself fall back again. *"Now it is no
longer important."* He remembered his nightmare and
began to tremble. "What do dreams mean? Do presenti-
ments mean anything?" He closed his eyes and the voice
spoke to him: "Hurry, you still have time."

"Time for what?"

He shouted out loud and got no answer. He had just
screamed at himself, and he burst out laughing. "It's absurd, but it's not the first time that something like this has
happened—I have lived these very same moments before,
not once but an infinite number of times since I was a
child. Deep within, I have always carried it with me: like
one of those nightmares in which you approach the abyss,
and, although you know that someone will push you from
behind, you stay there, quiet, waiting. There is something
that attracts you and you don't know what it is. Perhaps
at the core of each of us is just that, an abyss." He was
thinking half out loud, and he covered his ears.

"I have to do something," he said.

"Take it easy, take it easy. I'm behaving like a fool. If
someone were to see me now they would think me mad.
Or that I had a 'screw loose,' as the servants used to say,
referring to my grandmother. It's absurd, because I—"

"I don't care about anything," he shouted. "Nothing,
absolutely nothing." He had lost control of his nerves. He
picked up the glass of milk on the table and drank it down
in one swallow. Almost instantly he had to vomit. It was
sour. Besides, he wasn't thirsty. What he was was sleepy.

He closed his eyes and went back to sleep, but he did not really sleep. He did not know for certain what was happening to him. Then finally he was lost in sleep, until the damp contact of a hand awakened him. It was Eduardo Uribe.

"David," he whispered, "David."

Uribe had to sit down, to put his head against the pillow, and he held David by the sleeve. He had climbed up the stairs breathlessly, and as he had entered the room he had hit his face against something; a little blood trickled down his cheek.

"David, David. Listen to me. You must get up right away and go away."

He began to shake him with all his strength, and David let his head fall forward. Uribe passed his hand around his neck and forced him to look at him in the face.

"David, listen to me. Make an effort, and pay attention. I have just come from Agustín's studio, and there I found out everything that happened. I . . ." His voice hesitated; absorbed in itself, it faltered. "I wanted to tell you something, David. But you must listen to me. Oh, you must listen, David!"

He sat down on the bed and pulled David toward him. He noticed that his hands were trembling, and he felt filled with hatred for himself. "It's all my fault," he thought. "If it hadn't been for me nothing would have happened. I wanted to amuse myself, I was playing." He wished Raúl were there.

"Wake up, David, for God's sake, wake up!"

He saw David open his eyes, and his concern became even greater; David looked imbecilic; his face was expressionless.

"David, for the love of God, pay attention to me."

The boy made an affirmative sign, but then let his head fall forward, inert, close to Tánger's shoulder. Uribe thought he would go mad himself.

"David, please, wake up! You have to escape. I cheated in the poker game; I dealt you bad cards. I had drunk a lot that afternoon and Luis made me believe that it was just a joke. I thought that it was some kind of game. I was so sad that afternoon that I needed to cheer myself up, no matter how. I wanted to be bold and brilliant, so that you would all love me. I did not know that when they talked about killing they meant it seriously. I imagined that it was a game . . . you understand? Before we always used to play like that, and I thought it was just another joke."

David's eyes filled with gentleness, and his whole face seemed to grow beautiful with that look.

"I know it," he murmured.

He looked at him for just a moment before he closed his eyes again. Uribe felt his own eyes filling with tears.

"I swear to you that I did not know anything about it. I was very drunk and I could not conceive of Luis's doing such a thing. I wanted to be happy, don't you understand: I would have done anything in the world to be happy. I know that it makes no difference to you and that you won't want to forgive me. I— Spit on me, that's all I deserve."

His voice was choking in his throat and suddenly an absurd thought seized him. *"Exactly in your best moments."* He hesitated, terrified. A horrible doubt had taken hold of him, and, on offering his cheek to David, so that he might spit on it, he understood that, even now, he was playing a role. "Dear God, dear God, I love David, really I do. I'm not pretending. I'm not putting on an act." He felt himself victim of his own masquerading and broke down, crying desperately.

"I'm a son of a bitch, a complete son of a bitch. The whole thing's my fault. They want to kill you. They're coming right now, in a little while, to kill you. I was in the studio when they all left, and I heard them say it. I swear to you that I am not making this up. I swear that I wasn't drunk. I was lying on the mat, and I made believe I was asleep. But I heard everything. Agustín said that he had to kill you, and Luis was silent. He didn't tell him about the cheating, and I did not dare to tell him about it. I was afraid that they'd kill me, too."

His tears made him hold his eyes half closed, and his eyelids quivered without stopping.

"I heard everything. I was not drunk. Luis discovered that I was there and wanted to beat me up. He was like a devil, David. He had hit me once before that day, and I trembled with fear. But I heard it all. This very evening, they're coming after you. They are going to take advantage of the moment when the concierge goes to the Rosary, and then they'll come here and kill you. You have to escape right this minute. I'll look for a place where you can spend the night, and tomorrow you can go to Barcelona. Or, if you prefer, you can take the express tonight. I—" He put his hand in his pocket and took out some hundred-peseta bills. ". . . three, four, five. Five hundred. With that you'll have more than enough. I'll take care of everything else. But you have to go right now. The train leaves within a half-hour, and they're on their way here already. If they find you here, they'll kill you. Oh, David, David."

Once again David had fallen into a kind of coma and seemed not to be listening. Uribe took him by the shoulders and began to shake him hard.

"David, David, for God's sake, wake up. Pay attention to me. It's all my fault. Oh, I swear I'm not drunk."

David remembered the dream, and realized now that the cheating was of no importance. He said as much to Uribe, and his voice came from his throat, weak and choked.

"It's of no importance, Uribe, I would have failed in any case."

He closed his eyes, as though closing the incident, and Tánger felt his whole body break into a sweat.

"Good God, David, get up! I swear I'm not pretending. There's still time. You just have to get up."

Yes, thought David, I have to get up. I still have time. At last he knew for what he had time. Uribe continued to whisper it into his ear. "They'll kill you, David, they'll kill you. In just a little while they'll come up here and kill you." But he remained stiff, rigid, just as it had happened to him in the dream. The nightmare came back to him: Gloria, Juana, the pistol, the time limit.

"David, please, David."

Uribe spoke to him in a soft voice, right in his ear, caressing him, pleading, threatening. And David continued to lie there, unmoving, his chin resting on his chest and his white hands clasped over his knees.

"You've got to hear me, David. Promise me that you will pay attention to me."

Tánger was trembling like a leaf. In the moonshadow of the room, he had looked at the clock: it was just twenty minutes to eight. Agustín and Luis might show up any moment now. If they found him there, they would kill him, too.

"David," he whispered, "David."

He had just realized that he was going to leave, and he began to reproach himself for it. He looked at David, trying to detect some sign of life there, but he stopped with a sudden chill. "He looks like he's dead," he thought, "his face is as rigid as a corpse's."

"David," he whispered once again.

He spoke to him in a low voice, as though he now feared awakening him. He saw his own gestures reproduced in the mirror and felt himself being watched, scrutinized.

"They're going to kill you, and you have to get out of here now, right away. I have left you the money. Five hundred pesetas. The train leaves within a half-hour, but you can still catch it if you take a taxi. But you have to hurry. Hurry, hurry. . . ."

The voice was no more than a thread, and he realized perfectly well that now it rang false. But he could not help it. Something stronger than himself compelled him to lie, to prolong the odious moment.

"You have to go to the station, do you understand? In just a few minutes they'll be here. I've given you the money, see?" He gave him a little pat on the jacket and put the bills on the bed. "But you have to leave right now —otherwise, it will be too late."

He stopped and looked around him in astonishment, as though hypnotized. Through the open window he noticed the view that stretched over the rooftops where nothing seemed to be alive, and, in spite of himself, Uribe stopped, fascinated by the helpless look of those old houses. With a leaden bath of light the moon covered the jutting edges of the slate roof, the little puddles, and the oozing walls. He had the sudden feeling of being in an enchanted place, like something in a story book. Motionless under the prolonged magnesium light, the façades looked corroded, spent. And the smallness, the gracefulness of the dazzle and the fleeting reflection of the water that dripped seemed to have come out of a photographic plate.

Slowly he turned toward the mirror and analyzed his pale clown face. All movement seemed to cost him a super-human effort, as if by moving he had had to violate some physical law, and immediately he bent over his friend.

"David," he whispered, "I must leave you now, but you must remember everything I have told you, and, above all, you must leave in a hurry. If you hurry, you still have time. I have left the money there, on the bed. All you have to do is to take a taxi and go. Do you hear me?"

He had bent his head down to listen to David's heart-beat, and it seemed to him that David was asleep. A few seconds earlier the features of his face had become more fine, and a strange intelligence shone in his eyes. Uribe tried feebly to say a few words: "David, do you hear me?"

The boy's eyes were closed. His chest heaved as he breathed.

"David."

He stroked his forehead very gently.

"You're asleep, aren't you?"

He received no answer, and he got up. The mirror gave him back a white, fantastic image. He brought his finger to his lips.

"Hush! He is sleeping."

With his little finger he touched the tip of David's nose and said something in Esperanto: still no reaction. He picked up the blanket that had slid to the bottom of the bed and spread it over him very carefully, up around the shoulders, trying to cover him up the best he could. The boy was breathing hard, almost panting, and Uribe loos-ened the knot of his tie.

"Sleep. Sleep peacefully."

He remembered the money that he had just given him and slipped his hand under the blanket. He pulled out the bills one by one and put them back into his pocket.

"I have a few expenses," he murmured.

He stepped away from the bed furtively, walking on tiptoe, his finger still on his lips. The mirror continued to throw back the white image, and Uribe bowed to it, greeting it with a wave of his hand.

In the doorway he stopped. It had just struck eight and the church bells were calling the faithful to Holy Rosary. All his agitation had disappeared, followed by a magical calm.

"I'm crazy," he said softly.

But he felt no remorse. He went down the stairs two at a time and got into the taxi that was waiting for him at the door. The concierge had just left.

"Take me to a bar, any bar," he said, "tomorrow is the beginning of Lent, and I must get drunk tonight."

* * *

When Agustín and Luis arrived, David was still fast asleep. He heard the noise of their footsteps on the landing, and he woke up with a start. "They're here now."

He was overcome with the idea, somewhat hazy, that he had forgotten something rather important, and he tried vainly to recall it, as he got up out of bed. He wanted them to find him standing up; if possible, washed and dressed. Uribe must have shut the door when he left; he heard them hesitate before pressing the buzzer, and he hastened to turn on the light.

"All right! I'm coming."

He remembered that he had nothing to offer them in the way of a drink, and for a moment he thought of telling the concierge to get something. "But they're not coming to drink. They're coming to kill me," he said it in a low voice while he combed his hair, and he went to the door. Before opening it, he took a last look around the bedroom: everything was in order.

Agustín was the first to enter; he was wearing a white gabardine topcoat which David had never seen on him before and a loose necktie *à la bohème*, badly tied, hung on his chest like a rope. He wasn't wearing the gloves David had confusedly half seen in his dreams, and David felt grateful; the bare hands inspired more confidence in him. Luis was behind him and slipped in like a shadow.

"Come in. Sit down."

The window was wide open, and he closed it. Someone might see them. He lit the little lamp on the night table and turned out the ceiling-light. The room divided itself immediately into two zones, which the wave of light marked off with a precise line.

"I don't have anything to offer you, I'm sorry," he said.

"That's all right. It makes no difference."

David had a ghost of a smile on his face; he leaned on the armchair. He felt fatigued, vague. He no longer thought that they were going to kill him.

"I was waiting for you," he said in a soft voice.

Agustín standing before him looked at him with his eyes half closed.

"I preferred not to warn you by phone. I knew you would be waiting for us, anyway."

His voice rose hesitatingly. "Thank you, Agustín."

His hands traveled along his legs, white and thin as though he had been soaking them in a bathtub full of water for a long time.

"I have been sleeping since I came in," he said. "Last night I could scarcely close my eyes."

Agustín's expression was almost gentle, almost caressing. Before entering into the room, he had imagined the scene:

David, white and tall, smoking indolently, a being without nerves or blood. He had always thought they would end up this way. And the anxiety that he experienced before coming in gave him the measure of his affection.

"For a moment," explained David simply, "I was on the point of leaving. It was stronger than I. Then, the feeling went away, little by little."

"Naturally," said Agustín. "I, too, would have felt the same."

"You are very kind."

He said it in a very low voice, smiling at him from the shadows.

"Do you have a cigarette? It would make me feel better."

Agustín searched in his pockets.

"They're not very good, but—"

"That's quite all right."

They smoked in silence. David noticed that Luis was swinging his foot impatiently. Silent witness to the dialogue between two friends, he seemed excluded, as though he did not belong. "He is in a hurry," David thought.

He saw Agustín make a quick move, and the cigarettes from his case spilled all over. Instinctively David bent down to help him; Agustín, kneeling on the rug, stopped confused before David's burning look.

"Excuse me," he said.

The color had rushed to David's face, and, still filled with confusion, he picked up with both hands the pitcher of water on top of the table; the imprint of his fingers remained on the glass, like the hoofs of a strange animal, and then evaporated slowly away, absorbed by the steam.

He recalled the first day he met Agustín. He had the same look as now. He was leaning with his elbow on a marbletop table, stirring his coffee with a spoon. At that time, too, he was leaning forward, and his eyes had measured David with the same gentleness. "He is going to kill me." He felt a strange emotion take hold of him, as if his body were hollow, and he was afraid.

"It must be late," he murmured.

"If I did not have the courage to kill, won't I even have the courage to let myself be killed?" A sickly hope whispered in his ear: "Look at him in the face, David. If you look at him he will not kill you." And he felt full of hatred for himself.

His eyes were brimming with tears, and he turned his head to hide them. Soon. Please. Agustín took advantage of the moment: the target was less than two feet away, and the trigger responded to his pressure. The bullet sunk into David's chest very gently.

He did not have time to realize what had happened: he bent forward and slumped down, slow motion.

"Forgive me," said Agustín. "You know that it was necessary."

He turned around spontaneously, as if awaiting the protest of everything which for a long time had been a part of David's life: only a silence which was almost a sound. The noise had been like the lash of a whip. The body had fallen face down on the carpet; the hand contracted until it became stiff.

Standing above it, the body looked as though it were sunk in a deep sleep. The two arms were extended, following the line of his body, like a swimmer doing the crawl, and the motionless feet, heels touching, resembled the fins of some big fish. Only a moment ago it had been full of life, Agustín thought. Now from one of the sides blood began to run. The dark stain spread rapidly, already soaking the worn carpet.

Agustín stooped down over the corpse and with great

care turned it over, face up. David's eyes were open, askew, like the lifeless orbits of an expensive doll, and, with the head thrown back, they remained turned toward the light, like two bright dahlias. Awkwardly Agustín closed the eyelids. He put his head to David's chest. He was not breathing. Within a short time, the disintegrating germs in the air would penetrate without resistance this body of a friend and would start to disfigure him.

"He's dead," he pronounced.

He looked around. Luis was watching him with a shattered look, leaning with the palms of his hands on David's desk. Kneeling down beside the corpse, Agustín looked up at Luis long and hard, and the shadow of a smile distended his features.

"What's the matter with you?" he said.

All the boy's aplomb had disappeared at the sight of the blood. He brought to his lips the pitcher on which David had left his fingerprints, and began to sip the water.

"Are you sick?" he heard Agustín asking him.

Luis did not answer; he looked at the red stain slowly growing larger, and, in spite of himself, he closed his eyes.

"I thought you were prepared to see it through," said Agustín slowly.

Luis bit his lips. He felt choked up, powerless.

"And I have," he murmured. "But I don't like to see blood."

With great effort he managed to speak in a normal tone, and he was amazed to hear himself.

"You don't have to tell me," said Agustín. "I can see it."

Agustín looked at the corpse grimly, and he was filled with resentment. Obscurely he was blaming Luis for what had happened, and his whole being gave vent to his spite: "There's nothing better than a situation like this to get to know oneself," he said. "Some time ago when I flew to

London with my father, one of the motors stopped in mid-flight and the pilot thought that we were going to crash. As soon as the passengers realized it, they began to scream. I couldn't have been more surprised. I turned and looked at my father, somewhat shocked. There he was, right next to me, not even recognizing me, paying no attention to what I was saying. He, too, had stood up and was screaming. As you can see, nothing happened. We landed on an island, and nobody was hurt. But it was all very instructive. From then on, I have made a habit of dividing people into two categories: those who would have screamed and those who would not have." He paused, a smile fixed to his face, and added: "My dear Luis, I believe that you, too, would have screamed."

"Shit!" said Luis.

He brought the pitcher to his lips and started to drink. He hated Agustín, and he would have gladly killed him.

"Don't get excited, please. Have a little respect for the dead. It's in very poor taste. Moreover, you want me to shut up. And I do not want to. We have killed David, and it is important that you remember that and see it through with me. To the very end, understand?"

The words hammered in Luis's brain. He wanted to turn his back on him, for Agustín was kneeling next to the corpse, speaking to him. He had to turn around . . . he had to.

"Listen to me carefully," Agustín said to him. "We've undertaken this job together, and if they hang anybody, they'll hang both of us. Or we'll both escape. I have a border permit to go to Portugal in case things get complicated. But right now get this much straight. What you have just done is also murder. David is dead now. Look!"

He picked up one of the arms and let it fall, rigid, inert.

"He's dead, and you don't have to be afraid of him. Only

the living can harm us. The dead," he lifted the arm and let it fall again, "the dead cannot."

He kneeled down on the carpet and, using his handkerchief, removed David's watch. It had stopped. The hands showed a quarter to two. He stood up and glanced around the room. Luis, pale, his lips trembling, watched him.

"What are you looking for?"

Agustín paid no attention to him. He wound the watch and set it at nine. Then he picked up a heavy letter-opener and with the butt struck the face of the watch. The hands stopped dead, under the smashed face. Very carefully, he put it back on David's wrist again, and quickly took another look around.

"Come on, do something! Don't just stand there," he said scornfully. "This isn't how a room looks after a robbery."

He opened the drawers of the desk and emptied the contents onto the floor. He used a handkerchief for picking up things so as not to leave fingerprints. The pages of the diary fluttered over the rug, spattering the floor with white. Then he opened the door of the night table, messed up the clothes in the wardrobe. Luis watched him without doing a thing. Then he remembered that he had leaned on the desk, and he rubbed off his fingerprints with a handkerchief. He did the same to the water pitcher. And finally, he turned his back to the corpse and stood stock still; his face was bathed in sweat and he felt a damp cold between his shoulder blades, and in his armpits.

"Now," said Agustín, "all you have to do is hit him."

He had just emptied a drawer of clothes and was looking at Luis contemptuously.

"Hit him!" Luis muttered. "I don't understand."

"Let me explain it to you, then. We came here to rob him, and David tried to defend himself. We struck him, and when he resisted, we had to put a bullet through him. Got it?"

The boy's face had turned white. "But it's absurd. He's dead."

"Dead or not, you'll have to hit it. You promised."

"I said I would go as far as you did," replied Luis, "but this isn't part of the game."

"If you mean by that that I should go first, I'm ready to oblige."

He went over to the corpse and lifted his arm to strike it.

"Don't, for God's sake!"

The voice sprang from his throat, not human, like an animal's howl. A thick cloud closed in on Luis, and he felt like vomiting. He passed his hand over his forehead and stammered: "I can't, understand? I just can't— I beg of you— Not that." He stopped for a moment and added in an even hoarser voice: "I made Uribe cheat at the poker game."

"Cheat?"

"Yes. He gave him bad cards. I—"

Agustín's look was hard as metal. "And can you tell me what that has to do with your not being able to hit him?"

The confession had risen to Luis's lips against his will. But Agustín's response made him even more miserable.

"I— Now— No—"

"Now? You say: Now? You had to see him dead in order to confess? Or aren't you convinced yet that he is dead? If you wish—"

He repeated the same gesture he had made a moment before.

"No! Please—"

Luis let go with a flood of obscenities, but he stopped short. Someone was coming up the stairs. There was a second during which everything seemed to freeze, as if a movie projector had stopped in mid-action to permit the contemplation of the scene. Then suddenly the maddening buzzing of the bell fell like a stone in clear water —the waves radiating the length of the room, over the motionless furniture, the open drawers, the white sheets of paper on the carpet, and the corpse of the boy.

Luis's teeth were chattering. The need to cry out came to his throat as though driven through a syphon. He had to put his hand over his mouth and began to groan. Agustín put into his coat pocket the revolver which he had left on top of the table. He went over to the lamp and pulled out the plug. The buzzer rang again. In the darkened room only the slow dripping of the faucet in the lavatory and the impatient footsteps of the intruder on the landing of the stairway could be heard.

"Mr. David."

It was Doña Raquel. Agustín remembered that he hadn't barred the door, and stealthily he went toward the hallway. Behind him rose Luis's groans. He had made a move to escape when his foot had hit a soft object. *David.* He winced and clung to Agustín's shoulder.

"They're going to catch us. There's no way out."

Agustín struck him across the face. "Stay there! Stay back there, or I'll kill you."

He left him in the darkened room, with the corpse.

"No— No—"

Luis's voice was strangling him, but Agustín paid no attention to him. He closed the door to the room and continued toward the hall on tiptoe. Doña Raquel had used her key, and the front door opened suddenly. He had just turned on the light, and the woman stepped back.

"Oh, what a scare you gave me!" she said, recognizing him. "I knocked twice, and thought there wasn't anybody here. I was just bringing Mr. David's supper."

Arranged nicely on a tray were a plate of soup, some fried potatoes, sauce, and two veal cutlets. Agustín looked at it fascinated. *A meal for David.*

Doña Raquel took a step in the direction of the bedroom, but Agustín remained planted in front of the door.

"He's sleeping," he said. "It would be better if you left the tray. In a little while, if he does not wake up, I'll wake him and give it to him."

The woman looked at him uncertainly. There was something strange in the atmosphere. Her very entrance . . .

"Don't you want me to leave it on his desk for him?"

Agustín remained firmly in front of the door.

"Thank you. I think the two of us can manage alone. If he needs something I'll call you. David doesn't feel well. But, of course, you already know. . . ."

Doña Raquel left the tray on top of a little rickety table. She was fond of talking, and she grabbed eagerly at the thread of conversation he offered her.

"Poor boy," she said with great tenderness. "You know the scare he gave us the night before last. When we found him, he was yellow, looked just exactly like a corpse. So much so that I said to my daughter: that young man is going to die on us. What a scare, gracious! I think," she added lowering her voice, "that it's his father's fault. It isn't normal at twenty years old to have a heart like that child has. When I compare him with my girl . . ."

She was wearing a woolen bathrobe, and her dyed hair was an army of tiny curls.

"There's nothing like living as the good Lord commands us, don't you think? All the damage that could be avoided. If one is honest at heart . . ."

Agustín wasn't even hearing her. He was fascinated with the sauce. He turned around suddenly.

"When he has finished, I'll call you. Meanwhile, I want him to sleep for a while."

"Poor dear boy," said the woman, "poor child!"

She could not make up her mind to end the conversation, and she kept balancing herself first on one foot then on the other.

"If you need me, you know where to find me: it's just one floor down. I'll bring his custard up in about a half-hour."

"Don't worry about it; I'll tell him."

He had accompanied her to the door and then latched it behind her. For a few seconds he stood stiff, unmoving. The tray attracted him irresistibly: the sauce. The two broiled cutlets.

Never had he felt so calm as he did now. "So that was it," he thought. "So many years thinking about a thing like this, and then to have it turn out like this. It's incredible." He picked up the tray with his left hand and went back to the bedroom. Luis threw himself on him.

"What's going on?" he asked. "For God's sake, what's up?"

With great care, Agustín put the tray down on the table and knelt down in search of the light plug. Luis's groans could be heard. The waiting had driven him almost crazy, and his body felt like rubber.

"We've got something to eat," said Agustín in an empty voice.

Under the salmon-colored light of the shade, the sauce appeared even redder. Luis turned his head away.

"Aren't you going to tell me what has happened?"

He was close to the breaking-point, and it seemed to him he was going to faint.

"Calm down," said Agustín, "above everything else, be calm."

He sat down in David's armchair and studied the tray attentively.

"Just think," he murmured, "they've brought the supper. The supper of a dead man."

"Shut up!" yelled Luis.

"Looks appetizing. Don't you want some?"

"Shut up!"

He began to swear. The words came up out of his throat, sometimes forming a knot so that it was impossible for him to get them out.

"Well, at least let *me* eat."

He picked out, at random, a fried potato and bit off the end of it.

"Delicious!"

He drowned it in the sauce. The sticky, red liquid dripped onto the tablecloth. He brought it to his lips and swallowed it with obvious enjoyment.

"I haven't eaten such a well-cooked meal in years. Really, David knew how to live. This sauce is something—"

"Oh, shut up!"

He had turned his back on the corpse and was looking desperately at the machetes stuck into the wall.

"They've seen us! We've no alibi now. You should have— Oh, oh! What an imbecile— In your place, I'd—"

"In my place?" said Agustín.

"I would have killed her." He turned toward him and added defiantly: "Yes. That's what I would have done."

Agustín nibbled on one of the cutlets.

"Yes? And what would you have gained by that?"

"Saved us," he explained. "Yes, saved us. We're caught; we've no way out. They'll come and get us, this very night—"

"Keep quiet," said Agustín. "You're just talking without

knowing what you're saying. You're not cornered, and no one is going to catch you unless you want them to. You're just imagining things."

"I don't understand."

"I'll explain it to you, then, in a few words. The woman has seen only me. Therefore she has no reason to suspect that anyone's with me. You say we have no way out, but you should have spoken in the singular. I am the one who has no out. No one has seen you."

The cloud that a few moments ago had closed in on Luis disappeared as if by magic. The blood started flowing in his veins once more.

"You mean that—"

"Simply that you're free. Nobody has seen you come in. The woman hasn't seen you. She doesn't suspect anything. Her arrival has saved you."

Luis hesitated, caught between a maddening hope and the fear that Agustín might be joking.

"And what about you?" he managed to say at last.

"Didn't I just tell you that I won't say anything? Look, there's the door. Go whenever you please."

Luis swallowed his saliva. Agustín's calm terrified him, more than any outburst would have. He felt an immense desire to get out, but something stronger left him standing, immobilized, beside the corpse.

"I . . . I don't know how—"

"I couldn't care less what you think. Go on, now. Beat it!"

"And you?"

"Don't tell me that you're worried about me! I don't believe it."

"I—"

"Get going! Beat it!"

Luis started toward the door, stepping aside so as to

avoid David's body. As Agustín watched him, his eyes penetrated into Luis's back like darts.

"Get out!"

When Agustín was alone, he gave a sigh of relief. He had the feeling that now he was the only player left on stage, that at last he could talk alone with David. He remembered David's words: "What happened to us?" Now he could answer: "We are both dead."

He left the cutlet half eaten, and consulted his watch. "Within ten minutes," he thought, "no one will catch up with him." He took a look around. David, always a very neat boy, had detested any kind of disorder.

He began to pick up the pages of the diary which a few minutes before he had scattered all around the room. He put the drawers, the wardrobe, and the shelves back in order. In the washbasin he made a fire with all the pages of the diary that David had written on and watched them writhe, fragile and black like fragments of carbon paper. And it seemed to him that with them he had burned the final remains of David.

He lifted his friend's body up by the shoulders and carried him to the bed. He had stopped bleeding. On the carpet the stain was dark, almost black. He stretched him out with difficulty—he was already quite rigid—and rested the back of his head on the pillow. The face expressed a great peace, the kind of serenity that Agustín had never seen in David when he was alive, and, before leaving him, he kissed him lightly on the hand.

The room was in order again. Agustín cast a last look around before turning off the little lamp. The window was closed; he opened it wide, throwing the smashed watch out onto a neighboring roof, and left the bedroom.

The hall light was on, and he turned it off. Everything was to look as usual. Strangely he felt a great calm. He went down the flight of stairs that led from the garret to the third floor and knocked on Doña Raquel's door.

"Ah, it's you."

"I'm leaving now, but I think David needs you. Go up and keep him company. He should not be left alone."

"I'll go up right away, Don Agustín. I'll only be a minute finishing these dishes."

"As soon as you can. Good night to you."

He went down the stairs slowly, and he stopped in the doorway to light his pipe. The concierge had not come back yet. With his hands in his pockets, he walked over to the bar on the corner.

"It's curious," thought Agustín, "it's as though I had known it all along. There was always something about him that troubled me: the way in which he extended his hands when he sat down, his way of smiling, his apologetic look. If I had been asked the reason why, I would not have known what to answer. But I foresaw something from the very beginning."

The woman had put a bottle of gin in front of him and was smiling at him, resting her elbows on the bar. She was a fat, ordinary, loud blonde, whom he knew from his frequent visits to the place. She had made up her mind to save him from drink, and she fawned over him with a tenderness which was really tyrannical.

"Don't drink it all, my lamb," she said to him, opening the bottle. "You know it's not good for you."

She served him alcohol reluctantly, and one day when he had gotten very drunk, her solicitude had gone so far as taking him home to his studio. Emptying his glass, he studied her carefully. Her hair was hollowed out in tiny curls, and her face was covered over with a thick coating of powder. Her eyes were dark, jet black. He returned her smile.

He remembered everything with precision, and he felt extremely calm. He had just killed his friend, and now here he was, drinking. "Everything is pre-ordained from the start. My last lesson was to kill him and his, to let himself be killed. The two of us were playing a rehearsed scene, the kind of scene that ends up badly." He began to see things clearly. "If Ana had not come to see me, and if David had not been a friend of Gloria, and if Luis had not decided to play a dirty trick on him, and if Uribe . . . Always if . . . Coincidence. One can never be certain of anything." He drank four drinks, one right after the other. "Now I am a murderer, and in a little while they'll come and arrest me."

The woman winked at him from behind the bar. Her body was in constant motion, and her breasts stood out in relief from under the white of her apron. She set up a half-dozen glasses on the bar, filled them half full with crème de menthe, and then added a squirt of syphon water. The emerald green paled slowly. Through the glass could be seen darker spirals that rose to the top in rings; it was like the heavy mist that lifts at noon over the summer shores.

"You're drinking too much," she said to him as she passed.

She threw herself into a frenzy of activity, with the kind of self-conscious busyness that people always show when they feel they are being observed. She kept taking down bottles from the upper shelves, handing empty glasses to the boy, all the while carrying on two different conversations. The place was rather full, and there was a warm feeling of promiscuity among the people there. Snatches of conversation could be heard against a background of murmurs, of hand-clapping, of the hoarse squirting of empty syphon bottles.

At this very moment, he figured, Doña Raquel is probably arousing the whole house with her screaming. He continued drinking, almost without stopping. The bottle was going down noticeably, already below the halfway mark. An absurd idea had occurred to him while he was deciphering the strange figures on the label: "*The old man was nothing but a pretext.*" Every incident, all the varied events of the day, his conversations with Luis and with Ana, their need to compromise themselves irrevocably, seemed to exist merely on the periphery, completely disconnected from his principal line of action. "I needed all these detours in order to arrive at killing him." A strange fatalism had weighed on their friendship from the beginning. Now both of them were dead. He emptied the glass in one swallow. Dead. Beyond recall.

The woman was at the other end of the bar now. The waiters milled around him, broken down into an infinity of movements, like figures on a speeded-up reel of film. "There is something," he thought, "that makes us different from everybody else. An abyss that neither his parents nor mine were able to bridge. He had embarked on an adventure, and they had remained ashore. We could not go back, and they could not come near us. We lived too fast."

Suddenly he remembered the music teacher whom he used to visit every afternoon and who had tried to put him on guard against the demands of life. The teacher had spent his youth in a seminary, and he used to speak in a shrill voice about the effects of sin. "There is something much worse than fire and brimstone, worse than feeling oneself a live torch and remaining none the less incombustible; it is the lack of love—solitude, emptiness." His eyes had lit up like bubbles of dark water when he spoke to him of death and the devil. Agustín listened to him fascinated, enjoying, like a sick man, the discovery of his own symptoms. "I, too—" he would start. And one day he had had the courage to unburden himself. "I notice something. An invisible streak that makes me feel different."

The old man had stretched out his hands convulsively, gnarled like the claws of an eagle: "The devil."

From his table he waved for the woman.

"Sit down," he said to her, "it's about time you had a rest."

She made a sign as if to say "later," and launched into her work with renewed vigor.

On one occasion he had told David about the old music teacher: "He witnessed in horror the awakening of my senses. Every afternoon at sunset I would climb up to the garret where he lived and help him stir up the ashes of the brazier. I remember how he would take the poker from my hands. He was my well, my dumping-ground. The confidences had created a bond of horror between us. I was then fourteen years old, and at home they did whatever I demanded. That half-crazy old man supplied me with the kind of tension that I needed in order to exist, the tension I could not find among my own people: I listened to him talk of 'solitude,' of the 'Devil's trill,' of the 'fall.' One day he showed me the score of a Tartini sonata. From then on, I accompanied him on the piano when he played it. . . .

"It happens sometimes that you have an attachment for something, and suddenly you discover that it would be better to do without it. Since then I have sought thirst, and I can no longer turn back."

Exactly the opposite of David. "David looked for approval; when he no longer had the love of his own fam-

ily, he needed a substitute. . . ." Enriching one another
through their experience, they had grown up supporting
each other, like two real friends. Now David was dead,
and his death had not proved anything: on the rebound
Agustín had killed himself through David. "Oh, David,
David," he thought, "I have given you death, and without
knowing it I have killed myself."

Gin was no good. He would have liked a drug stronger
than forgetfulness. He turned toward the woman and
beckoned. Not yet; she had work to do. He looked at his
watch. At that very moment scores and scores of microbes
were feeding on David's body. "And mine," he thought.
"Am I by any chance any more alive than he?" In his
jacket pocket he had the letter of introduction which
would enable him to cross the border. "Flee? From what?
From whom?" He drank another gin. The bottle was almost empty. "In twenty minutes," he thought, "that's quite
a record." It seemed to him that his whole life had been
nothing but an impulse founded completely on the act of
killing, and that in the moment of carrying it out, the act
had left him empty, stunned.

A group had just sat down at the table next to his. There
were a half-dozen men, and although no one was aware of
his presence, Agustín had the feeling that they wanted to
tell him something. He waved to the woman and handed
her another bill.

"Bring me another."

"Another!"

She looked at him reproachfully and shrugged her shoulders.

"Bring six glasses, too."

"What do you want them for?"

"And one for yourself, my good girl."

He watched her while she uncorked the bottle and with a curiously timid gesture he tugged lightly at the sleeve of one of the men.

"Would you gentlemen do me the honor of having a drink with me?"

The man had a square chin and funny little Mongoloid eyes. He thought Agustín was joking, but he hesitated when he noticed the serene expression on his face.

"You're the one who is doing the honors."

"Help yourself, please."

He himself filled the man's glass for him while the woman left the others on the table.

"What's this?" she asked.

"This gentleman is treating us."

With a sober face, Agustín accepted their smiles and raised his glass at the toast, saying merely: "To David."

The bottle passed from one to the other. All the men were quick to take advantage of the generosity of the stranger, and only the woman looked with disapproving eyes on what, in her opinion, was mere squandering.

"Come, now. Don't drink any more. You've already drunk a whole bottle."

Agustín paid no attention to her. Once, during a nightmare he had had some years ago, he had dreamed that he was killing David with one of the daggers in his collection, and David hadn't offered the least resistance. And now he saw the dream again, in great accuracy of detail. David had curved his neck so the blade could go in more easily, and he had not uttered a single cry. Agustín told him about it the following day: David's mother, a very superstitious woman, had taught him as a child all about the prophetic nature of dreams. And he had never forgotten David's expression as he listened.

"That's odd," he had said to Agustín. "I, too, have

dreamed that very often." But then he had closed up like a clam with the modesty that was so characteristic of him, that always took hold of him immediately as soon as he began to open up to someone. Agustín had not thought about the incident again, and remembering it suddenly now made his heart beat violently. "So—" he thought. But the sound of voices, getting louder and louder, interrupted his thoughts.

Now.

An old woman, her hair all disheveled, had just come in and, with wild gestures, was pointing toward David's house. Most of the customers got up and rushed toward her. Through the door one could see people running and hear the confusion of voices outside.

"They've killed a young man. Yes, at Number 17. Raquel, the woman who lives in the third floor. . . . Yes, just a few minutes ago."

The men who were sitting at the next table went outside, where the commotion was getting worse and worse. Only the woman was left standing at the door, her hands on her hips; when she saw Agustín was alone, she motioned to him.

"Come now, don't you want to know what the excitement's all about?"

Agustín was thinking about David and felt a strange emotion welling up in his throat. He thought he saw him again: pale, with his golden hair uncombed, and with the sad smile on his bloodless lips. "You come up to me with a knife, and I don't run away. It's funny. I have had dreams like that ever since I've known you. If I were superstitious, I'd think . . ." Agustín had then made some coarse remarks on the hips of some girl he was dreaming about at the time. If only we had talked, perhaps . . .

Some of the men returned to sit down again at the table

next to Agustín's, and seeing that he had not moved from his seat, started to tell him the news.

"It's a student who lives at Number 17. Somebody just shot him. When the woman saw him she fainted, and now the police are taking her statement at the house. They won't let anybody go up."

The fine outline of Agustín's eyebrows traced a pronounced angle, like a circumflex accent.

"Yes," he said simply, "I was the one who killed him."

He reached into the pocket of his topcoat, and deposited the pistol on the table.

"And this is the weapon."

*   *   *

When Raúl walked into the room Planas, as usual, was buried in his studies. The light from the table lamp made a luminous circle over the desk and reflected on the pages of the textbook that Planas was holding in his hands.

"Uribe was in looking for you a little while ago," he said.

Raúl shrugged his shoulders, and began to take his jacket off.

"He left you a note."

"He did?"

"On top of the pillow."

Cortézar, who had just come in, too, picked up the envelope and handed it to Raúl: "They are going to kill David this very evening." His voice came out suddenly hoarse.

"When was he here?"

Planas drummed his sharp fingernails on the top of the desk; it was his way of showing that he was thinking.

"It must have been about an hour and a half ago."

"Was he drunk?"

Planas smiled: his smile was rather coy, like the smile of an old maid. With the bifocals that he wore when he was studying he looked like a clucking hen, a good-natured fowl.

"No. At least, not noticeably so. Well, you know how difficult it is to find him entirely sober. . . ."

"And this? When did he write it?"

"He told me to tell you that he had come to look for you."

"And didn't it occur to you to ask him what he meant?"

Against the light the talcumed face of Planas was no more than a series of white disks: chin, eyes, cheekbones.

"As you can understand, I did not read the contents," he said.

Raúl fingered his mustache nervously.

"Oh yes, I was forgetting that you are such an impeccable character."

Cortézar went up to him and took the paper from his hands, but Rivera was already putting on his jacket again.

"Let's go."

"Do you think?"

"Let's go."

Raúl felt irritated, filled with rage. When he opened the door, Planas got up from the chair.

"Anything wrong?"

Raúl spat out an obscenity and started down the stairs two at a time, with Cortézar panting along after him.

"Where are we going?"

Out in the street he caught up with Raúl and repeated his question.

"*I* am going to his house."

The answer hurt Cortézar, like a blow, and he felt the blood rush to his cheeks. The conversation that had taken place in the middle of the afternoon concerning David had lodged itself in his brain like a bat with wings spread. He continued running alongside of him.

"Taxi."

They got in, and the vehicle lurched forward noisily. Raúl did not talk, but Cortézar felt in his silence a rebuke much stronger than words.

"I trust that Tánger got there in time," Cortézar said.

A sudden chill made him shiver. "If only nothing has happened, if only, if only," he kept repeating to himself. He had forgotten all about the attempted assassination that morning; he seemed to be witnessing some monstrous game in which David was the prize.

I'm sure he arrived in time, he kept thinking until something compelled him to speak, and the words came forth in spite of himself: "In an hour and a half he could—"

He had turned toward Raúl, who was pointedly looking away from him.

"Oh, shut up!"

The taxi kept stopping for traffic lights. A feeling of guilt had taken hold of Cortézar as he thought: I shouldn't have left them. I might have known that was going to happen. He stared at the front seat. This was the end. On their very first job the group goes to pieces. And the certainty that everything had just tumbled down around him seized Cortézar like a terrible omen.

He consulted the luminous face of a clock in a jewelry store: a quarter after nine. His wrist watch showed only ten after: five minutes' difference, decisive ones, perhaps. Cortézar couldn't take his eyes off the clock: behind the round face the case was filled with little springs, steel wheels, minute gears. And perhaps at this hour David wasn't David any more; there would be another in his place, with his same features, usurping his position in space.

They had reached the Plaza de las Columnas and were headed in the wrong direction.

"Stop here," said Raúl.

He opened the door of the taxi and started running toward the house. Cortézar paid the driver and ran after him.

"Wait for me!"

A cold wind grabbed hold of people's clothes and ruffled the surface of the puddles. Raúl had forgotten his hat in the taxi, and his hair fell down in loose curls over his forehead. His cigarette, out, remained stuck to his lips.

"Don't run."

Although he was shouting, the wind whisked away his words like leaves, like birds' feathers, making them dance along with the leaves and feathers, around the gray base of the columns.

Cortézar felt a great oppression inside of him, the fear of facing the inevitable moment. In front of him Raúl walked with his customary swing, as if all his limbs moved by virtue of some invisible threads, which someone was amusing himself by pulling.

Turning the last corner, they stopped. Once they were protected by the walls of the buildings, they could breathe more easily. On the next corner crowds of people could be seen milling around; drawn, perhaps, to some street-vendor, they seemed to be listening with lowered heads, elbowing each other in order to see better. A street lamp threw a muddy light over their faces, and Raúl saw that they were arguing and talking.

As he drew near, he slowed down. This was no ordinary street crowd flocking around a hawker: it was a much larger, more silent group that spread out fanlike around the door of a bar.

"What's going on?" asked Raúl.

And by the tone of his voice, Cortézar knew what he was thinking.

"Look!"

He pointed out the entrance to Number 17: two uniformed police were on guard at the door. A few people forced and pushed, just like the ones at the door of the bar on the corner. And the busybodies visited back and forth from one side of the street to the other, exchanging opinions and comments.

"Did you hear what happened?"

"No. What is it?"

"Someone murdered a boy up there." He pointed out the doorway where the police and the inquisitive onlookers were standing guard. "And the murderer is in there, in the bar. Apparently, he gave himself up."

Raúl elbowed his way through. His appearance was so impressive that he was able miraculously to cut through the crowd—a path of arms, legs, hips, and human faces. Cortézar followed close on his heels.

"Where is he?"

"Inside there," said a fat woman. "But they won't let you go in. They made all the customers get out, and now they won't let anybody in."

"I saw the whole thing," said a little man who was holding her by the arm. "My friends and I—we'd just arrived, and the guy invites us to have a drink with him. He looked funny as hell. And then the business of treating a perfect stranger to a drink, it didn't seem right."

Raúl was not listening to him. Flattening his face against the glass, he looked inside. The proprietress was leaning over the bar, crying, and at the door in the rear three policemen were talking. Otherwise, the place was empty.

"And that's not the worst of it. The boy was a friend of his. The landlady had just brought up his supper, and this guy had the guts to stay there and eat it all up, right there in front of the corpse. You can't tell me. There are people who do things like that out of necessity, but guys like this—"

"I've lived in this neighborhood for ten years, and I've never heard tell of such a thing. Me—why I'd have that kind of man shot right away, without a qualm. When the case is so clear . . ."

"They say they both came from good families and had come here to study. Study what? I say. They never do anything; they get up in the middle of the morning. In my opinion there must have been something between them, and that monster . . ."

"A woman," she exclaimed. "Whenever something like this happens there's always a woman at the bottom of it. If it were up to me, I'd put an end to the good life of all those sluts who live by exploiting the young fellows. Sweet Jesus, to think how a mother watches and slaves over her sons, only to have them snatched from you like that!"

From the other side of the door the two waiters were staring at Raúl suspiciously. He had occasionally gone to that bar with Agustín and David, and their eyes now seemed to be lying in wait for him, like a watchful dog's.

"It's money," the woman was saying. "If, instead of getting it from their parents, they had to work their fingers to the bone . . ."

"When I first looked at him, I thought to myself this guy's a creep. Inviting you to a drink, like that, with no reason. Don't tell me it wasn't rather peculiar!"

Cortézar noticed the two waiters, too, and began pulling at Raúl's sleeve. The crowd was hurling angry threats and insults at the murderer, and they felt hemmed in.

"Let's get out of here," Cortézar said. He couldn't take any more, and he felt a cold sweat pouring all over his body. Raúl tried to tell him something, but his voice was drowned out by the shouting of the crowd.

"Look at him! Murderer! Murderer! Kill him! Kill him!"

One of the guards had opened the door to the bar. Agustín followed behind him, flanked by two policemen. His topcoat made him appear more robust than he really was, and an ironic expression hardened the features of his face.

Neither Raúl, nor Cortézar, standing up in front, had time to get away. A wall of bodies, fists, raised arms, cut off their retreat. The human wave pushed them forward. Agustín spotted them right away, and his smile reached them like an arrow.

The insults rained down on him: gestures of anger, incomprehensible cries, mouths open, like the mouths of fish gasping for air. Agustín stopped near the door while the guards tried to open up the way, and as he passed, Raúl and Cortézar lowered their heads, denying him, like Peter, amid the shouting crowd. And for those seconds they suffered agony and shame, wishing that the earth would swallow them up. Agustín went by without saying anything to them.

"It is as if by killing David we had killed ourselves, and as though by denying Agustín we had denied our very lives." A dizziness smothered Raúl like a thick blanket, asphyxiating him. He noticed that Cortézar had fled, lost in the crowd. They had just put Agustín into the police wagon, and the crowd began to disperse. In the doorway of the bar the two waiters still stood watching him suspiciously.

It seemed that all faces were turned upon him and that their scorn had left a mark on his face. He quickened his step. He had no reason for remaining there. David had died, and, with him, all his past. When he reached the square he stopped and searched in his pockets. He found a crushed cigarette in his pocket and lit it, protecting the flame with his hands. Then he resumed his slow walk, his hands buried in his pockets. Across the equestrian statue and the asphalt paving of the square, the moon shed its indifferent patina. Like a shadow, Raúl slid between the sleepy houses until he was lost in the gray reflection of the columns of the arcade.

JUAN GOYTISOLO was born in Barcelona in 1931 and lived in the Republican zone during the Civil War. He studied at universities in Barcelona, Madrid, and Paris. In 1951 he founded the "Turia" literary group; in 1952 he won the Joven Literatura prize for his story *The World of Mirrors;* and when he was twenty-one his first novel, *The Young Assassins,* was published.

Today "Juan Goytisolo is already considered an elder, the front rank man in the new literary generation," according to Daniel Mir in *Les Lettres Nouvelles.* Goytisolo divides his time among Paris, Barcelona, and his home on the Costa Brava in northern Catalonia, devoting himself to his writing.

A NOTE ON THE TYPE AND PRODUCTION

The text of this book is set in Caledonia, a Linotype face designed by W. A. Dwiggins (1880-1956), who was responsible for so much that is good in contemporary book design. Though much of his early work was in advertising and he was the author of the standard volume Layout in Advertising, *Mr. Dwiggins later devoted his prolific talents to book typography and type design, and worked with great distinction in both fields. In addition to his designs for Caledonia, he created the Metro, Electra, and Eldorado series of type faces, as well as a number of experimental cuttings that have never been issued commercially.*

Caledonia belongs to the family of printing types called "modern face" by printers—a term used to mark the change in style of type-letters that occurred at the end of the eighteenth century. It is best evidenced in the letter shapes designed by Baskerville, Martin, Bodoni, and the Didots.

This book was composed, printed, and bound by H. WOLFF, *New York. The paper was manufactured by* S. D. WARREN COMPANY, *Boston. The typography and binding were designed by* GUY FLEMING.